"Te

Taking her in his arms again, he lowered her to the ground and laid her on the blanket. Without a word he braced his arms on either side of her shoulders, leaned over her and kissed her.

This was not like the first kisses. It was much deeper, with that leashed ferocity, but also the tenderness she had felt in him before. His tongue ran along the inside of her lips, and a rush of warmth gathered between her thighs.

A normal response, she thought. But then she wasn't thinking about anything but the kiss, hesitantly returning it, touching her tongue to his.

Then she felt his teeth, and her muscles stiffened.

Timon drew back. "You're not ready," he said hoarsely.

"Will you...bite me?" she asked.

"Not unless you want me to."

"No," she said. "Not yet."

Susan Krinard has been writing paranormal romance for nearly twenty years. With *Daysider* she began a series of vampire paranormal romances, the Nightsiders series, for Harlequin Nocturne. Sue lives in Albuquerque, New Mexico, with her husband, Serge, her dogs, Freya, Nahla and Cagney, and her cats, Agatha and Rocky. She loves her garden, nature, painting and chocolate...not necessarily in that order.

Also by Susan Krinard

Harlequin Nocturne

Nightsiders Series

Holiday with a Vampire 4
"Halfway to Dawn"
Daysider
Nightmaster
Shadowmaster
Night Quest
Dark Journey
Twilight Crossing

HQN Books

Come the Night
Dark of the Moon
Chasing Midnight
Lord of the Beasts
To Tame a Wolf

Visit the Author Profile page at Harlequin.com for more titles.

TWILIGHT CROSSING

SUSAN KRINARD

ISBN-13: 978-0-373-13980-4

Twilight Crossing

This edition published by arrangement with Harlequin Books S.A.

For questions and comments about the quality of this book, please contact us at CustomerService@Harlequin.com.

Printed in U.S.A.

Dear Reader,

Love, and hope. Two of the most powerful forces in the universe. In the world of Timon, half-blood vampire, and Jamie McCullough, a young and beautiful human scientist seeking peace between two warring races, hope and love seem to be in short supply.

That's why Timon and Jamie must put everything on the line, even their growing, star-crossed love, to help end a plot that could end all hope of peace between humans and vampires forever.

I hope you enjoy the sixth book of my Nightsiders series.

Susan Krinard

Acknowledgment

Special thanks to Ginger Tansey, DVM, for her help with information on viruses and emergency first-aid treatment. Any and all errors are mine.

Dedication

With gratitude to my editor, Leslie Wainger, who exemplifies everything an outstanding editor should be.

During the fifty years following the post-War Armistice between the Opiri and humanity, the world slowly began to heal. As ruins crumbled and wilderness took the place of old towns and cities, both humans and vampires had to make difficult adaptations and hard choices.

In the earlier days of the "cold war," human Enclaves, usually built out of cities that survived the War, paid tribute to the Opiri in the form of "blood-serfs," criminals sent to the Opir Citadels in return for the cessation of blood raids on human communities. Citadels and Enclaves continued to spy on one another via half-blood agents—the Opiri's "Darketans" and the Enclave's dhampires—operating in the neutral Zone between cities, and skirmishes continued to break out between them, challenging the uneasy truce.

Over time, two significant trends put an increasing strain on the Armistice: the gradual reduction and eventual end to the practice of blood tribute, and the formation of new "mixed" colonies, in which Opiri and humans lived together in relative peace and cooperation.

This cooperation, however, was largely confined to these smaller communities, and communication between Enclaves and Citadels remained erratic until the rise of the Riders, a brotherhood of half-blood horseman whose work it was to carry messages and escort travelers across the western half of the former United States of America. Known for their skill in wilderness survival and fending off rogue Freeblood packs as well as human raiders, the

Riders gained a reputation for trustworthiness and complete neutrality. Facilitation of contact and travel among human and Opir cities led to new alliances and discussions of a permanent peace, one in which the "mixed" colonies would provide an example of coexistence across the entire western region.

Thus, the original Conclave was born: a meeting of delegations from every major Citadel, Enclave and mixed colony in the West. The Conclave was to be held in the neutral area of the former city of Albuquerque, New Mexico. It was to be the first such meeting since the signing of the Armistice, and the Riders were to take the role of peacekeepers and upholders of the Conclave's laws.

Though hope ran high for the success of the Conclave, there were many who resisted the idea of an ultimate peace and the cultural changes that would become necessary to sustain it.

—Alice J. Armstrong
Introduction to *A Matter of Blood: A History of the First Conclave*

Chapter 1

"Can you see who they are?"

Jamie McCullough squinted against the bright April sky, her eyes following Councilor Amos Parks's pointing finger. "They're on horseback," she said to her godfather. "They must be—"

"The Riders," Senator Greg Cahill said, talking over her. "It's about time they showed up here."

Here, Jamie thought. Far from the southern border of the San Francisco Enclave, even beyond the Zone that marked the no-man's-land between Opir Citadel and human territories.

But people *did* live in this land, where wild cattle grazed among the pre-War ruins, alongside deer and pronghorn antelope. Small colonies, well-fortified, with mixed human and Opir residents; pure human settlements, always ready to defend themselves against raiders both human and nonhuman. And human and Opiri who stayed on the move, hostile like the Freeblood raiders or unaligned like the Wanderers.

Then there were the Riders. Skilled fighters, neutral in their loyalties, always half-bloods and always male. They were the men who rode fearlessly across the West in their tight-knit bands, carrying messages and escorting travelers and colonists through the dangers of the wilderness, facing down rogues, raiders and wild tribesmen. Both humans and Opiri hired them, sometimes even to communicate with one another.

Today they were coming to escort the San Francisco Enclave delegation to the grand Conclave in the old state of New Mexico, a journey of a thousand miles. With the wagons and frequent stops, it would take about two months of hard travel to reach their goal.

But without the Riders' protection…

"They're coming fast," Greg said, his hand moving to the gun at his hip.

Too fast, Jamie thought. The thundering of hooves was shaking the ground under her boots. By now they should be slowing down, prepared to identify themselves. As they came closer, Jamie noticed that they were wearing hoods.

Riders weren't full-blood Opiri, who had to protect themselves from the sun. Most of them would subsist on blood and were faster and stronger than ordinary men, but in other ways they were very human.

These horsemen covered their entire bodies under heavy coats and cowls and gloves.

"Raiders," she said, her voice catching on the word.

"Freebloods," Amos said, speaking of the wild troops of masterless rogue Opiri. He signaled for the others in the party to retreat to the wagons, while the four armed soldier escorts, led by Sergeant Cho, moved forward to position themselves between the horsemen and the rest of the delegation.

"Jamie!" Greg said, dragging her down behind a wagon. "Do you *want* to end up as some vampire's meal?"

She winced at the pressure of his fingers on her upper arm. She mumbled an apology, but Greg had already moved away to shout orders as if he, not Parks, were in charge. The older man, grim-faced, caught Jamie's eye and nodded. She smiled at her godfather to prove that she wasn't afraid.

This wasn't like that *other* time. She wasn't alone. She wasn't a child. And she wasn't helpless.

Someone pushed a gun into her hand. "You've had training," Sergeant Cho whispered, crouching beside her. "Aim for the heart or between the eyes. Don't fire wildly—take your time."

"Don't worry about me," Jamie said.

Cho squeezed her shoulder and quickly moved away. Jamie's hand trembled on the grip. She wasn't a killer. This was a mission of peace. For it to be born out of violence…

She'd barely finished the thought when the first horse barreled past her, hooves kicking up clods of dirt as the air filled with the smell of horse sweat and leather, and a sharper scent she thought must be the Opir rider himself. He didn't stop to accost her, but a moment later she heard a cry and a shot. More horses flashed by; more shots followed, but the shouts were more of anger and defiance than pain.

Finally it was her turn. The horse reared up beside her, nostrils flaring, while its rider's eyes seemed to burn down on her from beneath his hood. She raised the gun, and the raider knocked it out of her hand with no effort at all.

"Please," she said, addressing him as calmly as she knew how. "I don't mean you any harm."

The horseman laughed. It was an ugly sound. He swept down and grabbed her arm, pulling her halfway into the saddle. His hot breath beat on the back of her neck. She closed her eyes, preparing herself for the bite.

It didn't come. He wheeled his mount around and rode away from the wagon, pinning her in place against him. When he stopped and let her slide to the ground, it was clear that the raiders had won.

Jamie counted. Five raiders, and ten in the delegate party. All ten were still alive, though one of the soldiers, Corporal Delgado, was lying on her side, nursing her arm. Three of the raiders were busy binding the wrists of their captives while the other two remained on their mounts, rifles resting on their thighs.

But Jamie saw no blood, except the little on the soldier's arm. The raiders had won almost without trying.

They're keeping us in good condition so that they can get the most out of us, Jamie thought, too numb to feel fear. This was a disaster of the highest order. Not only had the delegation been stopped before it truly started its journey, but now its members would serve as a food source for the raiders…kept alive for God knew how long, until they were too weak to keep donating blood. And then…

"This isn't necessary," she said, speaking clearly and loudly enough for everyone to hear. "We'll be happy to share our blood with you until our escorts arrive."

Her godfather, hands already bound, gave her a warning look. Greg's face was dark with anger, and the soldiers stared at her as if she'd gone crazy.

The presumed leader of the raiders, one of the two watching on horseback, turned the black circle of his hood toward her. "It is a great comfort to know that you're so willing to serve," he said mockingly. "We would not wish to force you."

"We *are* expecting others," she said, refusing to let herself be intimidated. "Riders. Perhaps you've heard of them. They call themselves the Brotherhood, and they're very good fighters. But there's no need for more violence, if you'll only accept our offer and then leave us in peace."

The leader of the raiders whistled through his teeth. "You speak for all these humans?"

"*I* speak for them," Parks said, his wispy gray hair floating in the breeze like a halo. "I'm President of the City Council of the San Francisco Enclave. We'll give you whatever you need."

Speaking a language Jamie knew to be rooted in ancient Greek, the leader addressed his mounted companion. The other Opiri gave an appreciative laugh.

"Put no faith in your Riders," he said to Jamie. He called

to his companions, who gathered up their human captives and forced them into a small space close to one of the wagons. She thought the raiders might take them on a forced march to whatever hideout the Freebloods kept as their base, but instead they left one guard to watch over the humans and retreated to the shade of one of the big oaks to the side of the track.

Waiting for night, Jamie thought. But they still could have taken blood from any of their captives, and did not. Jamie listened to the harsh breathing of the young medic next to her and tried to catch her godfather's eye. But there were too many others between them, and there was nothing he could have done.

From a place of detachment she had fostered long ago, she recognized her own terror. It was perfectly rational to be afraid, under the circumstances…even for someone who had never faced a hungry Opir before. Especially just after sunset, when one of the raiders came to untie her and lead her under the oaks.

He won't kill you, she thought, fighting panic as she was brought to stand before the leader. *It isn't in his best interest.*

But when he flashed his very sharp teeth at her, she shuddered in spite of herself.

"You said you'd offer us your blood," he said. "Is that all you're prepared to give for your freedom?"

Jamie tilted up her chin. "I will do whatever is necessary to avoid more violence."

"Quite a brave little human." The Freeblood sneered.

She took a shaky step toward him. "Do you know why we're here?" she asked. "We're on our way to a meeting among dozens of Enclaves and Citadels and colonies, a Conclave to reach a new agreement for peace among all humans and Opiri. If we succeed, you'll never have to hunt for blood again. There would be plenty of places where humans will give blood willingly, and—"

"You assume we want such a peace." The leader grinned. "Come here."

Jamie hesitated. Her escort pushed her toward the leader. She stumbled, began to fall, saw the leader jump up before he could catch her.

For an unknown period of time she lay on the leaf-littered ground, half-dazed. Again there were shouts and cries, hooves striking hard earth. This time there were no shots.

The others got free, she thought. But the voices she heard were not familiar.

A hoof stamped down next to her head, an inch away from striking her temple. She froze. The horse's leg moved away, and a boot came down in its place. A strong, very masculine hand descended to grip her shoulder.

"Are you all right?"

She looked up through her tangled hair. An uncovered face stared down at her, but all she could see were a shock of dark hair and vivid violet-gray eyes.

"You're late," she whispered.

Chapter 2

"Yes," the Rider who rescued Jamie said. "I apologize."

He helped her to her feet, brushing leaves out of her hair. Jamie put her hand up self-consciously and stepped back, making sure that her footing was solid.

There was just enough moonlight filtering through the tree branches for her to get a better look at her rescuer. His features were handsome from what she could see of their lines—his chin firm, his cheekbones high and his gaze direct and curious. He had a Rider's legs, firmly muscled, and his shoulders were broad under his shearling coat. He wore two knives: one in a sheath at his waist and a smaller one in his boot. His rifle was slung over his shoulder by its strap.

"Is anyone hurt?" she asked, trying to look past him at the wagons.

"Only the soldier who was wounded before," he said. He flashed her an utterly unexpected grin. "The raiders are gone, and they won't be returning."

"I have to see my godfather. Councilman Parks."

"Of course. I'll take you."

"That won't be—"

She didn't get a chance to finish. He looped his arm around her shoulder, half supporting her, and led her out from under the trees. There was no remaining sign of the raiders, except for a few abandoned weapons and broken earth where Opiri and half-bloods had struggled.

The night had grown dark, but her escort's steps were sure, and someone had lit lanterns by the wagons. Her godfather appeared before she reached the nearest wagon, his eyes filled with alarm. Her savior let go of her.

"Jamie?" Amos said. "Are you hurt?"

"No," she said. "I think I have this man to thank for that."

She turned, but the Rider was gone.

"Come and sit down," Amos said. "Our escorts have sent the raiders running, but they want us to remain together."

Peering into the darkness, Jamie tried to make out the newcomers. "How many have come?" she asked.

"Four," he said, guiding her to the nearest wagon.

"Almost evenly matched," she said.

"The Riders seem to be very good fighters, as promised," Amos said. "They didn't even use their rifles." He helped her sit beside the wagon. "I'll get you something to drink."

"You have other work to do, Amos," she said, squeezing his hand. "I'll be fine."

He crouched beside her. "You should never have spoken up as you did."

"It was worth a try," she said.

"You know better than anyone what they could have done to you," Amos said, cupping her cheek in his hand. "And in spite of your one experience with an Opir, you're still naive about so many things. I should never have let you come along."

"How many times have we discussed this, Amos?" she asked. "It's not just because of my mother. I'm a scientist, and I can't hide forever. Too much of the outside world is still unknown to us, and someone has to keep a record of what we experience and observe. Whatever I learn will help us at the Conclave, and afterward. I believe in this peace."

Amos sighed. "I know. But promise me that you won't do anything so foolish again."

She smiled unevenly. "I promise."

With a slow shake of his head, Amos rose and walked away. Jamie released her breath. She wasn't sure if she'd been truthful with her godfather. How could she be sure what circumstances would arise on their journey? Sometimes even a scientist had to take risks.

For her, even stepping outside the Enclave had been a kind of risk. She'd hidden herself away in her parents' lab since her father's death, avoiding all contact with the world outside the Enclave, missing even the most average social experiences most other young women her age took for granted.

Amos had called her naive, and maybe she was. But she had hope for the Conclave because of the words her mother had written in her journal—and because of what she had learned in the laboratory. A secret she believed might make all the difference at the meeting.

If she could present it at just the right time.

Rubbing her arms against the chill night air, Jamie found herself looking for her rescuer again. She caught a glimpse of him speaking to his fellow Riders, all four of them dressed in the same shearling coats tanned the color of wheat and with the wool side turned inward. He was tall and stood confidently, with an athlete's bearing, and the other men listened attentively.

He must be the leader, Jamie thought. And judging by the rugged, competent looks of the other Riders, that would mean something.

But he was also a half-breed. Half-Opiri, needing blood to survive. Expecting to take donations from the delegation to nourish him and his followers over the long weeks.

Her turn to donate would come, too. But she wouldn't think about that yet. For now she could honestly say to herself that this half-blood didn't frighten her. He was living proof that not all Opiri were violent hunters.

She reached inside her jacket to touch each of the two

hidden pockets, one containing her notebook, the other her mother's journal. She pulled out her notebook and drew a quick sketch of the Rider, trying to catch the firmness of his profile and the way his mouth curved up at the corners when he smiled at something one of his men had said.

About six-three, she wrote beside the sketch. *Lean and agile, but well-muscled. Darketan, with Opir teeth, human features and ability to walk in daylight. Hair dark auburn, eyes gray with violet tint; purple indicates Opir blood. Small scar above left eyebrow.*

And handsome, she thought, her pencil hovering above the page. She couldn't write *that* in her notebook.

She woke from her thoughts when the half-blood broke away from his men, clearly looking for someone, and stopped when he found Greg. The two men began to speak softly, Greg gesturing with obvious irritation.

Tucking her notebook away, Jamie inched her way toward Greg and the Rider leader. She was able to get close to them without leaving the partial cover of the wagon, and knelt beside the rear wheel to listen.

"…so late," Greg was saying, his voice pitched high. "Do you have any idea what they could have done to us?"

"I can only apologize again," the Rider said in a steady voice. "It was very bad timing on our part."

"And will you be ready the next time?"

A tense silence fell between the two men. Jamie stared at the Rider's profile. Moonlight rested on the planes of his face and shadowed his pale eyes.

Be careful, Greg, she thought. The Riders might be completely neutral, allied with no one group or race, but instinct told her that *this* Rider wouldn't suffer fools gladly. And Greg was acting like a fool.

"The Councilman's goddaughter was forced to go to that barbarian," Greg said, fists clenched. "He could have sucked her dry, or worse."

Light played on the Rider's lower lip as the corner twitched upward. "She's obviously a brave young woman. Have you spoken to her?"

Greg's jaw bunched. "I was just on my way to see her."

"Then I won't hold you up any longer." The Rider stepped gracefully aside, gesturing for Greg to walk past him. Jamie ducked under the wagon and crouched there, breathing a little fast.

Greg stalked away, but Jamie continued to watch the Rider as he scanned the camp and set off again with long, ground-eating strides. Jamie scooted out from under the wagon and followed him at a discreet distance.

Her godfather was talking with the two medics, Akesha and Don, when the Rider found him. Amos broke off with a reassuring smile and gave the half-blood his full attention. Jamie joined her friends, pretending to listen to their excited retelling of the attack as she focused on the other conversation.

"Didn't realize I was talking to the wrong man," the Rider said as he shook her godfather's hand. "The Senator gave me the impression that he was in charge here."

"He would," Amos said with a slight smile. "But it doesn't matter. It would be difficult to stand on ceremony over such a long journey."

"I'm glad you feel that way," the Rider said, releasing Parks's hand. "I didn't get a chance to introduce myself. My name is Timon, of the Kestrel Band."

"Timon," Amos acknowledged. "Needless to say, I'm very pleased to meet you. There's no danger of the raiders returning?"

"None." Timon glanced around him. "I'm told there were only minor injuries. Is there anything else we should know about?"

"It's all under control, thanks to your men. And I want to express my gratitude for what you did for my goddaughter."

Timon made a dismissive gesture with a gloved hand. "I did nothing but help her up after the raiders fled. She's a brave young woman."

"I wish I could send her back."

"Why?" Timon asked, cocking his head.

Jamie tensed, but she missed her godfather's next words when Don raised his voice to relate some particularly exciting moment of the battle between raiders and Riders.

"No one can be spared to take her back to your Enclave," Timon said when she could hear him again. "But she'll be all right. There are four of us now, and we expect three others to join us before we reach old San Jose."

"Rest assured that I won't be doubting or questioning your judgment," Amos said. "We're in your hands."

"Thank you, Councilman," Timon said, inclining his head in acknowledgment. "Given what's happened, I think we should wait for dawn before we set out...allow your people plenty of time to sort through their experience today. They'll be better prepared for the next occurrence, if there is one."

The next occurrence, Jamie thought. It wasn't as if they hadn't been warned. The volunteers had been drilled a hundred times. But it was one thing to imagine and another to experience.

Timon obviously knew that.

Jamie mumbled something to Akesha and Don and retreated back to the wagon. Its solidity, and the medical and laboratory equipment it carried, gave her comfort. People were building a small fire, and she observed the activity with a strange lassitude, as if it were happening in some other universe. She watched the other Riders move easily through the temporary camp as if it belonged to them. They had probably been in hundreds of such camps before, guiding and escorting travelers between Enclaves and colonies and even Citadels.

"You should be with the others."

Timon settled into a crouch beside her…he smelled of warm sheepskin and horse and something subtle but deeply pleasant. He smiled at her, his eyes searching hers with an intensity that took her aback.

"You shouldn't be alone right now," he said.

"There's nothing wrong with me," Jamie said, her heartbeat quickening. "After all, *you* said I would be all—"

She broke off, realizing what she'd been about to reveal. She didn't stop soon enough. Leather creaked as Timon shifted, and she felt rather than heard the rumble of amusement in his throat.

"I knew you were listening," he said. "You're not very good at hiding."

Her skin felt hot, and she barely prevented herself from raising her hands to her cheeks. "I'm sorry I eavesdropped," she said.

"No, you're not," he said. "What made you so interested in hearing what we were discussing?"

She swallowed her unease. "I've never met a half-blood before," she said.

Dark eyebrows lifted. "You live in an Enclave with dhampir agents, and you've never met one?"

"I've seen them, of course. But I never had any reason to be near them. And you're not a dhampir."

"No," he said. "I'm a Darketan. My mother was an Opir, and my father was human. With dhampires, it's the opposite."

"I know that." She felt hotter than ever. "I don't know much about the Riders," she said in a rush, "but you aren't all Darketans, are you?"

"We have a few dhampires," he said. "Does that make a difference?"

"Not at all."

"You're just curious."

"I'm a scientist," she said, as if that would explain everything. "I'm on this expedition to learn."

"What kind of scientist?" he asked.

"Biologist, among other disciplines," she said. "My mission is to observe as objectively as possible."

"Then you have no stake in the outcome of the Conclave?"

"Of course I do. I believe in what it stands for, what it will mean if it succeeds."

"I'd always heard that the San Francisco Enclave has had very poor relationships with the nearest Opiri communities."

"No Enclave has suffered more from the war than ours. We provided blood-serfs to the Opir Citadel Erebus for many years before it became impossible to continue. They have not accepted the change gracefully."

"Then why are you so sure the other Opiri want peace as much as you do?"

With an effort, she held his gaze. "You must know why we humans have hope. Opiri across the West have had to adapt to the lack of serfs as a source of regular blood. Many Citadels have gone from feudal societies where the strongest rule, to communities where resources are shared rather than fought over." She looked away. "You, surely, have seen this yourself in your travels?"

Timon shrugged. "I've seen every possible way that humans and Opiri have adapted. That doesn't mean that a change this massive will be easy."

"I understand that you Riders don't care if a lasting peace is achieved."

"We've been hired to act as security at the Conclave. Our neutrality can't be in question, but it's to our benefit if things go smoothly." He studied her face from the tip of her chin to the crown of her head. "How often have you been outside the Enclave?"

"What did my godfather say about me?"

"That you have little experience with the outside world. He'd like me to keep an eye on you."

"I don't need anyone to take charge of me."

He laughed, his white teeth gleaming. "It's no imposition, Ms. McCullough," he said lightly, removing his gloves. "Some things are worth looking at more closely."

Is he flirting with me? she thought in confusion. "What do you see now?" she asked, far bolder than she meant to be.

"Fishing for compliments?" He grinned. "You must know you're beautiful."

Oh, God. "I…" she stammered. "I wasn't—"

"Hasn't anyone ever teased you before?" He grew sober. "Maybe you don't even know it. I'll tell you something else about yourself—you're a brave woman. But that doesn't mean what happened didn't have an effect." He took her hand, and Jamie realized that her fingers were trembling.

"That's why you shouldn't be alone," Timon said, his thumb stroking the back of her hand.

She jerked free, alarmed by his touch. "When are you going to need us to donate blood?" she burst out. "I need time… I mean, you should warn people beforehand, so they have a chance to…"

She trailed off, deeply embarrassed. Timon looked at her in silence for a long time, as if weighing her words for some hidden meaning. "Are you afraid of me, Ms. McCullough?" he asked.

"No!" Jamie folded her arms across her chest. "Why should I be?"

With a soft sigh, Timon extended his hand again. "You'd better come with me," he said.

A cool breeze whispered past her ear, lifting a strand of dark brown hair. "Really, I'm—" she began.

"You're cold. You need the company of your own kind."

He squeezed her arm, the slightest pressure of reassurance. Jamie allowed him to pull her to her feet. Her initial unease at the contact had already begun to fade. In fact, the pressure of his fingers felt like something solid to cling to in a world that had lost its moorings.

Before she knew it, she was among the people already settled around the fire. They made room for her, and somehow a warm blanket found its way over her back. Timon's hands pressed into her shoulders briefly.

"Get plenty of rest," he said, his breath caressing her cheek. And then, as before, he was simply gone, and she was left bewildered and feeling not at all objective.

I've just met him, she thought as someone passed her a handful of hard crackers. *I don't know anything about him.*

Except that he was handsome and strong and brave—much braver than she could ever be—and that he'd taken care of her as if she were a friend.

When the others finally spread out their bedrolls to sleep, she pulled out her notebook.

He asked me if I was afraid of him, she wrote.

I don't know.

She closed the notebook and lay down on her bedroll. Before she closed her eyes, she saw Timon again, watching her from the other side of the fire. His gaze was the image she carried with her into sleep.

And into her dreams.

Chapter 3

At first light, Timon and his Riders gathered their charges and started south on the well-worn track parallel to old Route 101. The highway itself was buckled and pierced by shrubs and small trees, making travel over the old asphalt difficult.

The pace was slow, as Timon had expected. The horses drawing the three wagons moved at a deliberate pace, since the delegation had only one set of replacement animals for each, and the people walking their mounts beside the wagons were just as slow. It was better that way; Timon wanted them fit for the entire journey, not worn at the end of it.

He had been riding beside Councilman Parks for some distance, learning all he could about the delegation and the San Francisco Enclave. In all his time as a Rider, he'd never been part of an escort for the coastal Enclave, perhaps because the humans there kept largely to themselves.

Like Jamie McCullough.

Timon fell back, reining his horse toward the rear of the caravan. She rode quietly beside one of the middle wagons, constantly scanning the low, oak-studded hills and the marshes alongside the southern stretch of San Francisco Bay, occasionally jotting in her small notebook.

Keeping his distance, Timon considered what was wrong with him. From the moment he and Jamie had met beneath the oak, when he had helped her to her feet and looked into her wide blue eyes, he had felt a shock of attraction. It hadn't seemed to be such an odd reaction at the time;

she was stunningly lovely in spite of her seeming lack of awareness of her own attractiveness. Her dark, wavy hair hung past her shoulders, though she had worn it in a severe ponytail or braid since their first encounter; her face was a near-perfect oval, with full lips and slightly arched brows that ideally suited the shape of her eyes. She was petite, but her body was curved in all the right places, and she moved with a natural grace.

A scientist, he thought as he maneuvered his mount to the other side of the wagon. Officially, Parks had told him, she was both his aide and one of the medics accompanying the equipment that was to be the core of a human infirmary at the Conclave. The Councilman spoke with pride of her work in the laboratory, searching for cures for human diseases.

But she obviously *was* naive. She had no skill at hiding her feelings or guarding her words, and the way she'd behaved with Timon hinted at something more than mere inexperience with half-bloods. Her outburst about donating blood told him that either she'd been more deeply affected by her brush with the "raiders" than even he had guessed… or something else had happened to make her fear the act.

Many humans did, associating the giving of blood with slavery and compulsion. But it seemed personal with her, and he had no desire to make her more afraid of him.

There was no reason he should be riding so near her now, studying her profile and the way she frowned slightly when she made a notation. Especially when he considered the other women he'd known, in the settlements or among the Wanderers he and other Riders often met in their travels. The experienced, worldly women who were all too happy to accommodate his needs while he happily accommodated theirs.

If Jamie had been different, if she'd been anything like those other women…

But then there was Cahill.

Timon looked forward to where the Senator was riding near the head of the column as if he himself were leading it. He hadn't quite figured out the Senator's relationship with Jamie. Most of the time Cahill left her alone, but every so often he would ride back and lecture her as if she was obligated to listen to and obey every word he spoke. Cahill told her, wrongly, that she held the reins incorrectly; he chastised her for falling behind when she dropped back to the middle of the column. And there was an air of possessiveness about him that had aroused Timon's immediate dislike, though he shouldn't care one way or another what the humans did among themselves as long as it didn't endanger the party.

Realizing that he'd been glaring at Cahill's erect back, he looked toward Jamie again. The horse was still there, walking placidly beside the wagon, but the rider had vanished.

Timon reined Lazarus behind the wagon and rode around it, coming up beside Jamie's mount. She wasn't with the animal. He continued toward the rear of the column and Ajax, the Brother riding drag, searching for Jamie with a vague sense of alarm.

He found her crouched at the side of the track, her fingers picking through the green spring grass. She plucked a golden poppy and examined it with great concentration, then set it aside and made a quick sketch of it in her notebook.

With a whispered command to his horse, Timon slid out of the saddle. Jamie looked up as his shadow fell over her, scrambled backward and landed squarely on her rump. A deep red flush tinted her creamy skin.

"What is it?" she asked. "What's wrong?"

It took a moment for Timon to realize that he had been frowning. "It isn't wise for you to fall behind the column," he said, offering his hand.

She stared at it as if it were a striking rattlesnake. "I haven't fallen behind," she said. "I was only—" Her bright gaze flashed toward the last wagon, pulling away at a steady pace. "Oh."

He relaxed. "Being absentminded is an indulgence you can't afford," he said. "No matter how fascinating you find the local flora."

Ignoring his offer of help, she jumped to her feet. "I didn't intend to be so long."

"Are you always so caught up in your work?"

"I'm not really a botanist," she said, her voice rising with enthusiasm, "but there are only two in the entire Enclave, and they'll want to know—" She bit her lip and scooped up her notebook. "I won't let it happen again."

He wanted to laugh at her grave pronouncement, but he knew it would sound too much like mockery. "The only way we can protect you is if you stay together," he said.

"I understand." She brushed off her pants. "I tied my horse to the wagon. It won't take me long to catch up."

"Let's walk," Timon said. He gave a short whistle through his teeth, and Lazarus stepped up to thrust his head between Timon and Jamie. He nibbled on Jamie's hair, and she made a little sound of surprise.

"Lazarus likes you," Timon said. "That's quite a compliment."

"Oh?" she asked with a smile that caught him utterly off guard. "Is he so fearsome, then?"

"Only to enemies."

She cupped her hand over the horse's nose. "He's a very fine horse."

"Is that your vast experience talking?"

Her smile faded. "Are you teasing me again?"

"I know that you've spent your entire life in the Enclave, curing human diseases."

"Looking for cures, yes." She began to walk after the last wagon. "It's a very slow process."

"And you've been happy inside your laboratory?" Timon asked, falling in behind her with Lazarus in tow.

She stopped abruptly and met his gaze. "We don't know each other very well, Mr. Timon, but I don't imagine that my happiness can be of much concern to you."

"You value learning for its own sake."

She pushed her hair away from her face, leaving a smudge of dirt across her temple. It only enhanced her beauty. "You speak as if the desire to learn is a freakish aberration," she said.

He raised his hands in a gesture of surrender. "Easy," he said. "I didn't mean to offend you."

"You didn't," she said in an offhand manner that was far from convincing.

He brought Lazarus to stand beside her. "We're falling farther behind." He stretched out his hand. "Ride with me."

High color flooded her cheeks again, but when he looked into her eyes, he knew it wasn't from fear. He felt a jolt of awareness spark between them.

The feeling passed in an instant, but Timon knew in that instant everything had changed. Now he could hear the rapid beat of her heart, sense the blood pumping through veins and arteries; he felt drawn to her in a way he never had before, not even when he'd first met her. And she stared at him as if she had never seen his face, her tongue darting out to wet her lips, her eyes wide with sudden realization.

He was certain Jamie had never been with any man. But she was overwhelmed by feelings her rational mind clearly didn't comprehend. Yet her body knew the truth, on a very primal level that had nothing to do with logic. She was just beginning to grasp what it told her.

And she was fighting that knowledge with every scrap of determination she possessed.

Perhaps that was why she took his hand, let him pull her up behind him into the saddle and put her arms around his waist as he urged Lazarus into a gentle canter. She had something to prove to herself.

Timon could guess what it was. She had set herself the task of observing, of remaining objective. Any strong emotion—fear, anger, desire most of all—interfered with that task.

As they rode, Timon felt her breath on the nape of his neck, the press of her breasts against his back, the roundness of her thighs rocking behind his. He could smell her hair and her skin and her clothing, a rich mélange of intoxicating scents it was impossible to ignore.

He slowed Lazarus as they caught up to Jamie's mount, who nickered and tossed his head in greeting. Timon helped Jamie dismount and watched her climb into the saddle.

"You do that very well," he said.

"Thank you," she said, her voice perfectly steady. "The technique isn't so difficult to learn, once you understand it."

"And what do you do when you can't understand something?"

"I keep working until I do."

Timon wondered if she'd put so much effort into learning the joys of lovemaking. It would be another new world for her to explore, and the man who guided her through that world…

Would not be him. Jamie had far more sense than he did. He had no business lusting after a woman under his band's care, especially not one who might have some kind of obligation to another man.

Even an arrogant bastard like Cahill.

"Thank you," she said, calling him back to himself.

"For what?" he asked, keeping Lazarus well away from her mount as they rode side by side.

"For what you did last night. For making sure I was all right."

He looked straight ahead, ignoring the dust rising from the track ahead of them. "It's my business," he said.

"But I *was* afraid."

"You can't be brave without fear."

"You speak as if you know what that feels like."

The conversation was becoming too personal for Timon's liking. He began to pull ahead.

"Don't fall behind again," he called over his shoulder.

If she answered, he didn't hear. He kicked Lazarus into a gallop and shot forward along the column, past Parks and Cahill and up to the Rider who had taken the lead. Orpheus glanced at Timon, raised his eyebrows, and waited companionably for Timon to fall in beside him.

"Trouble with the humans?" he asked.

Timon schooled his features. "Nothing we can't handle," he said.

Orpheus tossed long blond hair out of his eyes. "It's true that I've never seen you have any difficulties with women before."

With a brief laugh, Timon scratched Lazarus between the ears. "If you're referring to Parks's goddaughter, you've lost your mind."

"She is rather beautiful, if you like the quiet type," he said. "Which, come to think of it, you usually don't."

Timon wanted nothing more but to set off on a hard ride well ahead of the column, just to clear his mind and feel the freedom of nothing but open space before him. "The problem with Ms. McCullough," he said, "is that she's inexperienced enough to be reckless with her own safety."

"Ah." Orpheus nodded as if he understood everything perfectly. "Well, we knew what we were getting into."

"I've seen no sign that any of them guessed that the raiders were our own people in disguise," Timon said.

"Why should they?" Orpheus glanced over his shoulder. "We needed a way of learning their secrets, and now they think they owe us their lives. They'll be that much more cooperative."

"It'll have to be done very carefully," Timon said, a bitter taste in his mouth.

"I've already spoken to most of the people in the delegation, and a few look promising. But if you have a rapport with the McCullough girl, you should exploit it. Especially if she *is* so inexperienced."

Timon wiped his mouth with the back of his hand. "I don't like it," he said. "Cassius never told us who hired us to spy on these people. That isn't what we do, Orpheus."

"I know." Orpheus shrugged. "Our first mission is to get these humans safely to New Mexico. If the San Francisco delegation means some harm to the Conclave, it's bound to become obvious over the next two months."

"The fate of the Conclave isn't our business."

"We're Riders. We don't take sides. But we can't pretend that a permanent peace won't affect us."

"*If* it happens, there's no point in worrying about it."

"And there's the Timon I know. I was beginning to think you'd turned into Cassius."

"He can have the leadership as long as we have our freedom."

"But we still have our duty," Orpheus said.

Timon wheeled Lazarus around. "We'll make camp in two hours. I'll send Bardas ahead to meet the three who are rejoining us."

He rode back the way he'd come, Orpheus's words echoing in his head. *If you have a rapport with the girl, you should exploit it.*

His duty. If he chose to exploit the intense attraction between him and Jamie, he would be turning her apparent innocence against her. Surely *she* couldn't know about any dangerous "secrets" hidden by the delegation.

But if she *did*…

He paused briefly to speak with Parks, ignored Cahill and looked for Jamie again. She was riding beside the two other medics, showing them her notebook as she chattered enthusiastically about some sketch she had made.

He had more than enough skill to seduce her, especially when she obviously had little defense against such attentions. Still, he didn't know if that was the best way to get close enough to her to question her without giving up the game. A game he most certainly didn't want to play.

He was bound by the Brotherhood's oath to protect her as well as all the others in the delegation. But who would protect her from *him*?

Chapter 4

"Stay away from him, Jamie."

Greg jerked on the reins, causing his horse to toss her head. Jamie pressed her lips together. Letting Greg have his say was usually the fastest way to get rid of him. And she didn't want to get into another argument with him.

Especially not over Timon.

"I mean it," Greg said. "These Riders may have a reputation for objectivity, but I don't trust this Timon as far as I can throw him. He spends too much time with you, and for no good reason."

Jamie lost her patience. "He knows the world, Greg, and I want to learn about it."

"The world? Oh, yes, they're worldly, the Riders. Everyone knows they keep lovers wherever they travel."

Her throat went dry. "It's nothing like that. He's curious about our Enclave, and—"

"What are you telling him?" Greg interrupted. "He doesn't have any need to know more about us than he already does. None of them do."

Watching a passing hawk cross the sky, Jamie sighed inwardly. This wasn't going to go away. And she wasn't going to change her behavior just because Greg was jealous.

Does he have reason to be? she asked herself. It wasn't as if she and Timon had ever discussed anything truly intimate. Yes, she'd managed to give away her unease about being bitten, but she'd never let on how attractive she found Timon, how he could draw her like a moth to a flame even when she feared what he was doing to her with every moment they spent together.

"It's only natural that he'd want to know about an Enclave he's never visited," she said, clearing her thoughts. "Every human city-state is different, and I have the opportunity to learn about the ones *he's* visited."

"This isn't about exchanging information," Greg said, extending his arm to grab her wrist. "I won't let you—"

He broke off, yelping in surprise as Timon rode up beside them, grasped his hand and lifted it from Jamie's. She already knew how strong the Rider was, part of his half-Opir heritage.

But he'd never used that strength against anyone in the delegation. Greg snatched his hand away and pulled his horse's head sharply to the side, earning a squeal of protest from the mare.

"Are you all right?" Timon asked Jamie.

Shaking with reaction, Jamie stared at him. "It wasn't necessary for you to interfere," she said.

"He was hurting you, wasn't he?"

"Not at all," she said quickly. "We were having an—"

"Argument?" Timon finished. "You seem to have them often."

"That's between me and the Senator."

"Is it normal in your Enclave for men to dominate their women with threats?"

"I'm not his woman," she said, flushing.

"But you have an understanding."

Somehow the subject of her relationship with Greg had never come up between them before. Jamie realized she had been avoiding it, as if merely talking about it would make it more real.

"I don't know what you would call it," she said quietly. "It's more of an—"

"Engagement," Greg interrupted, keeping her horse between him and Timon. "For the past two years."

Timon gave Greg a hard look. "Is that true, Jamie?"

She closed her eyes, shutting out Greg's angry face. "My godfather would like us to be married."

"But you don't want to be."

"How dare you," Greg spat. "My relationship with Ms. McCullough is none of your business."

"If there's trouble between members of the delegation, it *is* my business," Timon said. "It could jeopardize my mission."

"There's no trouble," Jamie said, recognizing that she had to put a stop to this irrational hostility.

"I want you to stay away from her," Greg said to Timon.

"You don't own me, Greg," Jamie said, surprising herself with her boldness. "And we *aren't* engaged."

Greg fell into a shocked silence. She had never spoken to him that way. She'd always let him win the battles, because it didn't seem to make much difference one way or another.

He'd been one of her few friends since childhood. And if he'd changed over the years, become more overbearing since his appointment as Senator, she'd accepted it.

But no one had ever told her his behavior was unacceptable. No one had ever interfered, until Timon.

Suddenly, Jamie felt a sense of freedom. It was as if Timon's words and actions had given her a glimpse into a part of herself she had left behind a long, long time ago.

"Excuse me," she said, giving her gelding a little kick. "I need some time to myself."

Neither of the men came after her as she rode forward, nearly to the head of the column where Timon's colleague Orpheus rode point. She stopped before she passed him, not wanting to call more attention to herself, and rode a little way off to the side, into the long, unsullied grass.

She let her mind drift as the gelding clopped along at an

easy pace. The sun was warm on her skin, and birds sang from the marsh at the southern end of San Francisco Bay. Ahead lay the extensive ruins of San Jose and its outlying suburbs; once the party had gone beyond them, they'd be following old Highway 101 another thirty miles until they reached the junction where they'd turn inland toward the great Central Valley.

But Jamie was thinking about the end of the journey, and the great work to be done there. Work Eileen would have done had she not died twenty years ago.

You would have loved this, Mother, she thought sadly. *We could have shared so much.*

At least she had the journal. It was close to her heart, the words inside it a comfort to her when she was sad or confused. As she was now.

That night she sat some distance from the fire, not quite cold enough to surrender her privacy. She could see her godfather casting several worried looks her way; she couldn't bring herself to tell him about her quarrel with Greg or Timon's interference. Amos would be so disappointed…

"Good evening," Timon said. He stood slightly behind her, making no attempt to sit, and gazed toward the fire.

Jamie knotted her hands together in her lap. "Hello," she said.

There was no particular encouragement in the word, but Timon remained where he was. After an awkward silence, he said, "Do you want to marry him?"

Her muscles went stiff. Timon had no reason to bring the subject up again. Greg was right about that; it wasn't any of his business.

"You won't have to worry about our arguing anymore," she said.

"You agreed to stay away from me?" he asked, his voice without inflection.

"That doesn't seem to be possible," she said.

"Do you want me to leave?"

She didn't. That was the problem. Even now she could feel his vital heat at her back, imagine his strong, agile body standing relaxed and yet ready for any danger, envision his eyes glittering in the darkness.

"I wouldn't have interfered if he hadn't been hurting you," Timon said.

"I understand," Jamie said. She rubbed her arms. "You might as well sit down."

Timon eased himself to the ground beside her, supple as a cat.

"Will you answer my question?" he asked.

"I don't know," she said.

"You don't know if you'll answer it?"

"I don't know if I want to marry him."

"What is he to you?"

"A very old and dear friend."

"Then you don't love him."

His statement was worse than just impertinent. He seemed to think he could see what was in her mind.

"What do you know about love?" she demanded.

Timon leaned back on his elbows, stretching his long legs out in front of him. "Marriage usually requires love, doesn't it?"

"Your kind doesn't marry, or even allow women to join your Brotherhood. I doubt that you're any kind of authority on the subject."

Low laughter hummed in his chest. "You're right," he said. "What I know I've picked up from a hundred missions to human Enclaves and mixed colonies throughout the West. But the love-and-marriage situation seems to be about the same in all of them."

"And why are you so interested in something that will never involve you in any way? Don't Riders usually stay Riders for life?"

"Yes."

"And *you* certainly don't have time to love anyone."

"We're not monks, Jamie."

His voice was amused, but the words were pointed, and Jamie's heart kicked inside her ribs.

"I don't think we share the same definition of love," she said, regretting the words as soon as she'd spoken them.

"But there can be so many definitions. You love your parents, don't you?"

"My parents are dead."

"I'm sorry."

He sounded as if he meant it. Though Darketans had originally been raised in barracks as soldier-agents in the Citadels, never permitted to see their Opir mothers or human fathers, that had changed in recent years. Matings that had once been considered shameful in the Citadels were no longer quite so rare, and many mixed couples fled the Opir cities to raise their children in freedom.

It was possible that Timon had lived with his parents, grown up in something like a normal family. Jamie very much wanted to know. She wanted to know everything about him, all the personal things they hadn't discussed.

But she wasn't prepared to risk giving too much in return for what she might get.

"Please don't interfere between me and Greg again," she said, rising to her feet. "I can deal with him."

"By letting him believe you feel more than you do?" Timon got up slowly. "If there's one thing I've learned about you, Jamie, it's that you don't play games. If you don't want the man, let him go."

They stared at each other, and Jamie could see a flame burning in the back of his eyes.

They'd known each other only a handful of days, spent a few hours riding together and speaking in generalities of her world and his. Until today, the question of any kind of love, carnal or otherwise, had never come up between them.

But Timon had made it very plain. *We're not monks*, he had said. Greg had warned her. If she'd had any doubts before she'd left the Enclave, Jamie understood now just how vulnerable she was to the same physical desires that drove most other people, human or otherwise. Desires she hardly knew how to act on. She knew that Greg thought of her as an innocent, even though as a scientist she was not nearly as naive as he guessed. She certainly felt something for Timon, but she'd never made any attempt to appear attractive to him. She had no idea how to compel a man's interest, let alone how to seduce one.

Even if it didn't make any sense to her, Timon wanted her. If she gave in, if she let him see her feelings, she knew exactly where it would lead. They would end up together behind some tree or in the remains of some ruined building.

I can't, she thought. She believed in logic, not in some kind of animal lust that couldn't be controlled.

"Don't be afraid of me, Jamie," Timon said, perfect comprehension in his eyes.

"No," she said, her mouth dry.

"Jamie, wait."

Turning awkwardly, she strode away from the fire and into the wild shrubs and low trees to the west of the track. If she could just break contact with him for a few moments, clear her senses and regain her composure…

A hand clamped over her lips from behind. Instinctively she struggled, but the grubby fingers filled her mouth, and the body that held her was far too strong.

Still, she kicked, and the man yelped. She was free for an instant before the world went black.

Chapter 5

Timon heard the attack before he saw it. He'd gone into the bushes after Jamie when the first shouts came, and he turned back for the wagons with his rifle in hand.

This attack was not fake. Timon's night vision showed him that the raiders bearing down on the delegates were almost certainly full-blood humans, tribesmen with long beards and animal-skin clothing. They rode toward the wagons with whoops and hollers, waving axes and a few rusted guns.

The battle was fully engaged before Timon joined it, and the delegate's human soldiers were fighting alongside the Riders. Timon crouched near one of the wagons and took careful aim, downing an attacker before he could grab the Senator's aide.

They're after the women, Timon thought as a second raider charged the young medic named Akesha. The male nearly had her by the hair when Orpheus slammed his horse into the raider's, knocking the bearded man from his saddle. Timon faced down the two raiders who were still threatening both women, circling like scrawny wolves around a pair of yearling fawns. He raised his rifle again, while Orpheus loosed one of his arrows into a raider's shoulder.

Then, all at once, the attackers were turning, fleeing, kicking their mounts into a frenzied gallop across the valley toward the hills in the west. The Riders chased them, firing their rifles and arrows, while Timon dismounted and plunged back into the brush where Jamie had disappeared earlier.

She wasn't there. But Timon quickly read the signs of struggle in torn earth and snapped branches. He followed hoofprints for a dozen yards and then stopped, cursing himself for his own stupidity.

The raiders had been after women. And Jamie had been alone.

Timon rode back to the column to take reports from his men. Akesha had been wounded but not seriously. The two other women in the delegation, the Senator's aide and one of the soldiers, were shaken but unharmed; Greg Cahill was berating one of the Enclave soldiers for failing to protect them well enough.

After gathering his gear and strapping it onto Lazarus's back, Timon assembled his men near the front of the column. Amos Parks ran up behind him, sweating and pale.

"Where is Jamie?" he panted, drawing his hand across his forehead. "I can't find her!"

"I think she's been taken," Timon said. Lazarus shifted under the pressure of his knees, and he tried to relax. "I last saw her off the side of the road, and there are signs of struggle."

"Then you must go after her!" Parks said. "Good God, what they might do to her—"

"They won't hurt her," Timon said through his teeth. "Women are highly valued by these human raiders."

"And how long do you think they'll leave her untouched?"

Not long enough, Timon thought. Not once they'd established who among their foul tribe would own and have the right to impregnate her. A deep and unfamiliar rage made the blood pound in his temples, and he remembered his own kidnapping when he was a child, terrified of the strange Freebloods who had taken him from his father.

"I'm going after her," he said.

"Timon, our brothers still haven't arrived," Orpheus said, controlling his own agitated mount. "If you leave, there'll be only three of us to protect the column."

"Our brothers may arrive anytime."

"Or not at all," Orpheus said. "Something has delayed them. They might even be dead."

"How likely is that?" Parks said, a note of desperation in his voice. "She's my goddaughter, but she also has skills valuable to the Conclave. You can't expect us to go on without her!"

Timon met the eyes of each of his men. They hadn't been blind these past several days. They knew this wasn't merely a matter of weighing the safety of the group against the life of one of its members.

But they also knew what their leader should choose. The mission was all-important. Nothing could stand in its way.

Except the woman he couldn't abandon.

"Orpheus," he said, "you're in command. Work with the human soldiers. You know what to do—take them through the pass to the Central Valley as quickly as you can, and watch for ambush. We'll catch up with you when we can."

No one spoke. Parks moved up beside Lazarus and gripped Timon's hand.

"Thank you," he said. "I know you'll find her and keep her safe."

Timon met his gaze. "Do as Orpheus says, Councilman Parks."

Without another word, he turned Lazarus about and set out toward the western hills.

He rode slowly through the dark, letting Lazarus find his way, and listened for any sound of men.

Once he reached the spring-green slopes of oak-covered hills, he took the path of least resistance along a creek bed. The shoeless hoofprints of the human raiders' horses were clearer now, pushed into the soft earth and leaving splattered mud to either side of a rough trail.

They obviously didn't expect anyone to come after them, Timon thought. Their tracks wound higher to the crest of the third ridge of hills and then sharply down into a narrow valley, a dry creek bed running along the bottom.

Timon dismounted under the cover of down-swept oak branches and rested his hand on Lazarus's muzzle to keep him quiet. There were horses below, and smoke rising from beneath the creek-side trees. He could smell cooking meat and the scent of infrequently washed bodies.

This was their encampment, then. If it was like most that Timon had seen in his wanderings, it would be a temporary dwelling with tents taking the place of permanent buildings and a rough way of life.

If he was right, these people were bent on increasing their numbers, and they were perpetually short of females. They would raid where they could, and when they'd exhausted their supplies of game and possible captives, they'd move on.

He knew Jamie was down there—afraid but undoubtedly defiant. But the sun was rising; it would be foolish for Timon to approach now, when the raiders would most likely shoot him on sight.

He couldn't get Jamie out by any direct approach. There would likely be a scout or hunter or two roaming around these hills, and if he could find one of them, he'd be able to gain more information about the camp and any weak spots. By sunset, he had to be ready to strike.

Mounting again, he guided Lazarus back down the hill and into another narrow valley, this one barely more than a cleft between two steep slopes. He fed Lazarus a little grain and then ground-tied the horse before climbing the hill again on foot. He lay on his belly and observed the camp through his field glasses, noting when people emerged from beneath the cover of the trees, men tending horses or patrolling the borders of the camp.

Timon only had to wait an hour before a mounted man left the camp and urged his horse to climb the hill on the opposite side of the valley. The sun was still angled low, and the shadows were long. Timon slid back down the hill, mounted Lazarus and worked his way up the side of the cleft until he reached the top of slope at the northern end. Seeking the cover of the nearest trees, he dismounted again and led Lazarus in the direction the scout had gone.

He found the man soon enough. The raider was tall and gaunt, festooned with leather and the furs of raccoon, fox and bobcat. Unlike most of the raiders Timon had seen, he was clean-shaven—a sign of lower status—and wore a deerskin hat with a fox's tail trailing down his back. His horse stood a little distance away, tied to the branch of a tall shrub.

As Timon watched from cover, the man removed a stick from his mouth and swung his well-worn rifle up to aim at some animal moving in the brush to the west.

Timon drew his knife and crouched low, stalking the man as the raider stalked his prey. The human never heard him. Timon grabbed him from behind, covering the man's mouth with one hand while batting the rifle away with the other.

The human fought back with wiry strength, biting down on Timon's hand with brown teeth. Timon's gloves took the worst of it, but the man's jaw was strong, used to eating tough and stringy meat. Once he freed his hand, Timon punched the raider in the face, snatched up the rifle and threw it as far away as he could under the trees. The raider opened his mouth to call out.

Timon struck him in the temple with the butt of his knife. The raider collapsed, still breathing but too dazed to fight. Timon sheathed his knife and dragged the man into the trees, then ran back to collect the human's uneasy horse.

Lazarus knew better than to greet the other animal with more than a brief touch of muzzles. But he had a soothing effect on his fellow horse, and Timon was free to concentrate on its rider.

The man stank, but Timon had been exposed to worse many times in his years as a Rider. It was the thought of Jamie in the clutches of a creature like this that fed his rage. He used rope from his gear to bind the man's hands and feet, and then waited for him to regain full consciousness.

Timon's knife was at the man's throat when he opened his eyes.

"Quiet," he said, careful to prick just the skin of the man's neck. "I need information from you. If you give it to me, I won't hurt you."

The raider puckered his lips and spat in Timon's face. "Bloodsucker," he whispered.

Timon wiped the spittle from his face. "A woman was brought to your camp," he said. "Is she all right?"

With an abrupt shift of his body, the raider tried to butt Timon's head. Timon leaned back, rocked forward again and gave the man another taste of his blade.

"You will tell me what I want to know," Timon said, shifting the knife much lower, "or I'll do worse than slit your throat."

As Timon had expected, the raider feared losing a certain part of his anatomy more than death. He talked.

Jamie was safe, for now. She was being held in the tent of the man who had taken her during the raid, but he was being challenged by several members just as eager to claim a mate.

She would have absolutely no say in the matter.

"*You* have no woman," Timon said to the prisoner.

The raider turned his face aside.

"Were you planning to challenge for her?"

Maintaining his silence, the man stared into the woods. But Timon understood his position perfectly. This young male's only chance of increasing his status was by gaining a mate.

If he hadn't challenged yet, it still wasn't too late.

Chapter 6

Night had fallen again by the time Timon rode into the camp, a deer's carcass slung over his borrowed horse's back. In the hills above, his prisoner had been bound and gagged. Lazarus, however little he liked being parted from his rider, remained where Timon had left him.

Timon was fortunate. The captive raiders' eyes were pale, like Timon's, the color difficult to make out in the torch-lit darkness, and Timon's hair was covered by the fox-tailed hat. His masquerade may just work.

The men gathered around the several campfires either grunted brief acknowledgment or ignored him entirely. He scanned the camp, noting the positions of the tents, and located the place where the raiders prepared their meat. He led his horse to the fire and, keeping his face averted, unloaded the carcass and hung it over a pole near the fire.

Almost at once a woman in a ragged dress came scurrying out of the nearest tent to examine the carcass. Timon took the opportunity to retreat, walking with the kind of uneasy familiarity of a low-status hunter. He tied his mount near the string of horses toward the rear of the camp and melted into the deeper shadows under the trees.

He took a deep breath, trying to sort the overwhelming scents from the one that belonged to Jamie. It was an impossible task, even for a half-blood with an excellent sense of smell. He looked over the tents, noting which were the largest and most prominently situated. Men gathered about the outside of several of them, like warriors standing guard in front of palace gates.

Only one of the smaller tents had a similar retinue, with the men outside looking far less like guards and more like a hostile force.

The challengers, Timon thought. Jamie must be inside, along with her captor.

It took all Timon's discipline not to rush straight at the tent and take on the six men. *Jamie hasn't been touched*, he reminded himself. She was far too valuable a prize, and if her captor moved on her without accepting challenge, he'd likely be torn limb from limb.

If only Timon could tell her she wasn't alone.

Even as he completed the thought, a short, muscular man emerged from the tent. He growled at his challengers, who muttered threats and brandished knives and axes.

Pushing his way through them, Jamie's kidnapper walked into the center of the camp and began to speak. The meaning of the rough words, Timon thought, didn't really matter; their purpose was to boast of his strength and his prowess, to scare off lesser challenges and reinforce his claim over the female.

Apparently there would be no waiting for the fighting to start.

Someone bellowed, and the first duel began. In spite of the earlier display of weapons, the two men fought hand to hand, viciously and with no apparent rules to constrain them. The men seemed equally matched in height and musculature, but it was soon obvious that Jamie's captor was stronger. Using little more than brute strength, he battered his challenger down to the ground and used both fists and feet to pummel the man into unconsciousness.

A heavy silence fell. The other challengers shifted and grumbled. A pair of boys dragged the unconscious man away.

Then another man, bearing a wicked-looking knife in

one hand, flung himself at Jamie's kidnapper. A knife appeared in the first raider's hand, and the second battle commenced with quiet and deadly ferocity.

It ended much the same as the first, but this time the challenger didn't get off so easily.

Again there was silence. Two of the remaining challengers withdrew, heads bowed. The victor shouted hoarsely, mocking the others for their cowardice.

Timon knew that he couldn't put it off any longer. Lowering his head under the hat and drawing up the fur collar of his coat, he stalked toward his opponent. The victor grinned, showing half-rotten teeth, and beckoned the man he believed Timon to be.

He obviously wasn't expecting much. He lunged at Timon with his large, long arms, as if he planned to break Timon's back. Timon slipped out of his reach, darted underneath the man's arms and butted him hard in the stomach. Confused by the suddenness of the attack, the man staggered back, holding his ribs.

But Timon knew it wasn't nearly enough. His enemy recovered quickly and punched at Timon's jaw. Again Timon was faster, and he landed a blow to the man's face and followed up by heaving the tribesman to the ground.

There were murmurs of surprise from the watchers, undoubtedly wondering at their fellow tribesman's unusual strength. Timon knew he didn't dare drag the fight out much longer.

As soon as Jamie's captor was on his feet again, Timon kicked his knees out from under him and dislocated both of his shoulders. Wailing in pain and rage, the man rolled onto his back. His efforts to rise failed over and over again, and after a time he lay still, his thickly bearded face a mask of fury and humiliation.

Checking to make sure that his hat was still in place, Timon turned to face the few remaining challengers. They looked from him to his opponent and, one by one, melted into the shadows. Timon turned and tossed back the tent flap, entering before any of the tribesmen could change his mind.

"Jamie!" he whispered.

She sat on the ground, bound to the tent pole, ropes digging into her wrists and ankles. Her lip was cut and bleeding, her hair tangled and wild around her shoulders. Her clothing was torn, and there was a heavy bruise on one cheek.

Timon swore, longing to charge back outside and treat her captor to a little more serious punishment.

"Timon?" she said, her voice hoarse. "Is it you?"

He was at her side in an instant, cutting through the ropes with his knife. "It's me," he said. "Are you all right?"

"They didn't hurt me."

Oh, no, Timon thought. The brutes had only handled her like a piece of livestock, hitting and terrorizing her with promises of worse to come.

But when he looked in Jamie's eyes, he saw determination. And hope.

"We're getting out of here," he said. "Can you run?"

"I heard fighting," she said as she rubbed her wrists. "Did you—"

"I defeated the man who captured you. He's off his feet, but there's no guarantee." He grunted and finished freeing her ankles. "No time to talk. We're going out the back, and hope they don't see us until we're out of this valley."

He helped her to her feet. She staggered against him, and for a moment he simply held her, feeling the rapid beat of her heart and the stirring in his own.

"Can you run?" he asked again.

"I can do whatever is necessary."

"Then let's go," he said. He ran to the rear of the tent and used his knife to cut a new flap in the patchwork of homespun fabric and deerskin. He went out first, paused to listen, and then grabbed Jamie's hand.

The tent was backed against the slope of one of the hills, partially sheltered by the twisted limbs of an oak. Timon pushed Jamie behind the wide trunk, took her hand again and began to climb, constantly listening for sounds of pursuit.

Jamie struggled but never gave up, her hands and feet clawing at the earth as she focused on the crest of the hill. She and Timon had almost reached the place where Timon had left Lazarus and his captive's horse when the cries started from the camp, echoing up into the woods.

Timon almost threw Jamie into Lazarus's saddle before taking the other horse, knowing that she'd have a better chance with a Rider's mount than that of a tribesman. His horse was about as gaunt as its former owner, but it felt Timon's experience and obeyed willingly as Timon gave Lazarus the command to run.

They crossed the ridge, the shouts of the men behind them, and plunged down into the next narrow ravine, splashing through a creek that still carried a trickle of water. Timon whistled to Lazarus, signaling him to take the lead, and he fell behind again, preparing his rifle.

After following the creek for a good quarter mile, Timon turned his mount up the slope. Lazarus climbed ahead of him, Jamie clinging like a burr to his back. The sounds of pursuit grew louder again. The horses galloped full-out along the ridge and into another dense stand of oak and underbrush. The wider Santa Clara valley lay below, a grassy expanse broken only by the occasional low hill or clump of trees.

The tribesmen knew these hills; they preferred the protection the higher ground afforded, but Timon had no doubt that they'd follow him and Jamie onto the plain.

He pushed the horses on to the foot of the final hill and

brought them to a halt beneath a single oak at the edge of the valley. "Stay on Lazarus," he commanded Jamie. "If we can't stop them here, you run. Lazarus is very fast and strong. He can outrun the tribesmen's mounts easily. You have to ride low and stay on until there's no one left chasing you. Cross the valley to the old highway and the pass through the hills to the east. Do you understand?"

"Yes," she said. "But I won't leave you."

"I've fought these kinds of men many times in the past. If they take you, your life will be slavery and degradation." He checked his rifle again. "I didn't come after you to see you fall to that."

"You shouldn't have come," she said, her thick, dark hair falling over her face. "You should have stayed with the others, to protect them."

"Get behind the tree, and be ready to run at my signal."

But he knew she wouldn't. She wouldn't abandon him because she believed she owed him her life. And so he would have to make sure that their pursuers lost their nerve before they got to the bottom of the hill.

Crouching behind a thorny bush, Timon took aim. The first of the enemy riders crested the hill and began to descend at a breakneck pace. Timon shot the ground just ahead of the first horse, who squealed and hopped to the side, unseating his rider. Another tribesman, close behind, took a shot at Timon, but the bullet fell short. Timon returned the favor by shooting the man in the shoulder.

After that, the rest of the world went away. Timon saw nothing but the enemy, felt nothing but the rifle in his hands. Bullets whizzed past him, some close enough to stir the air near his body. He continued to fire, aiming, as most Riders did, to wound rather than kill, scaring the horses into throwing their riders.

It took a moment for him to realize when the tribesmen began to retreat, some on foot with their horses temporarily lost to panic and fear. A few paused to help their wounded; one man screamed threats down at Timon and shook his fist ineffectually before plodding uphill.

Ineffectual for now, perhaps. But Timon knew that Jamie was too great a prize for the tribesmen to simply give up. They'd try again.

Setting his rifle aside, Timon crawled backward to the base of the tree trunk. Lazarus peeked around and nickered, his ears swiveling back.

Jamie was slumped on the ground just behind Lazarus, her wrist bent oddly, blood flowing steadily from the bullet wound in her outer thigh. Her eyes were closed. Timon dropped to his knees beside her and felt for her pulse. It was a little thready but still regular. He cursed steadily as he examined the wound. The bullet had passed in and out of muscle, and hadn't nicked any major blood vessels. But she was still bleeding freely, and her wrist appeared to be fractured, possibly a result of her falling out of the saddle. Only the luckiest of shots could have caught her without also wounding Lazarus.

He knew he had to stop the bleeding, bind Jamie's wound and splint her arm. He had his medical kit and oak branches littering the ground around him, but he'd only be able to do a quick fix under the circumstances. He needed to find them a place where he could give full attention to her injuries without fear of attack.

"Jamie," he said, stroking her cheek. "Can you hear me?"

She moaned softly, and her eyelids fluttered.

"Lie very still. You're injured, but I'm going to do what I can so we can get out of here quickly and find a better hiding place. It's going to hurt."

"I…know." She reached out with her good hand, and he gripped it gently. "Do what you have to."

She made barely a sound while he cut a long slit in her pants, carefully lifted her leg atop a heap of saddlebags so that the wound was above her heart and got the bleeding under control. Once the worst of it had stopped, he started a fire and boiled water to clean out the wound before bandaging it with more clean cloth and an outer covering cut from a bedroll.

Tears ran down Jamie's cheeks as he set her wrist, but she never flinched. He bound the wrist and lower forearm to straight, sturdy branches with additional cloth and fashioned a sling with the rest of the blanket.

It seemed little better than butcher's work to Timon, but at least now he could carry her on horseback without worrying that she might bleed to death.

"You're very brave," he told her, "and I'll need you to keep your courage up a little longer. We have to run before the tribesmen come after us again."

She nodded, her face drained of color. "I won't...disappoint you."

"I know you won't," he said. Overwhelmed by a feeling of gratitude and tenderness, he kissed her dirt-smudged forehead. "I'll get the other horse."

But the tribesman's horse had gone lame sometime during the chase, and the best Timon could do was leave him for his previous owners to reclaim. He loaded the saddlebags on Lazarus's back and returned to Jamie.

"Hold on," he said.

He lifted her in his arms and placed her in the saddle, then hopped up behind her. She collapsed against him. He wrapped one arm around her waist, gathered up the reins in his other hand and turned Lazarus toward the valley.

Chapter 7

As Timon had predicted, the raiders began to follow again when he and Jamie were halfway across the valley. But Lazarus had all the heart and courage of the Riders' specially bred horses, and he didn't slow until they reached the hills on the opposite side. The tribesmen never had a chance.

By the time the chase ended, Jamie was deadweight in his arms. Timon found a place in the hills just south of the pass through which the delegates and their escorts would have gone only a short while before. He laid the half-conscious Jamie down under a tree and reexamined the bandages around her thigh.

The wound wasn't bleeding heavily, but the pain would be excruciating, and he doubted she'd ever have experienced anything like it before. He was driving her body to move instead of rest when it had two injuries to heal.

He propped her head on his thighs and urged her to drink from his canteen. Most of the water dribbled down her chin, but a little got into her mouth, and she opened her eyes.

"Where are we?" she whispered.

"Away from the tribesmen," he said. "They won't find us now."

"Thank…God," she said. Her lips twitched. "And thank *you*."

Timon felt deeply uncomfortable with her gratitude. Protecting the Enclave delegates was, after all, his job. If he'd observed well enough in the first place, this never would have happened.

He didn't like owing anything to anyone, nor did he like others owing *him*. If she felt there was a debt to be repaid…

Then she'll trust you, he thought. *Isn't that what you want?*

"Lie still," he said. "Your body has suffered multiple shocks, and you need rest."

She moved as if she was trying to sit up, then fell back with a gasp. "We have to get back to my people," she said. "My godfather—"

"They know I came after you," he said. "We'll meet up with them when we can. But driving yourself now will only increase the risk of your becoming worse."

Jamie swallowed several times. "I understand," she said. "It's just… I wasn't prepared for anything like this."

"I know."

"The…man who took me told me what he was going to do to me, and what would happen to me afterward." Her words came out in a rush. "If I'd done enough research…if I'd paid enough attention, maybe I would have been ready to deal with it. I—"

"No. If I'd explained things more clearly—"

"It wouldn't have made a difference." Tears rolled from the sides of her eyes. "Even after the first attack… I couldn't have imagined such cruelty by humans against their own kind."

Timon didn't know how to answer her. He wet a scrap of cloth with the water and dabbed at the dirt on her forehead. Her skin felt cool, but that could change.

"You shouldn't talk anymore," he said. "If you'll sleep a little, I'll give you something to eat when you wake."

"Sleep?" She coughed out a laugh. "I'm sorry, but… I'm afraid I'm a coward. It hurts too much."

"There's nothing cowardly about you," he said, looking through his med kit for a packet of pills.

"How many of the humans living out here are like that?" she asked.

"Most aren't," he said, trying to ease the sting of her chagrin. "Most only want to survive peacefully, as you do." He picked out one of the pills. "This might help with the pain, but I won't lie to you. You're going to be uncomfortable."

"I'll take…whatever I can get."

He offered the pain pill with a sip of water, and then gave her an antibiotic. His supply was limited, and he had to be careful about the dosage.

"Thank you," she said. She looked into his eyes. "You could have been killed, fighting those men."

"I was lucky. I was able to pose as one of them."

Her nose wrinkled. "I don't think they…bathe very often."

For the first time since her capture, Timon felt like laughing. "I'll change," he said. "I have an extra shirt and pants you can wear, when you're able to put them on."

"You're twice my size," she said. "I can repair my own clothes, if you have a needle and thread."

"Later. Nothing matters now but that you're safe."

"Is it that important?" she asked, closing her eyes.

It seemed to Timon that she was asking herself as much as she was asking him. "*You're* important, Jamie. I know you have a contribution to make to the Conclave, maybe something no one else can."

Her eyes fluttered open, and Timon saw them spark with surprise. "How did you…" She clamped her lips together. "You couldn't."

"Couldn't what, Jamie?"

She fell silent. The sun had grown warm, but suddenly Jamie was shivering. Timon fetched a blanket and tucked her under it.

"No more talk," he said. "While you sleep, I'll keep watch."

"I'm sorry," she sighed.

"No," he said, taking her hand. "You have nothing to be sorry for."

She began to shake her head, exhaled slowly and drifted into sleep.

Timon held her hand a little longer, amazed by its delicacy and softness. It wouldn't be so soft at the end of their journey. Inevitably, she would lose whatever innocence she still had left. But her second capture, so soon after the first, had been a brutal way for her to experience the outside world.

He had lost his innocence much earlier, when he'd been kidnapped as a child by a power-hungry warlord. But even before that, growing up in a mixed human and Opir colony, he'd known how much danger lay beyond the seeming safety of the colony's walls.

But he would regret the hard lessons Jamie had yet to learn. He knew he couldn't afford to allow his personal feelings to get in the way, and yet he felt that if he could have kept Jamie in a bubble, protected from all unpleasantness, he would have done it.

He berated himself for his weakness. He couldn't allow himself to get emotionally involved. He could still take her back to the Enclave.

And she would resist him every step of the way. Fear wouldn't stop her from forging ahead, even though she had only one Rider to protect her.

A Rider who had ulterior motives. Even though he'd already come to hate the idea of manipulating her into giving up information he now had reason to expect she possessed.

This was the time to learn it. When she was vulnerable and dependent on him. When she had begun to trust him.

Rising quickly, Timon walked to the top of the hill. The grass in the valley rippled like water. It was very peaceful.

Timon's heart was not at peace. He had the overwhelming conviction that it never would be again.

Jamie woke at dawn. Timon had built a small fire, sheltered from view by the hills. He crouched beside it, the planes of his face carved of shadow and firelight, his big hands dangling between his knees.

Instinctively, Jamie felt her thigh. The pill had done some good, but the wound throbbed constantly, and her wrist wasn't much better. She felt weak and useless, worth no more than Timon's pity.

She watched Timon as he rummaged through his saddlebags. He wore a homespun shirt and pants with leather insets tucked into his boots, and even from a distance she could tell that the odor of his "disguise" was gone. Each of his movements was efficient and smooth, well-developed muscle working harmoniously and with no extraneous mannerisms.

Had he moved the same way when he'd fought for her in the tribesmen's camp, with such ease and grace? He'd overcome her captor, gotten her away, treated her injuries. She was completely dependent on him and his considerable skill.

Her face felt flushed, and she touched her cheeks. They were warm…with embarrassment, she thought. No matter how many times he told her she wasn't at fault.

"You're awake," he said, turning as he spoke. He smiled, and the strong lines of his face relaxed. "Are you feeling better?"

"Yes," she said, though she wasn't sure it was really true. Her stomach grumbled loudly enough for him to hear, and she winced. "Thanks to you."

"You've already thanked me," he said. He laid his hand

on her forehead, frowned and touched her cheek. There was nothing detached about that second touch. It was almost a caress.

She started in spite of herself. "No sign of the raiders?" she said, her lip cracking open as she spoke the last word.

Timon got up and returned with a small piece of gauze. He dabbed at her lip. "Nothing," he said. "They'd expect us to be long gone by now."

"We should be," she said, making an effort to rise. "We can't stay here."

His violet-gray eyes gazed into hers with a calm wisdom that made her feel self-conscious all over again. "We'll only move when you're up to it," he said, "and that won't be today."

Rising again, Timon fetched a tin plate filled with a kind of gruel and a strip of dried meat. "I'm sorry this is all I have to offer," he said. "But I was only able to bring my own packs with me, and I haven't had the chance to hunt. Do you think you can eat?"

Jamie nodded, her gut rebelling at the sight of the gruel. She let Timon feed her, though she began to resent every spoonful that went into her mouth.

"I still have one hand," she protested.

"I don't want you moving around any more than you have to."

"There are some things you can't help me with."

He grinned, showing his pointed cuspids. "I've lived most of my life on the move. Do you think something like that would bother me?"

"You only travel with men," she said.

"But I've known plenty of women," he said, an almost mischievous light glittering in his eyes. "Biology is biology. If you think you can manage it, I'll help you get up."

"You just said you didn't want me to move!"

All at once he was serious again. "I would rather you didn't."

With a feeling of queasiness, she imagined him cleaning up after her. *That* was out of the question. "Help me get over to the tree," she said. He half carried her to the tree and gave her a small measure of privacy, though she knew he was alert to the possibility of a fall. She was very careful not to fall.

Then he was easing her to the blanket again, laying her down with exquisite care, with something so much like tenderness that she almost didn't feel the increased pain as her arm and leg touched the ground.

"I'll give you another pill," he said, adjusting her head into a more comfortable position.

"I don't need one," she said with greater asperity than she'd intended.

"You kept insisting that you're a coward who can't stand pain."

"I am," she said, meeting his gaze.

He laughed softly. "Don't ever suggest such foolish things again."

"What—"

"That you aren't one of the most courageous women I've ever known."

"And you said you've known plenty."

She didn't know what had gotten into her. God knew she didn't want to hear the real answer.

"Do you want the details?" he asked, his eyes dancing.

Eager to change the subject, Jamie closed her eyes. "How soon will I be well enough to travel, so that we can catch up with the others? They can't be too far ahead."

"We have to make sure that the arm sets properly and the leg wound remains clean and healing. We'll find a more permanent camp, and stay there for a couple of weeks."

"What?"

"You need plenty of time to heal."

She began to sit up, but Timon was already pressing her down again. "That's too long!"

"Because you're anxious to rejoin your friends?" he asked. "Or is it the fact that you'll be alone with me?"

His bluntness surprised her, and she felt an unfamiliar heat swelling in her belly. "I'm not afraid of anything, remember?" she said.

"Good. Because the last thing I want is for you to have doubts about me." He leaned over her, a quiet ferocity in his voice. "I won't let anything else happen to you. All you have to do is trust me."

The emotions in his eyes were far too complex for her to read. She turned her head away.

"I do trust you," she said. "I don't have any choice."

His sigh told her it wasn't quite what he wanted to hear. "If that's true," he said, "I can suggest a way that might allow us to move a little faster."

She turned her head toward him again. "What?"

"It may not work. But there's a chance, Jamie." He touched her cheek with his fingertips. "All Opiri have a component in their saliva that can heal human wounds. Usually those are the small wounds that come with a bite. But sometimes..." He leaned closer, the subtle colors shifting in his eyes. "I'm only half-Opir. But some of us inherit the healing ability. If I bite you, I may be able to hasten your healing more efficiently than any antibiotic."

Her stomach began to roil with alarm. "Bite me?" she said.

"It's the only way to get the healing component into your bloodstream."

All at once his face changed, became that of a monster, eager to drain her dry. "No," she whispered. "Get away from me."

Chapter 8

Jamie flinched away as Timon jerked back. "Jamie?" he said. "What's wrong?"

All at once his face seemed to shift back to normal—though deeply concerned, uncertain, confused.

"You want to take my blood," Jamie said, anger rushing in to replace horror.

"Take your blood?" Timon backed away and crouched again, studying her face intently. "I didn't say that, Jamie."

"That was part of the bargain, wasn't it? Your Riders' escort for our blood to feed you along the way?"

"What happened when the first raiders took you? Did one of them hurt you?"

She couldn't answer. Though she knew he only wanted to help, the memories had been in her thoughts since the first raiders had captured the delegation. She looked at Timon's face now, and all she could imagine were his sharp, tearing teeth, the feel of them sinking into her flesh.

"Don't worry," Timon said, holding up his hands. "I won't touch you, Jamie. Not without your permission."

"Please, leave me alone."

Timon got to his feet and gazed down at her, his mouth pinched. "I'm going to leave you here for a short time," he said, "and look for a better camp, farther off the main track. Is that all right with you?"

Oak leaves overhead shifted with the breeze, letting through a beam of sunlight. Sunlight the real bloodsuckers couldn't tolerate.

"I'll be fine," she said, avoiding Timon's eyes.

"Don't try to move. Rest as best you can."

"Yes."

"Good." He hesitated, released his breath, and went to fetch Lazarus.

For a while, Jamie did nothing but listen tensely to every sound in her little haven: the slight rustle of fresh green grass just outside the circle of shade, the twitter of a bird, the chirp of an insect. There was no man-made sound anywhere within the range of her hearing, but she fought sleep as long as she could.

Then the dreams came. Timon was carrying her off, taking her away from her people just like the tribesman, his arm clamped around her waist and his expression grimly satisfied. He had claimed her for his own. He would brand her as his, with his body and teeth and his will, and no matter how hard she fought—

She didn't want to fight. God help her; she would give in to everything, anything he wanted. Fear was gone. The barriers of pride and modesty and obligation had fallen under Lazarus's pounding hooves.

"Jamie."

Her eyes flew open. She thrust out her good arm as if to fend Timon off and draw him closer at the same time.

He caught her hand between his. She felt the roughness of his palm, the gentle clasp of his long fingers.

"Easy," he said. "You must have been dreaming."

Her entire body went hot. "I…"

After laying her hand on her chest, he let go and stepped back. "Are you all right?" he asked.

She caught her breath, glad he couldn't actually read her mind. "Did you have any luck?" she asked.

"I found a good place for us deeper in the hills, with more trees and water nearby."

"Can we get there before sundown?"

"If you're up to it."

"Let's go," she said.

"I'll have to touch you, Jamie."

Heat rushed into her face. "I…didn't know what I was saying before. I'm sorry."

"Don't be. You must have good reason."

It had happened eighteen years ago, Jamie thought, and she should have been over it. To confuse Timon with *him*…

Irrational, she thought.

"It's all right," she said. "I'm all right."

She was very careful not to cry out when Timon lifted her into the saddle. Timon watched her face with acute concern, but she thought she managed to fool him. He kept Lazarus at a walk, and even the horse seemed to understand what Timon was trying to do; Lazarus avoided rocks and furrows with precise footwork that amazed her.

They reached the new encampment by midafternoon. Timon carried her to a large oak and positioned her with her back to the trunk, almost as if he knew that she couldn't bear another moment flat on her back. He arranged the remaining equipment nearby, unsaddled Lazarus and then offered her water. She was far thirstier than she remembered having been before and exhausted by the relatively brief ride.

But she said nothing of it. She was grateful when Timon checked her dressings and seemed satisfied. His lean and muscular body relaxed as if he felt more at ease in their new location.

"Tell me about your life in the Enclave," he said.

Startled by the abrupt question, Jamie looked at him. His profile gave nothing away, but she knew he didn't mean to make idle conversation. He was still looking for reasons for her strange behavior, and he wouldn't give up unless she distracted him with other topics.

"What do you want to know?" she asked cautiously.

"About your childhood. Your parents. What you were like when you were younger. What you dreamed of doing and becoming."

"My whole life story," she said, trying to laugh. "Believe me—it isn't very interesting. My mother was a biologist—a geneticist—and my father was a physician. They met while doing similar research at the Enclave Medical Center."

"What kind of research?"

"They never really talked about it. I know they were both interested in recovering the lost pre-War treatments for diseases humanity once thought were wiped out."

"And you carried on in their footsteps."

"I grew up around scientists," she said. "I only went to school until I was ten, and after that my father homeschooled me."

"You didn't have many friends."

It was a statement rather than a question, and Jamie winced. "There weren't many young people my age helping their parents in a lab," she said.

"You were lonely."

"I was too busy to be lonely," she said, irritated at his presumption. "My parents didn't deprive me of anything, if that's what you're thinking."

"But you had at least one friend. Greg Cahill."

She wasn't about to fall into that trap again. "My parents' closest friends were my godfather and Greg's parents," she said. "He always had ambitions to go into politics, and he was very successful."

"So it seems." Timon shifted his weight. "How does *he* feel about the Conclave?"

"He supports it, of course!"

"And you've dedicated yourself to it, even though you've never had to deal with Opiri."

"My parents advocated for a new peace for many years.

My mother spoke of it often, and wrote about it in the journal she left me."

"But you didn't grow up with open war. At worst, Opiri and humans have lived in a state of cold war for most of your life."

"The Citadels stopped claiming serfs from our Enclave five year ago."

"And that's why you think the Conclave can succeed."

"I know that not all Opiri are barbarians."

"In spite of your lack of experience?"

She wished she could stand up and pace away her anger. "Why are you asking these questions? Have we given you any reason to doubt our commitment?"

"I'd heard rumors that the San Francisco Enclave had reservations about this new effort."

"That's outrageous," she said, far more calmly than she felt. "You supposedly have no interest in the outcome of the Conclave. Is this some part of your job, to test how devoted we are to the Conclave's goals?"

His head came up sharply. "I only want to know more about you."

The intensity of his gaze made her feel dizzy and uncertain. "I told you," she said. "There isn't much to tell."

"I think you underestimate yourself," Timon said. "What did you do when you weren't in the lab? Did Greg take you out to dinner in one of your restaurants, or to walk by the Bay?"

Back to Greg again, she thought.

"You said you'd never been to San Francisco," she said, changing the subject.

"I did my research." He looked away. "Did you ever have fun, Jamie?"

"Of course I did. My parents were very cultured. My mother…" She swallowed. "Eileen saw the joy in everything, in every part of the world she saw in the lab or outside it. She died before my father, when I was still a child. He never told me how it happened, and he died when I was sixteen."

"I'm sorry. It must have been difficult to lose both your parents when you were young."

"And you…did you have a family, Timon?"

"I was born in freedom, outside the Citadel," he said. "My mother also died when I was very young."

"I'm sorry. Is your father—"

A muscle twitched in his cheek. "He and his second wife are still living."

"But you're not close to them."

"I'm a Rider. We put those relationships behind us when we join the Brotherhood."

"You ever see them?"

"Not in fifteen years."

She touched his hand. "When did you join the Riders, Timon?"

"I was seventeen." He slid his hand out from under hers. "It's not a very interesting story."

So he didn't want to talk about *his* past, Jamie thought. "Did you run away?"

"I was very young," he said.

Had something his parents done driven him away? Jamie wondered. Something trifling and foolish he'd never admit to? Or had it been a matter of youthful rebellion, the kind she'd never experienced?

Had he had a choice to keep his family, when she'd been robbed of hers?

"Your whole life is the Riders now," she said.

"Yes."

"Your freedom is very important to you, isn't it?"

"Yes. But we have our duties. Our leaders choose our assignments."

"And how do you choose your leaders? Do you fight for your positions, like the Opiri of the Citadels do?"

"We don't fight amongst ourselves," he said, flashing her a reproachful look. "It's a matter of consensus. Except in times of emergency, we hold elections. The highest-ranked Rider is called the captain. He arranges our hiring and holds ultimate authority over us."

"You're the leader of a band. Have you ever wanted to be more?"

"I wouldn't want the responsibility."

Jamie realized that he was being completely honest. He liked his life simple, uncomplicated by binding relationships or the desire to control others.

"Tell me more about your people," she urged. "I already know you serve whoever hires you, regardless of their politics or race. What happens if—"

Moving as quickly and effortlessly as always, Timon got to his feet. "If you're all right," he said, "I have another thing to take care of. It might require a little more time, if you think you can stay alone for a while."

"What is it?" she asked, sucking in her breath as she pushed herself a little more upright against the tree trunk.

"Horses. Lazarus can't carry us both for long stretches of time, so we'll need another mount."

"You plan to go back to the tribesmen?" she asked in alarm.

"No. I saw a small herd of horses not far from here. I'll bring one of them in."

"A wild horse?"

"I suspect they escaped from captivity not too long ago."

"And you think you can tame one well enough for me to ride it?"

"You'll be on Lazarus—when you're ready to ride." He went to saddle the horse and returned to her. "If I can't get one by sunset, I'll return."

Jamie gave no sign that she wished he would stay. Timon knew what had to be done, and she wouldn't be any more of a burden on him than she had to be. If she didn't want him to "heal" her with his bite, she had to do everything else possible to make sure they could move on a soon as possible.

She only wished her leg wasn't hurting quite so much.

"Are you sure you'll be all right?" he said, peering into her face.

"I'll just sleep," she said with a smile. "Good luck."

He accepted her reassurance with a brief nod. "I'll be back as soon as I can."

"Soon" proved to be much longer than Jamie had hoped. As the minutes passed, she began to feel warmer, and her leg continued to grow more painful. When she touched the bandage, it felt warm, as well.

An infection, she thought. That was no surprise, even with the antibiotics. The drugs hadn't really had enough time to work. Undoubtedly the fever and pain would pass in good time.

She closed her eyes and tried to sleep. Sometime later, she woke herself with shivering and pulled the blanket higher up to her chin. She drank from the canteen Timon had left for her and tried to go back to sleep.

The next time, she found herself in darkness. The steady clop of hooves approached from the north.

Timon, she thought, lost in a fog. The rider dismounted, and she heard him kneel beside her. A cool hand touched her forehead and then her bandages.

Jamie screamed.

Chapter 9

"Jamie, can you hear me?" Timon asked.

She tried to turn her head toward him, gasped and whimpered like a child. Timon couldn't tell if she could see him, let alone hear him; her eyes were blank, and the tremors racking her body made it impossible for him to keep her still.

You're delirious," he said, cupping his palm over her burning forehead. "Jamie, why didn't you tell me you were feeling worse?"

She blinked, tears leaking from her eyes. For a moment they focused on his.

"I'm…sorry," she whispered.

"It isn't your fault," he said, stroking her wet hair.

It was his misjudgment to leave her alone even for a few hours. Because he knew that she might have an infection coursing through her body, and without full medical treatment it could kill her.

He could think of only one answer. And he knew that she would fight it.

"Jamie," he said, "concentrate on my voice."

Her body shuddered again. She licked her dry lips, and he wet the last clean rag and placed it on her mouth, dabbing gently.

"You're very sick," he said, swallowing the knot in his throat. "Do you understand?"

She blinked several times.

"I can try to clean out the wound with the tools I have.

But your leg…" He closed his eyes. "You may lose it, even if you survive."

Turning her face away from him, she breathed sharply several times. "It hurts," she said hoarsely.

"I can help with the pain," he said. "Jamie, I want you to live."

She turned her head back, and her cracked lips almost formed a smile. "You…care about me?"

"Yes." He lifted her good hand to his face. "But you'll have to trust me. Can you do that?"

"Yes," she murmured.

Hating the necessity of what he was about to do, Timon took several of the pain pills out of his med kit and offered them to Jamie along with the canteen, supporting her head while she drank. Within fifteen minutes, she was asleep. He shifted her into his arms so that her body lay across his and he had full access to her neck.

His body betrayed him with sudden hunger, and he realized he hadn't taken blood since Akesha had shared with him two days before the tribesmen's attack. There had been nothing remotely intimate about his taking blood from Akesha. But he wanted Jamie in every way.

He suppressed his primitive instincts and concentrated on what he had to accomplish to make her well.

When he bit her neck, she didn't flinch. He was very careful to limit her bleeding, to give instead of take. Even so, he felt like a monster, remembering how she had reacted even to the idea of his biting her.

To the idea of being bitten, he reminded himself. She knew what she'd be facing as payment for this trip…that she'd be expected to donate her blood like the other human delegates.

Yet something or someone had hurt her in the past. The thought that he himself was not the object of her dread didn't ease his heart.

Timon finished, sealed her wound and helped her down onto the blanket. All he could do now was wait, stay beside her, tend her and hope. The taste of her fevered blood was still on his tongue, a part of her in him as part of him now worked within her struggling body.

All through the long night he watched over her, moistening her hot face, making her drink when she briefly regained consciousness, whispering words she needed to hear. He changed her dressing and packed the wound with antibiotic ointment. Her features were distorted with fever and pain, her hair was soaked with perspiration and her body was limp, and yet he still found her beautiful.

"Fight," he told her, again and again. "Fight, for me."

She did. Her crisis came with the dawn. Her body radiated heat, and Timon could feel her slipping away. He lifted her head into the circle of his arms and kissed her forehead and her cheeks.

"Stay," he said. "Stay with me."

And then he kissed her mouth, lips barely touching lips. She shivered violently and began to thrash, the tendons in her neck standing out, her lovely blue eyes staring into some indescribable horror.

"Don't hurt me," she whimpered. "I won't…tell anyone." Her head rolled from side to side. "Let me go. No. Don't." Her voice rose to a wail. "Don't! Please!"

"Jamie," Timon said, willing her to hear him. "It's only a dream."

"He won't let me go," she said. "His teeth! Hurts!"

Timon continued to hold her as still as he could, afraid to release her. "He can't hurt you now," he said. "I'm here to protect you."

She gave the shriek of a child in mortal terror and suddenly went limp. She gasped once, her breath draining out in a final sigh.

"No!" Timon said, panic flooding his body.

But it wasn't her last breath. Her fever broke all at once, and he knew it was over. Jamie would live.

He laid her down and stretched out beside her. When her breathing was deep and steady, he permitted himself to sleep.

When he woke, she was looking at him, her shadowed eyes filled with confusion.

"Timon?" she asked. "It doesn't hurt anymore."

He choked on a laugh, cupping her face in his hands. "You're getting better," he said. "We have nothing to worry about."

Slowly she raised her free hand to her mouth. "You kissed me," she murmured. "Why?"

Timon stiffened. If she remembered *that*…

"The antibiotics worked," he said, sidestepping her question. "But you'll still have to rest, Jamie. We won't take any chances."

"I'm very tired," she said. But she smiled as she closed her eyes. "I knew I could…trust you."

As she slept, Timon built up the small fire and realized he could never tell her the truth of what he'd done. Something ugly had happened to her, almost certainly in childhood, and it had to do with some Opir holding her against her will, biting her without consent. It was a trauma that had never healed, and in spite of all his good intentions, he also had acted without her consent.

It didn't seem possible that Jamie could have dealt so well with the Riders who had posed as Freeblood raiders. If one of them had threatened her in the interest of making the incident more convincing, she might just as easily have collapsed back into that previous trauma, as she had in her fever dreams.

What would she do when they reached the Conclave, and she was surrounded by many full-blooded Opiri, all in need of regular blood? She must be determined to fight her fear, at least consciously.

And who will help her if her courage fails? he thought. *Who will stand with her? Her godfather? Cahill?*

Did *they* know what had happened to her, before?

His chest tight with anger, Timon left Jamie just long enough to hunt for wild game and returned with the edge of his hunger blunted to a dull ache. He made a thorough inspection of Jamie's injuries and was satisfied they were improving.

But it would still take time. Time when he and Jamie would be alone together, and he would have to try to remain neutral after he had held her life in his hands, shared her worst fears and kissed her almost as if they were lovers.

He had to be her protector now, nothing more.

For the next few days, Jamie slipped in and out of consciousness, sleeping deeply as her body worked with the healing chemicals in her blood. On the fifth day she remained awake for several hours, and three days later she was eating normally and slept only half the day.

"Did I say anything when I was sick?" she asked Timon as he brought her a meal of gruel and freshly cooked rabbit.

He sat beside her beneath the wide-spreading oak. "You did mention that you'd like to see Cahill fall facedown in a mudflat," he said lightly.

Jamie smiled at him, weary but genuine. "You saved my life," she said.

"The drugs saved your life."

"Without your care, they wouldn't have helped."

"Even you must get tired of being grateful." He winced at the sarcasm in his own voice. "I'm sorry," he said. "I didn't mean—"

"I know you're restless," she said. "You aren't used to staying in one place for so long." She reached hesitantly for his hand. "I'm holding you back."

It was difficult to feel her touch and not want more of it, but he didn't withdraw his hand. "I'm doing exactly what I need to do," he said. "All you have to think about now is your own healing."

"Not a very interesting subject," she said with a slight laugh. She took a bite of the makeshift stew and ate it uncomplainingly. "How often do Riders have to play nursemaid to one of their charges?"

"A Rider has to be prepared for anything." He realized how pompous he sounded and grinned. "We can still be surprised."

"I'm surprised by everything," she said, stretching out her good arm. "I'm surprised at how much more beautiful the world is than I ever realized."

"Even after what happened?"

Her eyes brimmed with joy. "Especially because of what happened. Have you ever come close to death, Timon?"

Oh, yes. He knew that feeling. It did seem to change the world...but it could also make a person reckless, because there was too much new life bursting inside to hold back.

"Once or twice," he said quietly.

"I understand why you value your freedom," she said. Her gaze softened. "I envy you the life you've led."

"A life without roots, without a home to return to?" he asked.

"You must have one place where you all gather," she said.

"The Brotherhouse," he said. "But the only time all Riders are there at one time is when we elect our leaders, and that happens rarely."

"So you find companionship with your band." She flushed, looking away. "And the women you meet on your missions."

It was the second time she'd brought up the subject. He cleared his throat. "As you said. Companionship."

"In the places you visit? The colonies and Enclaves?"

"Sometimes. But—"

"Do you find lovers in the Opir Citadels, too?"

Curiosity, he told himself. She wanted to embrace all the knowledge she could gather.

Or it's something else entirely, he thought, and casually got to his feet. "Not often," he said. "Citadels may use our services, but few full-blooded Opir choose to associate intimately with half-bloods."

"Then you find humans more welcoming?"

Timon raked his hand through his hair. "It depends. Jamie—"

"What about children? Do you take precautions?" Her gaze followed him as he paced around the ashes of the fire. "Are you embarrassed to talk about it? You don't have to be."

"The one thing we never do," he said sharply, "is take partners from among the people we guide and protect."

"Never?"

He could have answered with a yes, if he weren't so obviously the exception to the rule in his desire to seduce Jamie.

But that was before she'd been injured. He was her protector, and he couldn't afford to forget that.

And the secrets she may carry, he thought. *The ones you still have to discover?* If they existed, they hadn't disappeared just because she had nearly died. But he would swear on his own life and freedom that she was innocent of any ill intent toward the Conclave or anyone, except perhaps the Opir who had hurt her some time in her past.

He would gladly have ripped that Opir limb from limb.

"We admit no females to the Riders because of the distractions and complications certain relationships would cause," he said at last. "No outsider has ever interfered with my duty."

Jamie was quiet for a long while, and Timon wondered

if he'd hurt her feelings. "I have to hunt," he told her, averting his face.

He didn't wait for her response, but saddled the new mare he'd caught, whom he'd named Chloe. She crowhopped a few times, just to remind him that she wasn't quite broken in, and then settled into a choppy trot.

He returned hours later to find Jamie on her feet, leaning heavily against the oak. The foot of her injured leg hardly touched the ground, but Timon could tell that the intense expression on her face was due to concentration, not pain.

"It doesn't hurt anymore," she said, smiling at him with unfettered happiness. He dismounted and approached her, his hands half raised to catch her if she began to fall.

"I'm glad the pain is gone," he said, "but you really shouldn't be standing yet."

"I really shouldn't be alive," she said. Her eyes danced. "Come over here, and help me walk."

"Jamie—"

But she was so lovely in her joy that he couldn't resist her. When he was just within reach, she nearly fell into his arms. He supported her under her good arm, her injured leg against his.

"We'll need a splint," he said. "Once we're sure you can consistently stand without pain or complications, we can work on strengthening your leg."

"I can ride," she said, "if we're careful."

The idea of leaving this place made Timon's breath come a little faster, but he suppressed his eagerness. "One move at a time," he said.

She tried to take a step, lost her balance and swung into him, hip to hip and chest to chest. Her face had regained its healthy color, and her lips were as inviting as they had been when he'd first met her. She laughed.

"I never was much of an athlete," she said. "And I don't suppose I'll become one now."

Afraid to let her go, Timon supported her around her waist. Her breasts felt firm and round, her body supple under his arm. She pressed her face into his neck and sighed.

"You're so warm," she said. "Are all Darketans as warm as you are?"

"It's my human half," he said, holding himself very still.

"You smell like horses."

Timon tried to maneuver her away from him without hurting her. "I'm sorry," he said. "You should sit down, so that I can check the leg again."

"Do you think I'm afraid of you now?" she asked, raising her head, her lips nearly touching his.

Her embrace was more than enough to bring his body to full alert. But she wasn't thinking clearly. And she wasn't in good enough physical condition to—

Jamie kissed him.

Chapter 10

For a moment Jamie felt Timon respond to her kiss; his lips firm and demanding, his arm tightening around her waist. She could feel the hardness of his erection against her, and she knew without a doubt that he wanted her.

But then he pulled his head back and lifted her away from him, setting her down gently against the tree. He unwrapped her bandages and examined the wound on both sides of her thigh. She could see that there was a slight divot in the front where there had been an ugly hole, the flesh pink and healthy, with only a little clear drainage.

"We'll be able to move sooner than I thought," Timon said, replacing the bandage.

She gazed at him steadily. "If you're trying to distract me, it won't work."

"You don't know what you're doing, Jamie," he said in an unconvincingly level voice. "Sometimes, after we come close to death—"

"Don't lie to yourself," she said, lifting her chin. "Do you think I can't tell you feel the same?"

Timon didn't look away. Jamie knew he was too honest to deny what she spoke the truth, but he didn't reply.

"One or both of us could die tomorrow," she said. "I know now what it is to feel life slipping away, to realize there are a million things I haven't experienced."

"You're barely functioning now," he said, touching her hair. "Jamie, we can't rush into something…"

"Why not? Is it because I'm not like those other women? Because I'm a virgin?"

She felt only a little embarrassed at speaking so plainly, but Timon actually blushed. "Cahill—" he began.

"The only thing between Greg and me is what he imagines," she said. She ran her fingers across Timon's cheek. "You and I both know what's been happening between us from the beginning. It's just that I had trouble acknowledging it, and I was afraid of these…things I hadn't felt before."

"You mean sex," he said bluntly, startling her.

But she was grateful for that bluntness. "Of course. I may be inexperienced, but I can recognize sexual attraction. I may need a little help—"

"Help?" he said with a short laugh. "You seem to be doing well enough so far."

"I'm no seductress. But you don't need games, do you?"

Abruptly he pulled her against him again, a storm brewing in his eyes. "Jamie, that raider who captured you just before I and my men arrived—"

"Is nothing like you. Whatever he might have done has no bearing on what you and I do together." She hesitated. "If it's pregnancy you're worried about, I had that taken care of before we left the Enclave."

"Is this so clinical to you?"

Jamie kissed him again. He reacted just as she would have hoped, with an added dose of suppressed ferocity.

"I told you," he said, his breath coming hard. "We don't become involved with the people we protect."

"I'm not asking anything of you but the chance to give each other pleasure," she said.

"As part of your thanks?"

She reached down with her good hand and cupped his groin. "Do you want this to stand between us for the weeks we'll be together on the trail? Do you think it'll just go away, Timon?"

He stared at her, searching her face, her eyes, looking for hesitation or doubt. Jamie knew he wouldn't find it. And he knew it, too.

"Teach me, Timon," she whispered.

Taking her in his arms again, he lowered her to the ground and laid her on the blanket. Without a word he braced his arms on either side of her shoulders, leaned over her and kissed her.

This was not like the first kisses. It was much deeper, with that leashed ferocity, but also the tenderness she had felt in him before. His tongue ran along the inside of her lips, and a rush of warmth gathered between her thighs.

A normal response, she thought. But then she wasn't thinking about anything but the kiss, hesitantly returning it, touching her tongue to his.

When she felt his teeth, her muscles stiffened.

Timon drew back. "You're not ready," he said hoarsely.

"Will you…bite me?" she asked.

"Not unless you want me to."

"No," she said. "Not yet."

She pulled him down again, and he kissed her with great gentleness. She wanted to weep, but he was already moving on to kiss her cheeks and her jawline and her neck, never so much as grazing her with his teeth. His tongue stroked the lobe of her ear, and then the hollow of her neck.

While she was savoring the remarkable sensations, his fingers moved to the upper buttons of her shirt. A moment of shyness overwhelmed her, but she didn't let Timon see it. She tried to help him with the buttons.

"Lie still," he said, "or I'll have to stop."

Swallowing a whimper, she let him take his time unbuttoning her shirt. She wore nothing underneath, and she knew he must have seen her naked body many times while he had cared for her. But this was different. He placed the palm of his hand between her breasts, as if he were checking for her reaction. When she remained still, he moved his hand to cup her right breast. His skin felt pleasantly rough, and when his thumb grazed her nipple she gasped.

"Easy," he said. He caressed her other nipple with his fingertips, expertly and thoroughly. Jamie closed her eyes and tried to remember that if she did anything to endanger her arm or leg, he would stop. And that she couldn't bear.

When his mouth replaced his fingers, the shock was delightful. His tongue curled around her nipple and suckled. His legs weren't touching hers, but she knew he would be as aching and hot as she.

He moved on to her other breast while he delicately pulled the tail of her shirt from the waistband of her pants. She felt no jarring of her leg or arm as he moved his mouth from her breasts to her stomach. His kisses burned like fire. She had never been so aware of her center of her body, or of the wet heat below.

"Are you all right?" he asked, his breath moving over her sensitive flesh.

"Yes," she said. "Don't...stop."

"Tell me if you feel even the slightest pain."

She couldn't imagine what pain felt like now, unless it was the discomfort of wanting more. Wanting everything she knew he had to give. He began to pull her pants down by tiny increments, exposing her upper thighs, kissing and licking what he laid bare. He went on to ease her pant leg past the bandage, then hesitated to examine it.

With her free hand, Jamie grabbed a handful of Timon's hair and pulled him down again. She already knew what was coming, and her body was leaping toward it with joyful abandon. When his tongue touched the sensitive crease of her vulva, she almost forgot she had ever been injured.

Wet warmth rushed between her thighs as he began to

stroke her with his tongue, caressing each satiny fold of skin and lingering on the nub of her clitoris with expert care. She knew that her gasps and moans of excitement must have sounded wanton, but she didn't care. There was no other way to express this incredible experience, this profound physical joy.

And when he found her entrance and circled it with his tongue, all she could think of was what it would be like to feel that emptiness filled. She lifted her hips, and his tongue penetrated her.

It wasn't enough. He withdrew for a moment, and she tugged at his hair again.

"Don't stop," she begged. "I want to feel you inside me."

He obliged by thrusting his tongue deeper, mimicking the act of love. She quivered, and then a great rush of sensation overwhelmed her, carrying her to heights of ecstasy she'd never known.

When she came down again, she knew exactly what had happened. But she imagined something else…something no other kind of lovemaking could imitate.

With strength that surprised her, she pulled Timon's head away with her good arm and tugged at his shoulder, eager to feel his body over hers. He braced himself on his arms and stared down into her eyes, his lips wet with her body's moisture. She felt for his pants, fumbling with the buttons, her fingers slipping in their impatience. His erection seemed barely contained by his clothing. It would take so little to free him…

His hand stopped hers. "No, Jamie," he said, a little breathlessly. "If I go on, I'll hurt you. Your body isn't ready."

"Then you get nothing?" she asked, her eyes welling with tears.

"I had everything I needed," he said, kissing her mouth. He pulled up her pants carefully, rebuttoned her shirt and caressed her hair. "Now it's time for you to rest."

He knelt beside her, his eyes closed, still touching her hair. She could almost feel him fighting his own desires for her sake.

"This wasn't what I wanted," she said.

He lay down beside her. "Sleep," he said. "When you're fully recovered, we can try again."

"Yes." She smiled and reached for his hand. "I understand now how all those other women must feel."

"Hush," he said, putting his finger over her mouth.

Jamie pretended to sleep, but her brain was on fire. Lassitude had overcome her body, yet she was aware of every heartbeat in her chest, every throb of the pulse in her throat.

It wasn't possible that it could happen so fast, she thought. It could simply be just another irrational feeling, brought on by her brush with death. Timon had been right about that; she hadn't been interested in what was sane or practical, only in the need to feel fully alive again. And to prove that Timon was nothing like the ugly Opir in her dreams.

But it hadn't quite worked out that way. He hadn't just given her pleasure, but something of himself, even if he hadn't realized it.

And now she felt more than curiosity, more than gratitude or desire or the need to be held. The knowledge she hid within her most private self could never be shared…not with Greg or Amos, and most certainly never with Timon.

There was no place for love in a Rider's world.

Chapter 11

Within the week, Timon decided that Jamie was fit to travel. There had been no more kissing or further intimacy during the intervening days; somehow Timon had always changed the subject when she suggested it.

Though Jamie still wanted him as much as ever, she didn't push it. There were still many weeks of traveling ahead, much of it through rough territory. Timon had spent the time before their departure preparing for the journey. He showed her the map he carried with its landmarks of old cities and towns, and the vast expanse of the Central Valley followed by the desert, miles and miles of it.

Once they entered the desert, on the other side of Tehachapi Pass, they would be relying on water from springs and wells scattered along their route. There would be little game. It was not the hottest time of the year, but it would be warm enough.

Timon did all he could to prepare Jamie, and she didn't doubt that he was genuinely concerned about her ability to tolerate the hardship without the wagon supplies. By now the delegation would be well ahead of them, but even considering the wagons' slow pace, Timon and Jamie wouldn't be in any position to move too fast with only two mounts and limited resources.

Still, Jamie found that little could disturb her happiness. Her leg no longer hurt, she wore only a simple sling over her arm now and she was eager to move.

Only one thing bothered her. Though Timon had obviously taken great pains to conceal what he was doing, she'd caught him taking blood from the game he was bringing back to camp. She'd known he must have been doing so all along; he hadn't once troubled her with his needs.

She'd tried to bring up the subject without asking Timon outright. He'd sidestepped the issue with vague reassurances that he was perfectly well and needed nothing from her.

He would have no reason to lie to her, she thought. He didn't know anything about what had happened in her childhood, and she wasn't ready to tell him.

They set off east through the long, winding pass leading to the great Central Valley of old California and, for the next several days, travel was easy and good, camping places abundant. They spent a great deal of time simply riding side by side in silence, while Jamie made notes and sketches of anything that caught her eye, from ruined towns to unfamiliar plants. It was a pleasant interlude, free of raiders or any creature more dangerous than a mountain lion she spotted watching them pass.

And still Timon showed no overt signs of either wanting her body or her blood.

When they broke out of the rolling hills into the wide valley, they followed the old Interstate 5 southward along a nearly dry canal once built to carry water to the thirsty cities of Los Angeles and beyond. Jamie observed vast herds of wild horses, cattle and pronghorn antelope, along with scattered groups of deer, pigs and turkeys. They saw occasional hunters from hidden communities of humans, but no Opiri of any kind. Once it was clear that her wrist was completely healed, Timon began to teach her how to use his rifle and gave her a small knife to carry in her boot.

"Very few people will notice it," he said. "Keep it well hidden. It may come in handy someday."

By the time they turned east again toward the mountain

pass that would lead them to the desert, they had made up half their lost days and Jamie had begun to develop skills she wouldn't have believed possible for her to learn. Still, Timon was extremely cautious when he touched her—no lingering caresses, no kisses, nothing that might be considered a sexual advance.

She'd asked if he wanted their mutual attraction to stand between them for their entire journey, if he thought it would just go away. Now it seemed as if nothing had ever happened between them…as if she had imagined his desire before.

She considered trying to seduce him again, or at lcast starting a frank discussion about mutual physical needs. But she had lost her confidence, and when they reached the base of Tehachapi Pass, there was already someone waiting.

At first Jamie thought it was the delegation column, somehow delayed at the pass. But as they approached, she realized these vehicles were very different, like moving houses with peaked roofs and painted doors. A small herd of horses stood passively in a makeshift corral, and a group of men, women and children gathered around a fire set safely away from the wagons.

"Wanderers," Timon said, aiming a grin at Jamie.

Immediately Jamie pulled her notebook from her satchel. "I've never met any before," she said. "Did you expect them?"

"No," he said, "but I'm glad to see them. They may be able to give us information about the delegation."

With a sharp whistle, Timon turned Chloe toward the Wanderer's camp. The people rose, men and women setting aside pipes and knitting to observe Jamie and Timon's approach. Children ran toward the horses recklessly, but both Chloe and Lazarus neatly avoided them without any prompting on their riders' part.

Timon was off his horse and helping Jamie down before

she could catch her breath. He greeted the Wanderers with obvious familiarity, and he shared embraces with several of the adults. Then he turned back to Jamie and introduced her with an air of pride that surprised and humbled her.

"This is Ava," he said, introducing her to an older woman with a brown, deeply lined face. "She leads this caravan."

"Riders and their companions are always welcome among us," Ava said, her long, colorful coat sweeping around her ankles. "We have just come out of the pass. You will have much to tell us of the Valley."

"And we have much to ask," Timon said.

"Food first," Ava said. She consulted with her people in an odd, barely comprehensible dialect of English, and asked her guests to sit by the fire.

That night, Jamie felt the warmth of that family all around her. Ava was a generous hostess, offering pipes to them both. Jamie tried one puff and quickly realized that she had better leave the smoking to Timon, who shifted between common English and the Wanderers' dialect as if he had been born in the caravans.

Timon insisted that she retire early, and she was given a bed in one of the wagons, a rare honor she was almost reluctant to accept. Timon stayed out with the others, speaking in a low voice of what he and Jamie had observed during their travels from the San Francisco region. Jamie lay awake, listening, until the party broke up and the Wanderers retired to their various wagons.

Jamie waited for Timon to come to her, hoping he would at least say good-night and she might finally try the techniques she had been practicing in her mind.

But he didn't come. She tugged on her clothes and crept out of the wagon. By the light of a waxing moon, she could see silhouettes between two of the wagons across from her own.

One of the figures was Timon, and he was feeding.

The woman had her head flung back, her cascade of hair tumbling down her back.

Shocked and startled, Jamie tried to retreat. But Timon heard her and looked up, dark liquid on his lips. His eyes glittered like a cat's in the moonlight…feral, hungry, predatory.

The woman laughed and pulled him back down. Jamie felt her way back into the wagon and fell on the cot, a sense of betrayal eating away at her soul.

She knew she had no right to feel this way. She had attempted to offer him her blood, but never explicitly enough. She had let her old fears blunt her determination. Hc had hidden this blood-taking from her, as if he thought he might hurt her by turning elsewhere.

And she had seen something ferocious in his eyes when he looked at her, as if he hadn't really seen her at all. A part of himself he had hidden, even when he'd fought the tribesmen in the hills west of the pass. The Opir half.

But she was done with waiting. Even if he didn't want or need her blood now, she could still offer herself. She would act—not rationally, but with emotion. And she would accept the risks with her eyes wide open.

Once again she crept out of the wagon, pausing to listen for voices or movement. All she heard were crickets in the grass. She descended the stairs and took a deep breath. Timon might be in a wagon, but she doubted it. He would sleep under the stars as he always did, one with the night.

She found him lying on a blanket close to the horses, his bare chest moving deeply with sleep. There was no one else nearby. She moved to the nearest wagon and began to undress, favoring her healing arm, slowly removing her shirt and her pants, her underclothes and boots.

Step by careful step she made her way toward Timon. He had ears like a fox, and she thought her chances of getting near without waking him were close to nil.

Incredibly, he didn't stir, even when she reached his blanket. She eased herself down beside him and pressed her cheek to the grass next to his head.

"I told you, Caridad," he murmured. "Not tonight."

Timon had said "not tonight" to the woman who must have offered herself to him? He'd turned her down.

She waited until Timon was breathing steadily and then brushed her hand down his chest, feeling the ridged muscle over his ribs. He sighed again. Her palm reached his hard stomach and ventured below.

Not even the rugged material of his pants could hide his arousal. She touched him tentatively and then traced his firm length.

Suddenly she was on her back, Timon's face staring down into hers with a look of almost comical surprise. But the expression changed when he came fully awake and realized who lay beneath him.

"Jamie," he said.

Chapter 12

Without thinking, Jamie lifted her knees and spread her thighs wide beneath Timon's hips. His cock pushed hard against her. He raised himself up on his arms, relieving the pleasurable pressure.

"What are you doing here?" he asked, though he must have known the question was foolish.

She raised her arms and linked them around his neck, pulling his head down. He gazed at her a moment, fire kindling in his eyes, and kissed her.

"Are you sure?" he whispered in her ear.

"Yes. I want this."

"You've never done it before."

"There has to be a first time."

His teeth flashed in a grin, pointed cuspids and all. "An experiment?" he asked.

"I'm not a scientist now."

"Aren't you?"

Jamie began to rise, pushing against him. "If you don't want me…"

"Want you?" He kissed her again, pushing his tongue between her lips, and drew back. "Do you need more proof, Doctor?"

"I feel it," she said, reveling in the pressure between her thighs. "But that isn't enough. I want—"

He silenced her with another kiss and rose on his knees, pulling off his pants with easy efficiency. For a moment her thoughts betrayed her, reminding her of all those other women he'd had in his travels.

But then he was naked, and she saw all of him for the first time, from the muscular breadth of his chest to the trim waist and below, where his desire was very much in evidence. She thought he must be rather large, but she had no means of comparison; she only knew that the sight of his hunger for her made her hot and wet, her body readying itself for penetration.

"Your arm?" he asked as he lowered himself over her.

"I'll be careful." She shifted her body, raising her knees higher, and felt the brush of his erection against her thigh. Her stomach tightened in anticipation.

He didn't enter her at once. He did as he had the first time, touching the tips of her nipples with his tongue and suckling them gently, each tug sending erotic sensation shooting down between her thighs. She felt beautiful, glorious, indescribably aroused. He kissed the underside of her breasts, and as he did he slid his cock along her thigh, creeping inevitably closer to its home. She reached down for him, winced at the pull on her healing wrist, and let him continue at his own, teasing pace.

Just when she though she couldn't bear it any longer, the tip of his cock slipped between her moist folds. Still he didn't enter fully, but continued to tease her, dipping in slightly and withdrawing, making certain that she was ready.

"Now," she said as he arched over her, bringing his face close to hers. He kissed her, and then he was all the way inside, one smooth thrust that pinched briefly and then became a kind of miracle. He withdrew, gazing into her eyes, and thrust again, this time with a little more force, and she flung her head back with a gasp. She felt the slight scrape of something sharp against her neck, there and gone in an instant.

Timon's movements became a steady cadence, entering and withdrawing, each time pushing deeper inside her. Jamie was filled as she had never been before, in a way she had barely begun to imagine. She wrapped her good arm around his back and locked her thighs around his waist, whimpering and moaning with no thought to who might hear. There was no logical, clinical part of her to count the minutes or worry about exposure. All that remained of her was raw passion and the desire to have Timon inside her forever.

But the end came unexpectedly in a burst of wild sensation, carrying her up and up to a pinnacle of ecstasy and then slowly letting her down again. A moment later Timon shuddered and moved more quickly, then lowered himself so that his chest grazed her nipples and his cheek touched hers.

Thought returned, and with it the memory of the graze of his teeth on her neck, a second of indecision, and then nothing but dizzy joy.

He hadn't bitten her.

He didn't need to, she told herself. He'd just fed that night. But she knew it wasn't only that. Something had stopped him.

She'd guessed that he'd recognized her fear of being bitten. But he deserved to know the reason, so he would understand that it didn't have anything to do with *him*… and that he could depend on her when they crossed the desert.

"It'll be dawn soon," Timon murmured into her shoulder. "You need to dress and return to the wagon."

"Are you afraid they'll find out?" she asked, running her fingers through his hair.

He brushed her lower lip with the pad of his thumb. "They'll know," he said, "but they'll be too polite to mention it." She gathered her clothing and began to dress. Timon pulled on his pants and shrugged into his shirt.

The predawn breeze had picked up, ruffling his hair and teasing Jamie's with agile fingers. Every nerve in her body was tingling, every sensation magnified. Timon's smallest touch, a brush of his hand against hers, made her long to fall back in his arms.

But logic and reason won out, and she did as he asked, retreating to her borrowed bed. She listened to the creak of wood and metal as people began to leave their wagons and prepare for the new day. Someone started a fire. She heard Timon's pleasant baritone among the other voices, making easy conversation.

After a while she wandered away from the wagon. She smiled at the children who were playing hide-and-seek among the wheels, greeted the adults who had made her and Timon so welcome the night before and paused to feel the rising sun on her face. It was as if she'd never truly felt its warmth before.

"Jamie," Timon said, taking her arm.

She opened her eyes, melting under his touch. He smiled and winked as if they shared a secret, and then led her down to the fire and a breakfast of biscuits and fresh eggs from the caravan's chickens.

They bid farewell to the Wanderers a few hours later, their horses well rested and their rations doubled. Jamie found herself a little sore when she mounted Lazarus, but it was an ache she didn't mind at all.

Once she and Timon were alone and had started up the winding, crumbled highway of the pass, she gathered her courage and broached the subject she'd kept to herself for so long.

"I'm sorry," she began.

Timon looked sideways at her, one brow lifted. "Why should you be sorry, Jamie?"

She flushed. "I'm not sorry about *that*."

He reined Chloe to a halt. "If I thought I'd hurt you—"

"*No.* It was the most—" She stopped before she made an utter fool of herself. "No. I'm sorry I made you feel you shouldn't ask to take blood from me." The horses began to move again, though neither Timon nor Jamie had given the signal. Timon frowned down at the saddle horn.

"I never gave it much thought," he said.

"Please don't lie to make me feel better," Jamie said. "I should never have acted the way I did when I was first wounded. It was part of the bargain we made with you and the Riders, so that you wouldn't be relying on animal blood during our travels. And here you and I have been traveling together, and you've been deprived of what you need to live."

He glanced up at her with a flash of white teeth. "Haven't I proven I'm very much alive?"

"I know you wouldn't die without my blood. But I also know you haven't been getting adequate nourishment, at least not enough to satisfy you. That's my fault."

"No," he said, pulling Chloe to a stop again. "It was my choice."

"Only because of my reactions," she said. "I know you would never force yourself on any unwilling human."

"What are you trying to tell me?"

"Last night…I saw you with that woman."

"Caridad," he said softly.

"You saw me watching," she said.

"I thought I saw someone. I didn't know it was you."

Jamie kicked Lazarus lightly, and he began to walk up the slope. "Seeing you feed from her made me realize how selfish I've been."

Chloe's tack jingled as Timon fell in beside her. "Caridad and I have known each other for a long time. We don't meet often, but—"

"Do you think I'm jealous?" she said with a light laugh.

"I'm only sorry that you had to go to someone else for what you needed."

"I don't accept your apology because I know you have good reason for your reluctance to share your blood, and I respect that."

"But I'm not re—"

"I know something terrible happened to you, and—"

"You *know*?" she asked, her head snapping up. "Did someone tell you? My godfather? Or was it Greg?"

Timon reached over and grabbed Lazarus's bridle. The horse stomped in annoyance, but Timon whispered a quiet word and he subsided.

"When you were very ill," Timon said, "you seemed to speak to someone who was hurting you. The things you said… I guessed it had something to do with a bad experience when you were much younger."

Jamie dropped the reins and covered her hands with her mouth. "I told you?"

"During your fever," he said. "I didn't think you intended to say the things you did, so I didn't tell you."

"Oh, God." She closed her eyes. "I should have been honest with you from the start."

"With a stranger?" he asked.

"A stranger who saved my life, who cared for me when I was helpless."

"Someone who was too much like the one who hurt you."

"Never." She leaned over to grip Timon's arm. "You're nothing like him."

"Maybe we should dismount," Timon suggested, taking her hand.

"No. It's easier this way." She gave Lazarus another little kick, and he snorted loudly before starting forward again.

"He doesn't think much of my riding habits," Jamie said. "I don't blame him."

"He's patient, but this little girl wants to be on her way."

"Let's not disappoint her."

They rode for a time in silence, and then Jamie began. She told him about the escaped Opir prisoner, how he had snatched her off the streets of the Enclave when she was with her mother and carried her to a dark place, where he'd taken her blood by force. After several days, the Opir had released her, but after she'd been restored to her family, she'd continued to have nightmares. They'd finally stopped in her late teens, but she'd never forgotten the terror of those days.

When she was finished, Timon was grim-faced, that feral light shining in his eyes.

"And he escaped?" he asked.

"Yes." Her throat felt tight.

"Your godfather and Cahill know about this?"

"Yes, they know. And I know I lacked the courage to tell you."

He jerked back on the reins and slid out of the saddle. With almost no help from her, he pulled her off Lazarus's back and into his arms.

He kissed her very gently and looked into her eyes.

"You were a child, Jamie," he said. "You survived. You went on with your life by refusing to let that Opir savage steal your future."

"Did I?" she asked. "I spent the rest of my childhood and young adulthood hiding in a lab."

"You're not hiding now." He set her back, his hands cupping the sides of her face. "You're not hiding from *me*." He kissed her forehead and let her go. "I wouldn't have put you through being bitten again."

"But I *want* you to." She smiled unevenly. "I'm not afraid anymore."

He caressed her cheek with the rough palm of his hand. "We'll see," he said. "When the time comes—"

"I will be ready." She took his hand and kissed his palm. "This will be the hardest part of our journey. We both need our full strength. We'll be together, Timon. In every way."

Chapter 13

Timon took a step back from Jamie. "Thank you," he said. "Thank you for telling me this," he said.

He helped her remount and leaped easily onto Chloe's back. They set out again, this time speaking only of simple things. Jamie felt as if an enormous weight had been taken off her shoulders. She had never told anyone but her father what had happened that day so long ago. Later, her godfather had learned the truth, and so had Greg. But neither he nor Greg truly understood just how deeply she'd been affected.

Now Timon knew, and understood.

The following weeks were as challenging as Timon had promised. Once they crossed the high pass they descended almost immediately into desert.

They met no raiders or settlements, and Jamie took copious notes to relieve the boredom when they traveled during the early mornings and late afternoons, after the heat of the day had passed. Sometimes when they camped at noon under the canopy Timon carried among his supplies, or when it was too dark to move the horses safely, she and Timon made love.

The first time he took her blood, he treated her like the virgin she had been that first night in the caravan. He made love to her as if she might break apart in his arms, and spent long minutes nuzzling her neck and licking the skin at the juncture of her neck and shoulder.

But he didn't take her blood until she asked him to, and

even then he hesitated. Only when she pulled his head down and held him there did he finally surrender.

She felt the slight pressure and pain of his bite, and then a flood of warmth and pleasure she hadn't expected. Sweet satisfation filled her body as he stroked her breasts and thighs and in between, and just as he finished she reached her climax and shuddered wildly while he closed the small wound with his lips.

"Was it all right?" he asked her afterward.

"If I had known how it could be..."

"With *me*," he said, a possessive note in his voice. "It might not be the same with others. When we get to the Conclave—"

"I'll be fine," she said, though she felt a little fearful. Timon was right. She couldn't know that it would be the same with another, that the bad memories wouldn't return. She wasn't sure she could share so much of herself with a stranger.

"They can't force you," Timon said, kissing her forehead and cheeks and lips.

"How can I expect peace if people like me won't freely offer what Opiri need to survive?" She trailed her hand over his chest. "You've made it easier. Thank you."

Timon pulled her into his arms and folded himself around her as if he could protect her from all the Opiri in the world. But she knew he couldn't. She didn't want him to.

When they crossed the Colorado River at the border of old California and Arizona, they found a small human settlement on the riverside. The colonists told them that the wagons they sought were only a few days ahead. Jamie and Timon rode on along Highway 40 west, crossing more desert and gradually entering scrubby grassland, broken by hills and mesas to the north and south. There were signs of the passage of groups of various sizes, on foot and horseback, along with the tracks of wagons. But they encountered no other travelers, hostile or otherwise.

One hundred miles from old Albuquerque and the Rio Grande River, they caught sight of another party's dust on the eastern horizon. Too eager for caution, Jamie kicked Lazarus into a run.

A sharp whistle brought the horse to a stop. Timon rode Chloe in front of Lazarus, blocking Jamie's way.

"We don't know who they are," he said sternly. "I'll ride ahead."

"They'll see us soon enough," she pointed out.

He removed his field glasses from his saddle pack. "At least we'll have a chance to run if they prove to be unfriendly."

Timon's proposal was reasonable, as always, and so Jamie hung back while he rode ahead to identify the other travelers. He paused once or twice to look through the glasses, and then continued on until he was lost in a haze of dust.

When he returned, his expression was neutral, but there was the slightest set to his mouth. "They're an Opiri delegation from the Citadel of Tenebris near the Los Angeles Enclave," he said.

"You spoke to them?" she asked.

"They wear heavy hoods and carry banners," he said, "and they have wagons. They wouldn't be out here for any purpose but joining the Conclave."

"Is there a reason we should stay away from them?"

"Not unless you prefer it. If you have any doubts—"

"We'll be seeing them sooner or later," she said. "Let's go on."

With a brisk nod, he turned Chloe around and led the way.

Timon watched Jamie closely as they rode up to the group. All eyes were on them as the column's leader brought the delegates to a halt, and two mounted, hooded and gloved Opiri split off from the others to meet Timon and Jamie.

One of them raised a hand in salute. "You are going to the Conclave?" he asked.

"We were separated from our party," Timon said. "My name is Timon, of the Brotherhood of Riders. My companion is Jamie McCullough of the San Francisco Enclave delegation."

"I am Dimitri of Tenebris," the Opiri said, "and this is Kyros." His eyes flickered to Jamie again. "Will you join us?"

Timon glanced at Jamie. There was no doubt in his mind that she felt uneasy. Timon maneuvered Chloe in front of Lazarus, blocking Dimitri's view of her.

"If you have water—" he said.

"We have water in the wagons," Dimitri said. "Please, share it with us."

"With gratitude," Timon said, inclining his head. He managed to keep his horse between Jamie and the two Opiri, and she made no objection, not even with a glance.

The Opiri moved ahead of them, and Timon reached surreptitiously for her hand. "All right?" he murmured.

"Yes." Her chin was lifted, her profile defiant. "Stop worrying about me."

She rode with body and head held high into the midst of the Opir delegation, smiling and acknowledging the reserved greetings offered by her hosts. Water was produced and shared with the delegation's guests.

But there was definitely a tension in the air that made the hair stand up on the back of Timon's neck. Something wasn't quite right here. Nothing overt; no hostility, no contempt of "lesser" humans and half-bloods. But a thread of anxiety seemed to run through the voices of the Opiri, as if they were waiting for something to happen.

Timon urged Jamie to take a rest in the shade of one of the wagons, though he remained standing beside her. After a while, Dimitri approached him.

"May I speak with you?" he asked Timon.

"It's all right," Jamie said, shading her eyes to look up at the men. "I'm fine here."

Not wholly convinced, Timon reluctantly followed Dimitri a little distance away. Dimitri's disquiet was palpable, and Timon balanced on his toes, ready to sprint back to Jamie's side.

"Please," Dimitri said, "do not be troubled. There is no danger here."

"Then why is everyone walking on eggshells?" Timon asked. "Why do you stare at Jamie as if you're ready to jump her?"

Dimitri flinched, a dramatic gesture in an Opir. "You and she are…"

"I'm her protector until we reach the Conclave."

"Then I will be honest with you, Rider. Some of us have not fed in several days. We did meet with your delegation two days ago, but the humans were weary and only half of us were able to take advantage of the Conclave agreement regarding the sharing of blood."

Subtly moving his hand toward his knife, Timon shook his head. "I'm sorry to hear it," he said.

"We have, of course, been subsisting on animal blood for much of our journey. But, as you know, there are some Opiri who do not do well in the absence of human blood."

"And that's why you're so interested in Jamie," Timon said, his muscles tensing to spring.

"I am sorry if we've alarmed you," Dimitri said, sounding as if he meant it, "but we are very concerned for one of our companions, Lord Nereus. He has been ill for the past two days, and will not take any animal blood."

"I can't speak for Jamie," Timon said when Dimitri was

finished. "She did take the oath, with the others, to provide blood to Opir delegates. But she has been keeping me in good health for many weeks, and I don't know if she is up to donating to anyone else."

"I understand," Dimitri said. "I only ask that you consult with her and explain the situation."

Easing his hand away from the knife, Timon returned to Jamie. She looked up, a question in her eyes.

He knew what he wanted to tell her. *Let's leave this place. They won't come after us.*

But he owed her more respect than that. He crouched beside her and relayed Dimitri's message without emotion, letting her make her own judgment.

She was quiet for some time after he finished. "It's only the one Opir?" she asked.

"So Dimitri says."

"But you think otherwise?"

Timon took her hand. "Some of these Opiri haven't had human blood in some time. They are civilized, but once they smell your blood, some may become aggressive."

"Aggressive enough to…" She swallowed. "To force themselves on me?"

"Not as long as I'm alive," Timon said, squeezing her hand. "If you want to leave, we can go anytime."

"No," she said, her jaw tightening with familiar stubbornness. "I'll do it."

His whole body on alert, Timon relayed Jamie's answer to Dimitri. The Opir seemed openly relieved, though his eyes were still hidden under his hood.

"Tonight," he said, "when we can move about freely, we will bring Nereus to her. Please extend our gratitude to Ms. McCullough."

"You can do that yourself," Timon said.

He joined Jamie again, sitting very close to her, listening to her heartbeat speed and slow as her emotions changed.

He wanted to sweep her up and carry her away, where childhood memories couldn't touch her.

But they weren't his memories to expel. Perhaps this experience, if it went well, would help her leave those old terrors behind once and for all.

If it went well. No one would be able to save this Nereus if it didn't.

Chapter 14

Night fell swiftly in the desert, the sun sinking behind the mesas to the west. Jamie leaned against the wagon, breathing deeply and steadily, only a slight twitch at the corner of her eye betraying her feelings.

As promised, Dimitri and two others brought Nereus to her. The Opir was, indeed, a little sickly looking, with shadows under his eyes and a strange way of jerking his head to one side. When he saw Jamie, his lips lifted away from his teeth in an instinctive reaction to the smell of her blood.

Timon stepped in front of Jamie to face Nereus. "I warn you now," he said softly. "If you cause Ms. McCullough any hurt, I will stop this."

The Opir's gaze darted to Timon's. "I understand," he said in a harsh whisper.

"I am ready," Jamie said, bracing herself against the wagon.

The other Opiri took a step back as Nereus approached Jamie. Timon remained within touching distance, heedless of the Opiri custom of keeping a good distance from a feeding. Nereus put his mouth to Jamie's throat. She stiffened and then tried to relax as Nereus, the tendons standing out on his neck, bit into her skin.

Timon almost grabbed the Opir to fling him aside. A wild possessiveness gripped him, though he knew he had no right to the emotion. Jamie did not belong to him.

No right, he told himself over and over again. *No right.* But every muscle in his body was ready to move, and he had to look away while Nereus lapped up Jamie's blood. He looked back in time to see Jamie staring at him out of the corner of her eye, carefully concealing her panic from everyone but him.

He was ready to put an end to it when Nereus finally finished and withdrew. The bite mark was only a red patch on Jamie's neck, but Timon had to fight all an Opir's most primitive instincts to keep from attacking Nereus. The human in him despised his other half, the part that took and took without giving back.

Pushing Nereus out of the way, he put his arm around Jamie and led her apart from the wagons. She stumbled once, and he carried her to a tall juniper bush.

"Are you feeling weak?" he asked.

She brushed hair out of her face. "No. Just a little—" She broke off. "I'm fine."

Timon clenched his fists behind his back. "You were very generous to Nereus."

"It was good practice." She reached up to touch her neck but let her hand fall without making contact.

"Does it hurt?" he asked. "I can help."

"Really, I'll be all right."

Timon felt more pride in her than he could express. "I'll bring the horses here, and we'll stay in this spot for the rest of the night. We'll leave first thing in the morning."

"Do you think some of the others might expect to—"

"No. But we should stay apart from them, just in case."

"In a few days we'll be in a camp full of Opiri."

"And humans," Timon reminded her. "*Your* people."

She closed her eyes. "My people. Can I really call them mine when I've been keeping secrets from them since before we ever left the Enclave?"

Forgetting to breathe, Timon pretended a calm he didn't feel. *Secrets.* Like the ones he'd been asked to uncover in a mission he had deliberately ignored over the long weeks of their journey? The ones he'd nearly convinced himself didn't exist?

"I don't know what you mean," he said.

"I didn't know who to tell," she murmured. "Not even my godfather knows. I found the old research, buried away in a basement storage area no one seemed to remember. When I saw it, I knew it could make all the difference in this Conclave."

"What research, Jamie?"

She met his gaze. "I've learned to recognize my own mortality, Timon. I could die tomorrow. If something was to happen to me..."

"Hush," he said, pulling her into his arms. He kissed her forehead with no regard for any Opiri who might be observing. "Nothing will happen to you, now or later."

She rested her cheek against his. "I told myself when I left the Enclave that I would do everything within my power to accept the shared humanity of all the people I would meet, including the Opiri. I'm afraid I didn't do a very good job of living up to my principles."

"Shared humanity?" Timon asked, genuinely puzzled.

She moved to face him, taking both his hands in hers. "That is what I learned, Timon. That we're all related. Opiri, humans...we're all of the same stock. Sometime thousands upon thousands of years ago, the line of our ancestors branched off. One branch continued to develop into humanity as we know it today. But the other branch..."

"The other branch," he said with wonder, "became Opiri."

"Yes," she said. "I don't know how the pre-War anthropologists missed it. Why, over hundreds of years, they never found the remains to suggest the presence of vampires and parallel evolution. But during the War, someone studied Opiri prisoners. They did extensive DNA tests, with advanced technology we don't have full access to today. And these scientists uncovered facts so startling that they must have known what could happen if everyone knew the truth."

"If anyone would believe them," Timon said, still dazed by her revelation. "Are you sure they *did* learn the truth?"

"I saw the records of everything they'd done. It all added up, Timon. It explains why humans and Opiri can have offspring, like you half-bloods. Why Opiri and humans are alike in so many ways."

"Do you have these records?"

She touched her jacket. "I couldn't carry all of them, but I have the extensive notes I took, stitched inside the lining."

"Why are you telling me this now?" he asked cautiously.

She gripped his hands more tightly. "Timon, you can see what this would do if it came out in the wrong way. It will be a great shock to many, many people on both sides. This information could ensure the success of the Conclave. That's what I hope."

"I see you have to plan it carefully," Timon said, his mind racing. If this was the secret Captain Cassius had wanted so badly, how did it support the idea that the San Francisco Enclave might intend some mischief at the Conclave? This was Jamie's information alone, and she wanted it to be used for good.

"What happened to the scientists who discovered this?" he asked. "It's possible they're still alive, even if they're elderly. Have you tried to find them?"

"Of course," Jamie said, her gaze distant. "But I could find no trace of them in personnel records, or locate anyone who knew or remembered them. It's as if they just vanished."

And they might have, Timon thought, *if someone wanted to quash this incredible discovery.* Jamie was right; it wouldn't be only certain Opiri who wouldn't want this getting out. Hatred was an emotion that fed on itself, like a flame that never died.

"I have to get this information to the right people," Jamie said. "Not politicians who might use it the wrong way. Scientists, men and women who will understand and could interpret it for the Conclave when the time is right."

She had no idea what she was talking about, Timon thought. She could never be sure that the people she told, even scientists like her, wouldn't be careless with the information, or even misuse it. Someone could decide to eliminate the one who carried the proof.

If something was to happen to me... she'd said.

"You can help me, Timon," she said, her words cutting into his grim thoughts. "You said the Riders would be handling security. You can watch and listen where I can't, and help me decide who to approach."

With a bitter inner laugh, Timon thought of what he should do as soon as they reached the Conclave. He would have to report to Cassius and share the very information Jamie had entrusted to him. That was his duty.

And he should tell her. Explain that they had to confide in someone immediately—someone neutral like the elected leader of the Riders, whose job it was to keep the Conclave peaceful, playing no favorites. A man whom Timon trusted with his life.

But what would Cassius do with the secret? Report back to those who had hired Timon's band to find it, employers Cassius had never revealed and whose motives remained unknown?

It isn't your responsibility to make these decisions, he told himself. But he had made Jamie his responsibility. Whatever he chose to do, he would be betraying someone close to him. Cassius—like a second father to him, and to whom he owed his first loyalty—or Jamie, who trusted *him.*

"I'm telling you this now because I know we'll be going our separate ways," she said, unaware of his inner turmoil.

"Now that you know what I know, maybe I won't feel so alone."

Timon looked away. "We never spoke about how things would change when we reached the Conclave."

"I thought about it many times, but I never had the nerve to bring it up."

"Our being here doesn't have to mean we'll never see each other," he said.

"You mean we can still be lovers."

It sounded almost crude, even to his own ears. But he wanted it. He wanted it very badly.

"It won't be like our time together during the journey," he said, turning back to her.

"No. We'll have to hide it, won't we?"

"Do you think I'm ashamed of you, Jamie?"

"Will you tell your captain about us?"

"He'll assume I took your blood."

"Yes."

"He may assume the rest, as well."

"But you'd rather not give him confirmation."

"It's none of his business, as long as it doesn't interfere with my duties at the Conclave."

Yet even the thought of her interferes with my duty. The idea of giving her up was intolerable. But if she chose to break it off, he'd soon be with his own kind again.

A world without Jamie.

Chapter 15

The tent city was immense, stretching in a lopsided circle a half mile in diameter. Along the flattened western border ran the Rio Grande River, with its winding bosque of tall cottonwood tree on either side; to the east, beyond the perimeter of the encampment, stood the high Sandia mountains, and between lay a wide stretch of desert dotted with juniper bushes, scrub, sturdy wildflowers and scattered ruins.

Jamie's first thought at seeing the city was that it was almost a colony in itself, though there were no walls to keep enemies at bay. Instead there were rows upon rows of smaller tents inhabited by the various delegations, grouped in smaller "camps." Solar panels had been set up everywhere, and a wide central thoroughfare ran between the two distinct halves of the encampment: one human, one Opir. At the center of the camp lay the "Hub," containing the administrative offices, Assembly tents, Administrative Committee chamber, human medical clinic, mess hall, donation booths and the security headquarters. The biggest tents included the meeting place where the delegates would determine the course of the future.

A little in awe, Jamie glanced toward Timon. He, like her, was taking it all in, but she sensed that he was seeing the camp differently; for him it was a place to maintain peace among the delegates, not to help formulate a new way of life.

Soon he would be leaving her, reuniting with his own

people. Jamie had known this moment would come, but she found it difficult to accept. She took comfort in the fact that Timon shared her secret, and that it bound them as much as their weeks of lovemaking and blood-sharing.

"Jamie."

She came back to herself to find Timon staring at her, brows raised in inquiry.

"I've asked around and learned where your delegation has settled," he said. "They arrived only a few hours ahead of us."

Trying to clear her head, Jamie nodded. "How do I find it?" she asked.

"I'll escort you," he said.

His voice was a little distant, preoccupied, but still held a touch of warmth.

They rode along the thoroughfare amid the chaos of neighing horses and bawling livestock, people of all kinds rushing to and fro, tents and banners and dusty paths, as busy as any city. Humans and Opiri, in their long, hooded daycoats, mingled in the lane and near the Hub, speaking with one another like civilized beings.

Nevertheless, Timon stayed protectively close to Jamie, and she was glad of his company. Like all the delegates, she would have to learn her way around the tent city, but her mind wouldn't hold such details now. Seeing a few Opiri earlier hadn't prepared her for the vast number here, or for the way humans and Opiri interacted peacefully.

"I can see that humans and Opiri are on opposite sides of the encampment," she said to Timon. "But where are the mixed colonies and settlements?"

"Scattered on the outskirts, if the map I saw was accurate," Timon said.

"Along with the other half-bloods?" she asked as Lazarus just avoided colliding with an oblivious human.

"We Riders have our barracks next to Security Headquarters. It's possible that a few non-Rider Darketans are here with the Opiri, and most other dhampires would be with the colonies or Enclave delegations."

"Living proof," Jamie murmured.

"Yes," Timon said, a little more distance creeping into his voice. "This way."

They turned into an alley between tents flying Enclave banners unfamiliar to Jamie. But it didn't take long before she saw the San Francisco wagons, two of the soldiers leading the horses away as Amos and Greg supervised the distribution of the supplies.

Amos spotted her first. "Jamie!" he called, jogging toward her. She dismounted and went to meet him, returning his hug with relief.

"Thank God you're all right," he said. "When you and Timon didn't catch up with us, we feared the worst."

"Timon saved my life more than once," Jamie said. She glanced toward Timon, who had also dismounted and stood by, quietly watching. "I was very ill for a while, which is why it took us so long."

"Then I owe you a great debt," Amos said, extending his hand to Timon. "I know you went well beyond your duty."

"Not at all," Timon said, gripping Amos's hand. "It was both my duty and my pleasure."

The tone was formal, but the final word sent a chill through Jamie's body. Amos was no fool. He glanced between her and Timon with a sharp, assessing look, and then smiled.

"Whatever your reason," he said, "I would gladly offer you whatever I can in gratitude for saving her."

"There is no need," Timon said formally. "We've already received payment."

"Then I'll owe you a debt," Amos said, as stubborn as Timon.

"Individual Riders aren't permitted—" Timon began,

stopping as Greg Cahill charged up to them and pushed past Amos.

"Jamie!" he said, taking her in his arms. "My God, are you all right?" Before she could answer, he turned to glare at Timon. "You took your time about bringing her back to us."

"Greg!" Jamie said, jerking away from him. "You have no idea what it was like, what Timon had to do to get me here in one piece."

"And what *did* he have to do?" Greg asked, still looking at Timon. "Take your blood?"

"Yes," Jamie said. "It was the least I could do, and it was part of our bargain with the Riders."

"Bargain," Greg muttered. He grasped Jamie's arm. "You need to be properly examined."

Jamie held fast. "Greg, you can't—"

"Jamie is no child," Timon said, moving close to them. "I suggest you stop treating her as one."

The two men stared at each other, and Jamie could feel the heat building between them.

"I'm all right, Timon," she said, taking a step away from Greg. "Thank you. For my life, and for everything else."

Timon took her offered hand and squeezed it gently. "I'm glad I could be of service."

The words were impersonal, but the moment was intimate. Greg and Amos seemed to disappear. After a long moment, Timon released her hand.

"I'm sure we'll meet again," he said. "Take care of yourself."

"You, too," she said, her heart knotting in her chest.

He smiled, took Lazarus's reins and remounted Chloe. With a brief nod to Amos, he rode back up the alley and vanished.

"You're too thin," Amos said, throwing his arm around her shoulder, "and you obviously need rest. The medics will be accompanying our equipment to the clinic tents, but you can check that out later."

"Thanks," she said, suddenly weary. Amos took her to the Enclave tents, Greg clumping along behind them. She endured the expected greetings from the other members of the delegation, and reassured everyone that she had come through her ordeal safe and sound.

Amos had barely left her at the tent she would share with Akesha when Greg barreled in.

"What happened?" he demanded. "Who took you?"

She told him about the tribesmen and how Timon had rescued her. She answered his other questions succinctly, explaining how she'd been shot and how Timon's healing skill had saved her.

"His skill?" Greg asked, pacing around the small tent. "What other skills did he use on your journey?"

Jamie sat on the edge of her cot. "We were intimate, Greg. I'm sorry to break it to you this way, but it's not fair to let you go on believing that you and I would have been married. It was never my idea, and I tried to make you realize—"

"You slept with that half-blood?"

"I didn't mean to hurt you."

"I thought better of you, Jamie," Greg said stiffly. "I didn't take you for a slut."

Rising quickly, Jamie met his gaze. "You've always wanted me under your control, ever since we came of age. But I'm not yours, Greg. I never was."

Greg laughed. "You think you love the bastard, don't you?"

Her throat closed. She should answer with the truth, so Greg would realize she meant every word she said.

But she couldn't. Speaking the words would make her feelings too real—loving a man who belonged to another world.

"I've said all I intend to say."

"Yes," Greg said, contempt in his eyes. "You've said more than enough."

He turned on his heel and left the tent. Jamie sat down again, breathing heavily and feeling more than a little ill. She'd known it would be uncomfortable with Greg, that she should have come right out and rejected him before they left the Enclave. He was too arrogant to take even the broadest hint.

Now she was free of him. And Timon was gone.

But we can meet again, as he said, she thought. *We could still be—*

Lovers? Snatching brief moments together on the sly, hiding from everyone?

If that was the price, Jamie would savor every one of those moments, even though she knew they'd be stolen from two separate and very different lives.

Chapter 16

"Timon!" Cassius said, grabbing Timon by the shoulders as he entered the Riders camp. "We had almost given up hope."

"On me?" Timon said with a grin, returning Cassius's gesture of affection. "When have I ever disappointed you?"

The captain of the Riders dropped his hands and smiled, his light violet-brown eyes crinkling tanned skin under the close-cropped gray hair. "I should have known better," he said.

The other Riders not currently on duty crowded around Timon in the barracks, slapping his back and welcoming him with grins and relief. For a moment Timon was disoriented, surrounded by men—his brothers—after so long alone with Jamie.

But the strange feeling passed quickly. He was among his own kind, sure of his place. He greeted each of his brothers in turn, paying particular attention to the members of his band…explaining what had happened when he'd left them to go after the stolen San Francisco delegate.

He left out a few small details.

Orpheus, the last of the Riders to approach him, cast Timon a sly look. "I doubt it was too terrible for you," he said. "You had very pleasant company along the way."

"The human female is well?" Bardas asked.

"I wouldn't be here if she wasn't," Timon said.

"Jamie," Orpheus said, drawing out the name. "She must have been very *grateful*."

"A burden, surely, if it took so long to get here," Bardas said with a faint smile.

Soon enough Timon recognized that his attempt at discretion was useless. The brothers assumed that he'd slept with Jamie, and that she'd shared her blood with him; the hints became ribald jokes, and Timon began to feel very protective of Jamie's reputation.

"Enough," he said with a forced laugh, pushing his fellow Riders away. "I'd appreciate a little privacy to clean up." He looked at Cassius. "If you can spare me."

The captain smiled with a father's warmth. "You've had enough work for one day. Tomorrow we'll discuss assignments for your band." His gaze swept the small crowd. "The rest of you, back to your posts."

With the efficiency of habit, the Brothers dispersed, leaving Timon alone with Cassius.

"Is it true?" the older man asked. "Was she so grateful?"

Timon shrugged. "The circumstances were unusual," he said.

"It was a foolish thing to do," Cassius said, taking one of the camp chairs and gesturing Timon to another. "There's a reason why we discourage even temporary relationships between Riders and our charges. It weakens us, loosens our cohesion and makes us forget where our true loyalties lie."

Timon stopped in the act of sitting down. "Forgive me," he said. "But you have no idea of what occurred between Ms. McCullough and me, what we discussed or what we felt."

"And what *did* you feel, Timon?"

Had it been any other Rider, Timon probably would have ended the conversation there and then. But, in spite of what he'd told Jamie, he owed Cassius at least some measure of the truth. If anything represented home to Timon, it was Cassius.

"Jamie was brave, cooperative and steadfast," he told his

mentor. "She nearly died after her capture by patriarchal tribesman, but she recovered when I bit her. After that, she regularly provided me with blood."

"As she should have done," Cassius said, a frown in his voice. "And what of the other matter?"

"I'm here with the Brotherhood," Timon said. "That should answer your questions."

"It never occurred to me that you would leave us," Cassius said. "You did not develop any emotional attachment to this human?"

"Admiration and respect," Timon said. "And some affection, yes. But she has returned to her delegation, and she has important work to do."

"Work that does not concern you."

"How could it?" Timon said. But his ribs seemed to push in on his heart, and he knew then that he'd already made his decision. He wouldn't tell Cassius about Jamie's discovery.

"I only wish to confirm that your neutrality is not in question," Cassius said.

"It isn't," Timon said, wondering whether or not he was lying, to Cassius or himself.

"Then I am satisfied," Cassius said. "Is there anything else you wish to report?"

"I do have a request."

The captain nodded. "If you want more time to rest…"

"No. I'd ask that my band be assigned messenger duty throughout the camp, rather than patrol the perimeter or the human or Opir precincts."

"Why?"

"My men have just completed a difficult assignment, traveling farther than any of the other escort bands. I think they've earned a job that gives them a little more freedom, at least for a while."

"And you deserve it, as well."

Cassius's statement was a challenge, as if he'd seen through Timon's ploy. Timon smiled ruefully.

"I admit that after spending weeks with one human woman, I wouldn't mind a little variety."

Relaxing in his chair, Cassius steepled his fingers under his chin. "There is one other matter you have failed to mention."

"The supposedly threatening secret held by the San Francisco delegation?" Timon shook his head. "No, I learned nothing of it. The girl certainly had no knowledge of any interest to us." He wrapped his fingers around one of the tent poles. "Did any of the others in the band—"

"No," Cassius said. "They had no success."

"Then maybe this secret doesn't exist," Timon said, dropping into a chair. "Who hired us, Cassius?"

"That must remain confidential. Suffice it to say that the concerns of our employers are probably justified."

Concerns of our employers, Timon thought. Again he wondered what they actually suspected, and if they would consider proof of common ancestry a threat. That thought troubled him deeply.

"How do you plan to proceed now?" he asked.

"I am still considering our options," Cassius said, rising. "Go to your tent and rest. If you need blood—"

"Not yet," Timon said.

"Then spend the rest of the day as you wish. I will make assignments tomorrow, keeping your request in mind. The first informal meeting of the delegates will occur in two days. We will all be needed there."

"How much authority do we have?" Timon asked.

"Our goal is to maintain the peace without resorting to physical interference, but we are the only people here permitted weapons any larger than small knives. Any use of force will have to be justified to the President of the Administrative Committee."

"Understood," Timon said. "With your permission?"

Cassius waved him away. Timon looked through the two barracks tents and found the section assigned to the Kestrels. He left his gear beside his cot, checked briefly on Lazarus—who was being groomed by one of the novices not yet fully accepted into the Brotherhood—and went in search of the nearest bathhouse.

The bathing tent was open to all comers, segregated by sex primarily for the comfort of the human delegates. Water was pumped into overhead showers. All but one of the booths was occupied.

Beginning to strip, Timon was almost to the booth when someone emerged from the women's section. Jamie stopped with a jerk and stared at him, her lips slightly parted, her wet hair tied up in a loose knot atop her head.

"Timon," she said. "I didn't expect…to see you again so soon."

Timon drank her in, noting the way the damp fabric of her clean clothes clung to her body. It didn't seem possible, but it was almost as if he were recognizing her beauty for the first time.

As if he were reliving every moment they had spent together.

"You're well?" Timon asked.

"I'm much better now that I'm clean," she said.

Her words only put Timon in mind of her standing under a showerhead, her naked body slick with moisture, drops of water quivering on the tips of her nipples and the soft curls between her thighs.

"No problems with Cahill?" he asked.

Jamie glanced around as if she feared they'd be overheard, then squared her shoulders. "He's accepted that he and I have no future together," she said.

"I'm glad to hear it. Have you been resting?"

"I'm fine." She hesitated. "What about your Brothers? I

was told that all the members of your band returned safely with the rest of the delegation."

"Yes."

"Good." She smoothed her hair. "You'll begin your duties soon?"

"I've asked to have my band assigned as messengers to carry information across the Conclave. We'll have greater freedom of movement, and that might be useful."

Her lovely eyes sparked. "Yes," she said.

Timon's pulse jumped. She was relieved, as if she'd expected him to abandon her. He wanted to take her in his arms and reassure her again and again until she couldn't catch her breath.

But touching her here would certainly attract the attention of the other bathers, and if one of his brothers should walk in…

"It was a pleasure to see you again, Ms. McCullough," he said. "I hope your work here is a success."

"I'm sure it will be." She licked her lower lip, holding his gaze. "Goodbye, Timon."

She fled from the tent, her towel streaming behind her. Timon ducked into the shower stall and shed the rest of his clothes. Even being near her had made him hard, and it took several moments of meditation to clear his mind and settle his body.

He wondered how he could ever be near her as a "neutral" Rider when anyone with eyes could see how much he still wanted her.

Chapter 17

Jamie had thought she'd seen amazing things when she'd first entered the tent city of the Conclave, but seeing the main Assembly tent made her realize the wonders had just begun.

Twice as large as the second-biggest tent in the camp, the space was filled with people. The risers that would serve as chairs during the formal negotiations had been pushed to the very edges of the tent to provide room for the hundreds of delegates, informally mingling and introducing themselves as they drank clean spring water and smiled with teeth pointed or flat.

"Remarkable, isn't it?" Amos said, tucking Jamie's hand through the crook of his elbow. "Nothing like this has been seen since the War began half a century ago."

"Yes," Jamie said, seeking out the one face that meant more to her than anyone else's in the room. But if Timon was present, he wasn't in plain view.

Just as well, she thought. She was here as an aide to her godfather, not as a moonstruck lover. And if she was lucky, she might even acquaint herself with other scientists at the Conclave, people she could trust with her secret.

As she'd rightfully trusted Timon.

She smoothed her gown and patted self-consciously at her hair. She wasn't used to this kind of gathering or the need to dress herself so glamorously. The dress was the only one she'd brought with her, and she was relieved she wouldn't have to make the choice of what was appropriate for which event.

"You look lovely," Amos murmured. "Ah. Good evening," he said to an Opir lord in a long tunic and high boots. "I am Amos Parks, President of the City Council of the San Francisco Enclave."

The Opir examined him minutely, and Jamie began to bristle. As if he'd sensed her mood, the Opir tilted his head to stare at her.

"Lovely, indeed," he said, showing his teeth. "I am Lord Charon of Irkalla Citadel. You have come a long way to join us."

For a moment all Jamie saw was Charon's teeth. Then she smiled. "It was well worth the journey," she said.

"Indeed," Amos said with a brief glance at his goddaughter. "It is our city's fervent hope that this Conclave will be a success."

"As it is ours," Charon said, his gaze still on Jamie. "Miss—"

"McCullough," Jamie said. "Aide to the Councilman."

Charon took her hand and kissed the back of her fingers. "Charming," he said. "I trust we will meet again soon."

"That is also my wish," Amos said.

Once Charon was gone, Amos whistled under his breath. "I'm proud of you," he said to Jamie. "If you feel up to it, we have other guests to meet."

Jamie accompanied Amos as he approached the leaders of other delegations, gravitating naturally toward the humans. They had come from old Texas, from Colorado and Arizona and, of course, old California, as well as surrounding areas. While Amos spoke to the head delegates, she occupied herself with looking over the other members among their ranks.

Frustratingly, she soon discovered that lesser members

of the delegations, such as the scientists, had been left behind in camp or outside the tent, like the Enclave's soldiers.

"Good God," Amos muttered, gripping her arm. She looked up to see another Opir delegation approaching, three richly dressed Bloodlords who moved with such arrogance that Jamie disliked them on sight.

"Ah, Councilman," the lead delegate said, inclining his head to Amos. "We were pleased to hear that you reached the Conclave safely. So many dangers along the way."

"And your journey from Erebus was also successful, Lord Makedon," Amos said, an uncharacteristically cold note in his voice. "I trust you found sufficient nourishment?"

"Ah," Makedon said, his gaze shifting to Jamie. "We met few humans who believe in sharing, as you do. And of course we had no supply of our own to bring with us."

Jamie clenched her teeth. He was speaking of human serfs, the Enclave "convicts" who had once been sent to Erebus to provide blood and status to the lords of the Citadel. That supply had been cut off at the source years ago, but it was well known in San Francisco that many older serfs still remained in a state of slavery in Erebus, and that some Opiri, in defiance of the old agreement, bred their own human slaves.

But Makedon was pretending that such serfs no longer existed. Staring fixedly at the heavy pectoral necklace worn by the Opir lord, Jamie lost her grip on her previous feelings of hope. It would take considerable pressure to make the Erebusians give up their serfs and their traditional way of life. With Opiri like them to deal with, was there any chance that a lasting agreement could be reached?

"Ms. McCullough," Makedon said. "We hear that you were kidnapped by barbarian humans and were separated from your fellows. You came to no harm, I hope?"

"No lasting harm," she said. "Thank you for your concern."

"It would have been such a waste of beauty," Makedon purred. "And blood."

Jamie froze. That Makedon should be so blatant astonished her, but she didn't dare react.

"It didn't go to waste," she said. "The Rider who saved me had free use of it."

"She's generous with her friends," a familiar voice said. Jamie turned to find Timon at her side, wearing a light jacket and clean, well-fitting clothes. He smiled, all teeth, at Makedon, who narrowed his eyes.

"Friends?" he said. "I wasn't aware that Riders had such relationships outside their Brotherhood."

Oh, Timon, Jamie thought. She experienced a deep sense of pleasure that he wanted to protect her from a perceived threat, but at the same time knew he'd just compromised his own neutrality. She couldn't let that stand.

"*Friend* is one word we use for allies," she said. "I know the whole concept is difficult for some Opiri to grasp."

"Then the Riders have allied with humans?" Makedon asked.

"We're here to prevent open conflict between delegates and their parties," Timon said, following Jamie's lead. "We have no other interest in this Conclave."

"Since there is no conflict here," Makedon said, "surely you have more vital things to do."

Timon flashed a glance at Jamie, inclined his head and retreated. But Jamie could feel that he hadn't gone far, and she was certain that he was still watching.

"Pardon us," Amos said, drawing Jamie away. His face was pale and set, and Jamie wondered if she was going to get an earful for speaking so frankly.

"I'm afraid you haven't fully recovered from your experiences after all," he said, guiding her toward the tent's main entrance. "I'll have Cho escort you back to our camp."

"Councilman," she said formally, "I assure you, I won't—"

"Ms. McCullough."

An Opir Jamie recognized walked up to them, interrupting her reply to Amos.

"Councilman Parks," she said, "I think you've met Lord Dimitri of Tenebris."

Amos took the Opir's offered hand. "Of course," he said. "Good to see you again." He glanced at Jamie. "Are you two acquainted?"

"Indeed," Dimitri said, smiling at her.

"My Rider escort and I met with the delegation from Tenebris not long before we arrived at the Conclave, Councilman."

"And Ms. McCullough was kind enough to share her blood with Lord Nereus," Dimitri said.

"He was still ill after we met with you?" Amos asked in obvious surprise.

"Your generosity was much appreciated," Dimitri said, "but it seems he required more."

Looking past Dimitri's shoulder, Jamie glimpsed Nereus, who seemed no better than he had when they'd met before. In fact, he looked about as sickly as any Opir could, with deep hollows under his eyes and cheekbones and skin that looked as thin and fragile as tissue. He looked at her as if he didn't really see her.

"I'm pleased that Ms. McCullough was able to be of help to you," Amos said smoothly.

"It was my pleasure," Jamie said, carefully concealing the lie with a smile.

"And perhaps a small step toward peace that will be duplicated many times here at the Conclave," Amos said.

"I've no doubt of it," Dimitri said. He bowed to Jamie. "Ms. McCullough."

"Lord Dimitri."

The Opir and his party moved away as Amos took her arm again and continued toward the entrance.

"You didn't tell me that you'd shared blood with anyone but Timon," he said.

"I couldn't very well let a sick Opir die if I could do anything to prevent it," she said, remembering Nereus's empty stare. "The Tenebrians told us they'd already met you."

"I wish you'd spoken of this earlier," Amos said, "but you have clearly won over at least one Opir delegation."

"You did just as much for them," she said.

"It will not only be the lead negotiators who actually work to earn the trust of our former enemies," Amos said. "Strange, though, that Nereus still required blood again so soon after we offered ours."

"He still looks unwell to me."

"Indeed," Amos said. "Very strange."

He led her out of the tent and craned his neck, looking for the Enclave soldiers. "I still want you to go back to the camp and rest. I'll be returning in a few hours."

"I don't need an escort," she said, looking for Timon out of the corner of her eye.

"Do you expect him to pop up again?"

"What?" Jamie shook herself. "You mean Timon? I don't know why he—"

"I'm an old man, but I'm not blind, goddaughter. I suspected that a close relationship had formed between you and the young Rider, but I didn't realize it would continue beyond your arrival here."

"I—I—" she stammered.

"Have you met with him, aside from today?"

"We...ran into each other at the showers. We can't pretend we've never met."

"Can't you?" Amos said. "He might at least avoid inserting himself into private conversations."

Flushing, Jamie looked away. "That was a mistake," she said. "I'll have to talk to him about it."

"Is he imposing on you? I can speak to the Riders' captain."

"No," she said. "I'm sure he knows that what he did was foolish."

"As you know how foolish it would be if you were to continue seeing him." Amos sighed. "I know you have good intentions, Jamie. But it's obvious that this Timon isn't going to ignore you, in spite of his commitment to the Riders and their neutrality in these negotiations. He obviously has some kind of attachment to you that he hasn't let go."

Jamie's heart began to pound, but not only with anxiety. *He hasn't let go*, she thought. *And neither have I.*

"I'd hoped that you would remain close to Greg," Amos said. "He has the power and will to protect you from any harm, and he loves you."

"What would he need to protect me from in the Enclave?" she asked. "I know you've always worried about me, but I've already made my decision about Greg. We wouldn't suit, for so many reasons."

"Jamie," Amos said, taking both her hands, "I want you to listen carefully. You heard Makedon's accusation about a Rider alliance with humans. Timon's friendship with you can only appear to be favoritism toward our delegation. The situation here is too delicate to risk any such speculation."

"I don't understand what a single Rider's attention could to do benefit one delegation over another."

"I don't know, but I don't want to find out. Stay away from him, Jamie. Don't give him the slightest encouragement, and this will pass."

Jamie stared at the ground. "You're right," she said.

"That's my girl." He released her hands. "Ah, here's Sergeant Cho. He'll see you back to our camp." He exchanged nods with the soldier. "We'll speak more when I return."

Her steps heavy, Jamie was just turning to accompany Cho when she looked up to see Timon with another man in Rider's clothes: older than Timon, gray-haired and forbidding in appearance. His gaze met Jamie's across the crowd, and she flinched at the hostility in his eyes.

Was this Timon's captain? Was he giving Timon the same lecture Amos had given her?

Afraid to catch Timon's eye, Jamie let the sergeant take her arm and guide her away from the Assembly tent.

Before today's encounter, she'd already decided to keep meeting with Timon. But she couldn't openly *seem* to disobey her godfather or do anything to put the Conclave at risk even in a way that appeared insignificant to her.

She'd need to arrange to see Timon in private, to make things clear between them. To make sure what had happened in the Assembly tent never occurred again and remind him to keep their future rendezvous absolutely secret.

That would have to be enough…just as the sex would have to be enough, if she couldn't have the one thing her heart yearned for more than anything else in the world. Even more than the success of the Enclave itself.

Chapter 18

Jamie lay awake with her thoughts, Akesha asleep in the other bed, when she heard scratching on the side of her tent. She knew it was Timon before she heard his voice.

"Jamie?"

She crept to the front of the tent and slipped out, unnoticed. The night was dark, lit only by the torches scattered about the human half of the tent city. Timon waited for her at the back. He took her hand and pulled her away from the Enclave camp, hurrying her along until they reached the nearest bathhouse.

At this time of night it was deserted even by the Opiri, as good a secure meeting place as any in the Conclave. Huddled together in a shower stall, neither of them seemed willing to speak first.

"Timon—" Jamie finally began.

"Jamie," Timon said, speaking over her. "I'm sorry for what happened at the reception. I had no right to interfere."

Jamie took Timon's hand and held it between hers, basking in his warmth. "You know it was dangerous," she said.

"I could have compromised the Riders' neutrality," he said. "How bad was it?"

"We didn't speak much to the Erebusians after you left," she said, "but I don't think any serious damage was done."

"Your godfather…what did he say?"

Jamie thought of what Amos had really said and pushed the thought away. "He knew about our relationship," she said. "He wasn't happy, and he doesn't want it to continue."

"My captain guessed, as well," Timon said.

"And he doesn't approve of our seeing each other."

Timon gave her a rueful smile. "No. But as long as I use my brain next time, it shouldn't be a problem."

Jamie looked down at their interlaced hands. "We both need to keep our heads. And our secrets."

He pulled his hands from hers so gently that she almost didn't feel the motion. "Did you learn anything useful at the reception?" he asked.

"It seems the people I'd like to meet weren't there," she said. "What about you?"

"I have my eye on two scientists from other Enclaves," he said. "They seem like reasonable people. If I think they're suitable, I can arrange a meeting."

"Wonderful," Jamie said, wishing she could kiss him. "How will you get a message to me?"

"I'll leave a note under your pillow," he said.

"My pillow? How can you get into my tent unnoticed?"

"Riders are taught many skills," she said. "I can avoid being seen."

Jamie believed him. "All right," she said.

Awkwardness fell between them, and Jamie felt more confusion. She couldn't read Timon's face. Was he trying to pull away from her, or being cautious? He knew how foolish it would be to do anything other than talk here, in the middle of the encampment.

So did she. But her heart gave her the courage to reach out and pull his face down to hers, to kiss him with all the passion she couldn't seem to express in words.

His tongue plunged between her lips, and the very air around them seemed to crackle with desire.

"Jamie," he said, breaking away. "This isn't wise."

"I don't care," she said, breathless. "I don't care about anything but us."

"The success of the Conclave—"

"Can go hang," she said, no longer bewildered by the sudden change in her priorities. "How can there be any peace if people who…care about each other can't be together?"

Timon froze, and Jamie understood why an instant after she had spoken. Were even the words *care about* too much for him, even though he'd proven his concern for her a hundred times in the past two months?

"Jamie," he said, taking a step away from her. "You honor me with your trust, and your—"

She covered his mouth with her hand. "Not now. You're right…this isn't the place or the time." She ducked out of the stall and moved cautiously to the bathhouse entrance. "There's no one out here. We can—"

She broke off as she saw a figure race past the bathhouse, the woman's hood half fallen off her gray-laced brown hair. She glanced at Jamie as she went by, her mouth forming an O of surprise.

Then she was gone. Jamie slipped back into the tent, Timon right behind her.

"What is it?" he asked.

"I don't know," she said, deeply unsettled. She peered outside again, just in time to see another figure—male this time, and obviously Opiri—running in the same direction as the woman. He didn't look at her, but she caught a glimpse of his profile.

The Opir was one of Lord Makedon's aides, from the Erebusian delegation.

"Something's wrong," she said to Timon. "An Opir was chasing a human woman."

She showed Timon the way the runners had gone, and by unspoken agreement they walked in the same direction, Timon constantly watching for observers. Twice they had to hide when Opiri passed by, presumably on nightly strolls.

It soon became clear that they weren't going to find any

trace of the runners. They were already approaching the border of the Opiri precinct, which Jamie couldn't enter without permission.

"Why do I have the feeling that the Opir was deliberately chasing the woman into his territory?" she asked.

"Don't even think about it," Timon said. "I don't want you going anywhere near the Opir precinct unless you're with your godfather or one of your guards."

"Or you," she said.

He didn't look at her. "Let's go back," he said. "If I hear anything about a problem between Opiri and humans, I'll let you know."

"What if he was chasing her for her blood?"

"I'll do what I can to find out," Timon said. He took her hand and led her by roundabout ways back to the Enclave camp, where he left her in front of her tent. He vanished before she could say good-night.

Timon ran.

He didn't care who saw him, or what they thought of his flight. He raced through the human precinct and kept on going to the very edge of the tent city, beyond the colony camps to the place where vendors and locals had gathered to serve the needs of the delegates. He ran into the area set aside for the Wanderers with their brightly colored vehicles, where small fires burned down to ashes as the people of the wagons sought their beds.

A horse in the nearby corral lifted its head and whinnied softly as Timon approached the wagons. No one stirred. Timon wove his way among the vehicles, looking for the one he knew so well.

Caridad sat up in her bed when he entered the wagon, her black hair tousled and her eyes heavy-lidded. They widened when she saw Timon, and her full lips curved in a smile.

"I wondered if you'd come looking for me," she said.

Timon leaned against the door. "I didn't know if you'd be here so soon."

"Our horses are very fast and strong," she said. "We left the camp at the foot of the pass not long after you did and arrived just this afternoon."

"Then I should let you rest," Timon said, his hand on the doorknob.

Caridad leaped out of bed and cornered him, her hand on his arm. "I am not tired," she said. "I would welcome the company and the tale of the last part of your journey."

"It wouldn't interest you," Timon muttered.

"Then there are other ways to pass the time." Her hand slid down to his and pulled him toward the bed. "Sit, and I will brew us some tea."

Clearing his throat, Timon perched on the end of the bed, aware of Caridad's rich, warm scent on the tangled sheets. He had shared that same bed dozens of times over the course of his years as a Rider, whenever he and Caridad's troupe of Wanderers met during their travels. He knew what to expect when she invited him to her wagon, and he never left it without feeling well satisfied both physically and emotionally.

He didn't know if that was possible now. He had come to find out.

The sweet-and-spicy smell of Caridad's tea filled the wagon, and she let it steep as she returned to Timon and knelt to untie his boots. He let her do it, though his body was taut as a wire.

Caridad would know how to relax him. She knew how to work the knots out of his muscles, how to tease away his cares without demanding more than he was willing to give in return.

"You are troubled tonight," she said, tugging off his boots and setting them aside. "Was your expedition so terrible?"

He was certain she had already guessed. "There was no trouble," he said as she pressed her fingers into his shoulders.

"Then the girl is here with her people?"

"Yes."

"I wonder what she would think if she saw you here with me."

Timon's muscles twitched. "Why should she care?"

Caridad gave a rich, throaty laugh. "I should say she cared when she saw you taking my blood before."

"She was only surprised."

"You hadn't taken *her* blood yet?"

"She had suffered unpleasant experiences in the past."

Digging her fingers more deeply into his trapezius, she leaned her head close to his. "I'll bet she wanted you to do it, after you and I were together."

Timon kept his face blank. "Why are we talking about Jamie? I came here for…to—"

"Get away from her?" Caridad purred. "Stop thinking about her?"

"Where do you get these ideas, Caridad?"

"I keep my ear to the ground." Her lush black hair spilled over his neck as she spoke against his cheek. She moved around and began to unbutton his shirt.

"What are you hearing?" he asked, pushing her hands away.

"Oh, nothing important. As you said, let's forget about her." She knelt before Timon and resumed unbuttoning his shirt. She slipped her hand inside to lay her palm on his chest. "Your heart is beating fast. I hope it is for me."

To prove to himself that it was, Timon kissed her. He knew it was wrong the instant his mouth touched hers.

Caridad ended it before he could. "Ah," she said, disappointment in her voice. "It doesn't beat for me, after all."

"Caridad—"

"Don't apologize. I know it is beyond your control."

"I shouldn't have come here tonight. I'm not myself."

She got up and walked away, trailing her fingertips across his hair. "Indeed. My wild Rider has vanished, tamed by a woman."

"I'm not a horse to be broken."

"But you have fallen in love with someone else, have you not?"

Chapter 19

Timon jumped to his feet, fumbling at the buttons of his shirt. "Is it possible that you're jealous, Caridad?" he demanded. "Is that what's making you see things that don't exist?"

"Is it possible you don't even realize it?" She turned to face him, sipping a cup of tea. "I can have my pick of any man, human or Opir, in this encampment. If you choose to seek your entertainment elsewhere, I won't try to stop you."

Finishing with his shirt, Timon yanked on his jacket. "I'm sorry to have disturbed you."

"It's always a pleasure to see an old friend."

Caridad opened the door for him, and he hopped down the stairs. He could imagine her watching him with a mocking smile, but when he looked over his shoulder he saw that her expression seemed almost sad.

Fallen in love. He clenched his teeth and strode back into the camp, wondering why she had spoken to him with such spite.

Because you hurt her, he thought. Because even if they'd been naked in her bed, he couldn't have followed through.

It isn't love, he thought. *It's only—*

His thoughts came to a sudden stop when he saw the three men standing in the deep shadows under one of the outermost tents. All wore hoods. One, his senses told him, was human, while the others were Opiri. One of them moved, and Timon caught a glimpse of the Erebusian sigil on his belt. Timon thought nothing more of it until he saw the human's face.

City Council President Amos Parks, Jamie's godfather. Why would he be meeting in secret with Erebusians at the edge of camp?

He had no answer, but he was not to be left to his own speculation. As he walked farther into the camp, Greg Cahill strode out of the darkness to meet him.

"Stay away from Jamie," the human said, stopping just a few feet from Timon.

Timon laughed. It was either that or knock Cahill down and cause an incident that would reverberate throughout the entire Conclave.

"I'm honored," he said with a mock bow, "that you came so far to find me, Senator Cahill."

The man worked his mouth as if he were ready to spit. "I know you've been seeing her privately," he said.

"You've been following her?" Timon asked, his fingers working into fists.

"I've been protecting her," Cahill said.

"Why? Has she complained about me?"

"I know what you Riders are, and how you've convinced Jamie that you care for her."

"You're mistaken, Senator."

"Do you think she didn't confess to me what you did while you were traveling here?"

"I know she did."

"So you have her confiding personal conversations to you. She might even jeopardize our mission, if you continue to compromise your people's neutrality."

To hear such a suggestion from his captain was one thing; to endure it from this foul-tempered human quite another.

"Accusations like that can be dangerous," Timon said.

"To me?" Cahill grinned. "You'd like to take me down, wouldn't you?"

Timon only stared at him, unwilling to take the bait. "Does Jamie know you've come to speak to me?"

"No. But she knows I've forgiven her indiscretions. You've twisted her loyalties and taken her away from us. Her godfather is deeply concerned." Cahill's strident tone softened. "She is one of us, Rider...our kind. Human. For you, she's only a way to pass the time."

Timon struggled to find the right answer. Caridad's words still echoed in his mind. *Fallen in love.* She claimed he didn't even realize it.

But that wasn't possible. He had never intended to steal Jamie from her world. He cared for her...enough to keep from poisoning her relationships with her own people. And to keep from leading her on when she thought she loved *him.*

"I am not ashamed of the time Jamie and I spent together," he said. "But it's over."

Cahill's face cleared. "Then you *will* stay away—"

"I won't avoid her, Cahill. But I won't seek her out. My responsibility is to the Brotherhood, wherever that takes me."

Jamie clamped her lips together and breathed through her nose, swallowing the soft protest that bubbled up in her throat.

He doesn't mean it, she thought, grasping at fading hopes. *He's trying to disarm Greg.*

But she knew it wasn't true. He hadn't even denied that he'd "twisted her loyalties" or that he regarded Jamie as "only a way to pass the time."

Damn him, she thought. He'd led her to believe...

Nothing. He'd never been anything but honest with her.

She got to her feet and snuck away from her hiding place, praying that Timon didn't spy her out in the shadows. She wasn't worried about Cahill; he'd never so much as sensed her presence even when she was nearly within touching distance.

Unable to bear the thought of returning to the Enclave camp, she skirted the edge of the tent city, keeping to the human side. No one called after her. She walked blindly, ignoring the few people she passed, and found herself moving toward the Rio Grande. Cottonwoods rustled overheard; the river itself spoke in soft hisses and gurgles, gliding around fallen tree trunks and sandbars.

Jamie sat on the bank and tossed stones into the water. Reflected stars shone like mysterious lights under the surface. Her eyes burned with unshed tears, but she refused to give in.

The snap of a twig brought her head up sharply. She scrambled to her feet, searching for the source of the noise. The sound didn't repeat, so she brushed off her pants and slowly started back toward the Enclave camp. She wasn't prepared when the arm closed around her neck and a man dragged her back among the riverside shrubs. She gasped and tried to pry his arm away; he only pulled harder, nearly choking her.

Abruptly he let her go, and she fell. It was difficult to see his features in the darkness, but something in the gauntness of his face, the hollows under his eyes told her who had taken her down so easily.

Nereus.

He bared his teeth in a grimace that seemed more mad than threatening. She subdued her terror and held up her hands.

"Nereus," she said softly.

The Opir blinked as if he hadn't expected her to speak. The whites of his eyes were so bloodshot that they were nearly red.

"What's wrong?" she asked, scooting away from him. "Can I help you?"

"Hungry," he said, his voice like rocks clashing against each other.

"You need blood?"

His eyes widened, and he licked his lips. Jamie weighed her options. There was obviously something very wrong with Nereus, just as there had been earlier during the reception. His fingers were like crooked sticks, and in spite of his Opir strength he moved like an old man. His veins showed clearly through his skin.

If she gave him blood, he might calm down. He would have no reason to injure her; she'd cooperated with him before, and if he'd meant to kill her he'd have done it already.

"You can have my blood, Nereus," she said. She got to her feet, suppressing her shivers, and held out her hands again. "There's no need for force."

But if Nereus understood her, he gave no sign. He bared his teeth again and lunged toward her. She hurled herself to the side and tried to rise, but a tiny forest of branches plucked and pulled at her clothes.

Then his hands were on her, long fingernails scraping her skin, teeth snapping at her neck as he grunted like an animal. She wasn't able to make a sound.

"Nereus!" someone shouted.

The Opir hesitated, his fangs grazing Jamie's neck. Hands clamped around his shoulders and yanked him backward, dragging him off her and throwing him to the ground.

"Run, Jamie," Timon said.

Chapter 20

Jamie didn't run. She stumbled well out of reach of both men and looked around for a stick big enough to club Nereus with.

For Timon had his hands full. Nereus was on his feet seconds after he hit the ground, his fingers curled into claws and his eyes aflame with madness. He launched himself at Timon, who ducked and threw Nereus over his shoulder.

Again Nereus jumped to his feet, and this time Timon was obviously prepared for violence. He fell back, gathered his body and met Nereus in midleap. The two men grappled fiercely, Nereus's nails seeking to rake Timon's face, but Timon kept his head just out of the Opir's reach.

Searching with both eyes and hands, Jamie found a thick tree branch and inched her way closer to the men. Timon flung Nereus away, but not before his opponent's fangs tore a piece out of his shirt.

Darting toward Nereus, Jamie swung at his head as hard as she could, and he grunted as the branch made contact. It barely seemed to affect him, but Timon was on him as soon as Jamie lifted the branch for another blow. He pinned Nereus to the ground with his hands around the Opir's neck and his teeth just above Nereus's throat.

"Stop!" he commanded. "Lie still!"

Nereus thrashed under him. Timon bore down with his hands until Nereus's struggles ceased and then closed his teeth lightly on Nereus's neck.

"No," Jamie whispered, sucking in her breath. But

Timon didn't bite down, and Nereus didn't move. His eyes closed, and he shuddered as if he were in the midst of a seizure.

"There's something wrong with him," Jamie said, dropping the branch. "He's ill, not just physically. His mind—"

Timon lifted his head. "Are you all right?" he asked, his voice rough with worry.

"I'm fine. He didn't really hurt me." She ventured closer. "Is he unconscious?"

Timon studied Nereus's face. "He seems to be. But I didn't do it."

"It must be part of whatever's wrong with him," she said. "Look at his face."

Sucking air through his teeth, Timon shook his head. "I've never seen an Opir look like that," he said.

Reality hit Jamie all at once, and she sat down hard. "I can't see why he'd attack me if he was in his right mind. I gave him blood willingly before."

"And blood is available from volunteers in donor stations all over the Conclave," Timon said. He reached inside his jacket and pulled out a thin but strong-looking rope. "I should take him to my captain immediately."

"Wait," Jamie said. "What would your captain do? Confine him until he comes out of it? What if he doesn't?" She hesitated. "I think we should take him back to his own people, to Lord Dimitri, and try to find out what's wrong with him first. Then you can take him to the captain."

Timon cocked his head, weighing her words. His gaze lingered on her, moving from the top of her head to her knees, as if he were verifying that she hadn't been hurt. His eyes held a peculiar expression, perhaps reflecting his memory of what he had told Greg, even though he wouldn't know she had overheard.

"All right," he said after a long silence. "I'll take him to his delegation and question them first."

Relieved, Jamie got to her feet. Her heartbeat had nearly returned to normal, and she felt safe even before Timon rolled Nereus over and lashed his wrists together behind his back.

"We'll stop by your camp on the way back," he said, looking away from her. "As long as you're sure you don't need medical attention..."

"I don't," she said. "And I want to come with you."

"If he returns to consciousness—"

"I'm not worried," she said. "But I have a particular interest in this situation. And I'm a scientist. There aren't many illnesses that afflict Opiri, and I'd like to know what it is."

"*If* it's an illness." He frowned. "I don't like having you go into the Opir precinct."

"You don't really have any say in the matter."

Timon sighed. "I suppose you have the right," he said. "And you're on good terms with the Tenebrian delegation."

"How will you get him there?" she asked.

Without a word, Timon got up, dragged Nereus to his feet and slung the Opir over his shoulder with seemingly no effort at all. Jamie wondered how she could have doubted his strength.

They made their way through the rows of human tents and across the central thoroughfare and Hub to the Opiri side. Opiri wandered here and there, pausing to stare as the human woman and half-blood Rider walked by.

In spite of herself, Jamie shivered. Timon shifted Nereus's weight and continued unerringly toward one of the clusters of bannered tents. A pair of Opiri stood outside one of the peripheral tents, deep in conversation. They stopped as Timon and Jamie approached. Timon lowered Nereus to the ground, where he slumped on his knees.

"What is this?" one of the Opiri asked.

"One of yours seems to be having a little problem," Timon said. "We need to speak to Lord Dimitri."

"What did you do to him?" the other Opir demanded.

"He attacked this woman without provocation," Timon said, staring into the Opir's eyes.

With an exchange of glances, the Opiri split up, one entering the tent, the other disappearing around the corner. Jamie could sense Timon's impatience as they waited, and she felt on pins and needles herself. Only part of it was due to being surrounded by Opiri.

The rest was Timon.

Stop it, she told herself, squeezing her eyes closed.

"What has happened?" a familiar voice said. She opened her eyes to find Lord Dimitri, flanked by two of his aides, standing very close to Timon. Threateningly close.

"Nereus attacked Jamie," Timon said bluntly. "There was no provocation. He wanted her blood and was prepared to hurt her to get it."

That wasn't exactly the way it had gone, Jamie thought, but she wasn't prepared to argue the point here and now. "I'm all right, Lord Dimitri," she said, "but Nereus was behaving very strangely, and we thought we should discuss it with you before Timon takes him to Security."

One of Dimitri's aides moved to take Nereus, but Timon blocked his way and kept a grip on Nereus's shoulder. "He committed a crime, to which I was witness," he said. "He is still bound for a cell, but if you have some explanation for his behavior, it will be considered."

Dimitri's nostrils flared, and the pleasant aspect he'd shown Jamie before was replaced by barely veiled hostility. "Nereus would never attack anyone," he said.

"But he did," Timon said. "And it's not likely to be a coincidence that he attacked the same human woman who volunteered her blood in the past."

"That is precisely why he would never harm Ms. McCullough," Dimitri said.

"He didn't appear to be completely sane. His behavior was that of an animal."

Tense silence fell as more Tenebrians gathered behind their leader. "He has been ill," Dimitri admitted grudgingly.

"What kind of illness?"

"We do not know. We were watching his condition closely."

"Then how did he come to be hunting Ms. McCullough?"

"We did not realize that he had left our camp," Dimitri said. "Give him to us, and we will make certain that he causes no further trouble."

"I'm afraid that's impossible."

The Tenebrians crowded closer. The hair rose on the back of Jamie's neck.

This was not good. She was prepared to bet that the Tenebrians wouldn't simply let Nereus go with Timon, and the Rider wasn't going to let the Opiri have him. If Dimitri's party attacked one of the Riders, there could be nasty consequences.

"Wait," she said. "I will not press charges against Nereus, as long as you keep him confined and let the medics examine him."

"Human medics?" an aide said, his upper lip twitching.

"Some of whom have considerable knowledge of Opiri physiology," Jamie said. "And humans understand illness as most Opiri do not."

"We can promise to confine him," Dimitri said. "As for the other—"

"Rider Timon," Jamie said formally, "I do not wish to press charges."

Timon narrowed his eyes. "Ms. McCullough, it isn't your decision to make."

"I was the injured party," she said. "But I'm afraid I no

longer remember much of the incident. If you question me, I may not be of much help."

Sweeping the gathering with his gaze, Timon seemed to be making a quick calculation. Jamie knew him well enough to believe he'd reach the same conclusion she had. Punishing Nereus, when he obviously wasn't in his right mind, was not worth the conflict that would arise if Timon didn't remand the Tenebrian into the custody of his own people.

Timon released Nereus with a slight shove, and the Opir began to fall forward. Several of the Tenebrians rushed forward to take charge of him.

"If I see Nereus outside your camp again," Timon said, holding Dimitri's gaze, "I *will* arrest him."

Lord Dimitri inclined his head, and Jamie imagined she saw relief in his eyes. Timon took Jamie by the arm and pulled her away from the Tenebrian camp, taking long strides that she could barely match.

"I hope you're satisfied," he said.

"I'd hoped to learn more," she said.

"We just let a possible future killer go free."

"But you knew what would have happened if we didn't."

"I would have taken him in if you hadn't been there."

Jamie dug in her feet and forced him to stop. "I wasn't afraid of them. I only wanted to make sure—"

"I should never have let you interfere."

"You are not my personal guard, Timon. I don't need your constant protection."

"Maybe Cahill and Parks will start taking better care of you."

"I realize that you've had to save my life several times, but you know I'm not a child."

"Oh, yes. I know."

A pulse of desire ran through Jamie's body. Then she remembered that Timon would expect her to learn of his conversation with Greg once she returned to the San Francisco camp, and *he* wouldn't have to tell her that he was through with her.

Tamping down her anger, Jamie jerked her arm free and walked beside Timon, careful not to touch him.

"Are you all right?" he asked.

"Obviously," she said.

"I don't mean physically," he said, stopping abruptly. "This must have felt a lot like the attack you suffered in the Enclave as a child."

"I think I've finally put that behind me," she said. "What have you put behind *you*, Timon?"

They gazed at each other. Timon looked away first. They continued to the San Francisco camp, where Timon left her without a word.

Chapter 21

Timon didn't report the incident. But he relived it, again and again…imagining what would have happened if he hadn't been there to stop Nereus.

Jamie didn't want his protection. She'd said so. But he could no more ignore any danger to her than he could give up his place among the Riders. Whatever he might feel—or *not* feel—about her didn't change that.

He'd known that Jamie was right in wanting to give Nereus back to the Tenebrians; now all he had to do was hope they'd hold to their promise and keep Nereus under strict control.

But he'd betrayed Cassius in not doing his job as he should have. For Jamie's sake.

His thoughts bleak, Timon reported the incident of the Opir chasing the human woman, leaving the problem in the hands of Cassius's investigators, and went in search of one of the donor stations, where humans volunteered to provide Opiri delegates with blood. He entered one near the Rider headquarters, pausing to examine the small signs above each of the closed stalls. They indicated the gender of the donor, and whether said donor was already engaged.

He chose one of the female booths and found an older woman with a round and pleasant face and graying hair pulled up on a knot. She smiled at Timon and indicated the seat next to hers.

Timon hesitated in the doorway. "How often have you donated today?" he asked.

"Twice," she said in a soft, musical voice. "You will be my last." She tilted her head. "You needn't worry, you know. They don't expect us to donate too much in a day, or too often."

"I know," Timon said, entering the booth.

"You're a Rider, aren't you?" the woman asked, patting the seat. "My name is Maggie. I'm from the San Antonio Enclave."

"Timon," he said, taking the seat. His seat and hers stood side-by-side, facing in opposite directions to facilitate feeding from the front of her throat. Timon was grateful that Maggie was so pragmatic about it, when he knew not all humans were so easy about donation.

"You seem worried," Maggie said in a sympathetic voice. "I know the Riders have the job of security for the entire Conclave. It must be quite a burden."

"Everything's been peaceful so far," Timon said, seeing no reason to share the complete truth. "How does your delegation stand on the Conclave's goals?"

He had no right to ask, but Maggie seemed unperturbed. "They're for peace, of course," she said. She bared her throat. "We're really all the same in the end, you know."

As Jamie said, Timon thought. Here was one human who wouldn't resist the truth when it finally came out. But so far, he hadn't done a damned thing to help Jamie arrange to share the information.

"You *have* done this before, haven't you?" Maggie asked, gently teasing.

"It won't be painful," Timon assured her.

"Please go ahead."

After another few moments of hesitation, Timon accepted her invitation. He leaned into her and placed his mouth close to her throat. He could feel her pulse, hear her steady breathing.

He bit carefully, numbing the area as soon as his teeth pierced her skin. She sighed. He began to drink.

He'd hardly taken a mouthful when he realized that something was wrong. The blood tasted sour, almost tainted, and he stopped immediately. He withdrew, healed the small wounds and got to his feet.

"What's wrong?" Maggie asked, rubbing her neck. "Why did you stop?"

"I don't know," Timon asked, dazed and off balance. "Something's not right."

"With my blood?" She searched his face. "The other two had no problem with it."

"I have no explanation," Timon said, nearly stumbling over the chair as he made for the door. "I'm sorry."

Maggie rose. "Are you ill? Is there something I can do?

Timon shook his head, unable to speak. He nodded thanks to Maggie and rushed out of the booth, stopping to lean heavily against one of tent poles.

What was wrong with him?

His body aching with newly aroused hunger, he looked for another booth. The last one was open. A much younger woman waited inside, a pretty, almost fragile-looking female with deep brown eyes.

"I'm Clary," she said with a smile.

"Timon," he said. He sat without any of the previous niceties and leaned toward her. Her heartbeat increased, and her breathing quickened.

He knew the signs. She was sexually aroused by the act of being bitten, but he wasn't in any state to back out. He heard her gasp as his teeth touched her, feeling her body shudder as he began to feed.

Then it happened again. Nearly spitting, Timon reared back and wiped his mouth. Clary stared at him in confusion.

"I'm sorry," he said, backing away. "It isn't your fault."

"But I—"

He left without hearing the end of her sentence. The first rays of morning sunlight struck the tops of the mountains to the east, and for a moment he was blinded.

Still pierced with hunger, he strode away from the donor station. Every human he came across was a potential source of blood, but he felt nothing but revulsion.

It was only when he found himself standing outside the San Francisco camp that he realized what he was seeking.

Jamie's blood. The only blood he wanted, just as she was still the only woman he wanted, regardless of his inability to return her deepest feelings.

There were several possible explanations for his need for her blood alone. But Timon feared the worst. Time would tell; if he continued to reject all other donors, he'd know that something profound had happened between him and Jamie on their journey.

It was almost certain that they'd formed a blood-bond, and no other blood would ever satisfy him again. And if that was true, he'd become utterly dependent on her.

He couldn't accept that. It would be grossly unfair to her, and intolerable for him. There must be another explanation. He would have to keep trying. And if the worst happened, he would simply have to overcome it.

And Jamie could never know.

For two weeks, Jamie heard nothing from Timon.

She saw him often enough, riding through camp, he and his band carrying messages from one delegation to another, or from the Conclave administration to other departments responsible for running the huge encampment. Sometimes she caught him looking in her direction, and it seemed he passed the San Francisco camp a little more often than he ordinarily might. She got the strong impression that he was protecting her from a distance, keeping an eye on her as his duties permitted.

But he never stopped to speak to her. She heard nothing more about the scientists he'd met and promised to put her in touch with. There was an emptiness inside her, an emptiness that seemed to curse her insistence on loving a man who couldn't return that love.

She turned her concentration to her role as aide to her godfather. The negotiations in the Assembly tent had begun in earnest, and Jamie could see early on that they would not be easy ones. On a personal level, some of the delegates could seem friendly, even charming; during the opening statements they revealed their true feelings in dry language that held a wealth of emotion behind it. Many of the Opiri were arrogant, their sense of superiority impeded only by the fact that they needed new and regular sources of blood; some humans were distrustful, wary, even hostile toward the Opiri, remembering years of slavery under the old system of serfdom.

Jamie's primary duty was to fetch and carry for Amos, as well as take copious notes. But she kept two notebooks, and in one she recorded little observations, informal ones, that might be vital later on: certain subtle signs from this or that delegation that indicated a willingness to compromise, or hinted that the delegation in question would take a great deal of convincing to make a new peace.

In between sessions, she looked for levelheaded scientists with whom she might share her secret, but every time she found one, she couldn't bring herself to make a move. If her judgment was wrong, as it had been so wrong with Timon…

"Are you all right, Jamie?" Amos asked, taking her elbow as the latest session broke up. "You've seemed out of sorts lately."

"There's a lot to think about," she said. "I never imagined myself in a place like this."

"I don't think any of us did." He guided her through the crowd. "Have you heard anything more from that young Rider?"

Jamie started, wondering if Amos had spoken to Greg. Greg had come to her after his conversation with Timon, making it clear without actually repeating the words that the Rider had gone his own way and that he had simply used Jamie for his own convenience. Greg, on the other hand, had fully "forgiven" her.

He still loved her. She could still marry him, as Amos wanted. They could have a future together.

But Jamie knew it would never work, and she wasn't so certain that a happy future was sure for anyone. She could only be grateful that no one besides her, Timon and the Tenebrians seemed to know about Nereus's attack.

"Jamie?"

"No, I haven't," she said, belatedly answering Amos's question.

"It's just as well," he said.

Jamie didn't reply. She went along quietly until they reached their camp and retreated to her tent. She sat cross-legged on the bed and opened her mother's frayed journal, reading some of the old, familiar passages and the dense notes so few others could understand.

What would Eileen have said about Timon? Would she have encouraged Jamie to forget him? She had loved her husband… Would she have understood that you couldn't just solve a complicated relationship and file it away like a mathematical problem?

Jamie set down the journal and stared at the plain blanket that served as her bedcover. It couldn't go on this way. She wasn't going to let Timon off so easily. She'd find him and make him tell her to her face. Tell her it was over, that no lingering trace of affection bound them together.

She swung her legs over the side of the cot and noted the time. Just after sunset; maybe not the best hour to wander around the tent city, but she wasn't going to let the memory of Nereus's attack stop her.

Pulling on her jacket, she left the tent and walked to the front of the Enclave camp. She was startled when Sergeant Cho rode up to Amos's tent, dismounted and rushed inside.

With a sense of dread, Jamie waited at the side of the tent, listening to anxious voices, catching partial sentences and piecing together the subject.

"Dead," Cho said. "…found the body."

"Who?"

"…know… Nereus…Tenebris."

A body. Nereus. Tenebris. Had Nereus killed someone, when she and Timon might have stopped it?

Without considering the consequences, Jamie caught Cho's horse and mounted hastily. She rode onto the central thoroughfare toward the Hub, keeping her eyes and ears open. Humans and Opiri were walking or jogging in the same direction.

She followed the tide of the crowd to the western boundary of the tent city, not far from the place where Nereus had attacked her. She used her mount to push her way through the observers who had already gathered around something on the ground.

A body. It lay on its back, mouth agape, face so horribly sunken that Jamie could barely recognize it. There were no marks of any kind on the body, no blood, no apparent broken bones.

Nereus. She released her breath, relieved that he hadn't found another victim. But why was the Opir out here, and how had he died?

She dismounted and led the horse to one of the cottonwoods, loosely tying him to a convenient shrub. The rumble of hooves marked the arrival of the Riders, ten in all, who scattered the crowd as they approached the body.

One of them was Timon. He leaped from Lazarus's back and knelt beside the dead Opir.

"Did you know him?" his captain said, dropping down next to him.

Jamie saw Timon hesitate, his expression impossible to read. "We met," he said.

"There's clearly something wrong with this Opir," Cassius said. He looked up suddenly, and his eyes unerringly met Jamie's. "The Tenebrians are on their way. If you have anything to report, Timon…"

"I saw him," an Opir said, stepping out from the crowd. He pointed at Timon. "I saw this Rider arguing with the dead man. Maybe *he* killed him."

Chapter 22

The accusation of murder silenced the crowd instantly. Jamie left the illusory protection of the trees and started unthinkingly toward Timon, a protest already on her lips.

Timon rose and stared toward the Opir who had made the claim. Jamie didn't recognize him; he wasn't from Tenebris, and she'd never seen him during the assemblies. She could tell from Timon's expression that he'd never seen the Opir, either.

"Who is speaking?" Cassius asked, getting to his feet.

"The Rider threatened him," the Opir said, lowering his head so that his hood hid his face. "They were ready to fight."

"Step forward," Timon said, his fists clenched. "Show yourself."

But all at once the crowd shifted, and the Opir was swallowed up again. Riders dismounted to search for him, but they returned empty-handed.

"He's disappeared," one of the Riders said.

"He was lying," Timon said. "I had nothing to do with this Opir's death."

"*Did* you argue with him?" Cassius said, stone-faced.

"Because of me," Jamie said, stepping forward. She met Cassius's unfriendly stare. "I am Jamie McCullough, of the San Francisco delegation. This Opir, Nereus, attacked me without provocation two weeks ago. Timon stopped him but didn't harm him."

The buzz of the crowd started up again. Cassius turned his gaze on Timon.

"You had an altercation with this Opir and did not report it?" he asked.

"It's my fault," Jamie said. "Nereus was obviously sick, physically and mentally. I suggested we take Nereus back to his own people."

"So you let an aggressor attack one of our human delegates without informing me?" Cassius asked Timon.

Timon lifted his head. "I did," he admitted. "The lady declined to press charges. The Tenebrians agreed to keep him confined."

"Clearly they did not," Cassius said. He turned to Jamie again. "It was not your decision to decide the fate of one who attacked you, miss."

"She was the victim," Timon said, his voice rough.

"And yet you said that this Opir was sick. The highly unusual circumstances should have been enough to merit a report." He glanced down at the body. "And now a man is dead."

"I did fight him," Timon said, "but he was alive when I left him with the Tenebrians."

"I'm sure they'll confirm it when they arrive," Cassius said. He called to several of his other Riders, and they moved about to dispel the crowd. Reluctantly, the observers drifted away.

"I can also confirm it," Jamie said.

Cassius's expression remained anything but friendly. "You didn't see the dead man again after this incident with Ms. McCullough?" he asked Timon. "Perhaps out of concern for her safety?"

"No," Timon said.

Jamie wondered if he was lying. It wasn't impossible that Nereus had escaped confinement, and that Timon had run across him.

But he wouldn't have killed Nereus. Or try to hide the fact.

"I think it would be wise to temporarily relieve you of duty," Cassius said. "We'll speak more of this at headquarters."

Timon seemed to freeze. He looked at Jamie again, and she saw a flare of something like panic in his eyes. Not fear that he would be blamed for Nereus's death, she thought, but that he would be barred from doing his work with the Riders.

He broke away from Cassius and strode toward Jamie. As he got closer, she could see that he, too, had hollows under his eyes and cheekbones, and that his eyes seemed to burn with a strange light. They softened as they met hers.

"Are you all right?" he asked.

Jamie wet her lips. "Yes," she said. "I heard about Nereus in camp, and I came… I was worried that—"

"You thought I was involved?"

"I didn't know what to think."

"I didn't have anything to do with it, Jamie."

"I believe you. I'll testify to everything that happened. This is all my fault."

"No." He raised his hand as if to touch her, and then lowered it again. "Cassius has reasons to doubt me, which is why he's suspended me from duty."

"Why should he doubt you?" she asked. "Because you didn't make the report?"

Timon looked away. "It isn't that simple. But I won't be able to speak to you for a while."

"It's already been two weeks, Timon," she said, keeping her voice level.

"I know." He made a helpless gesture with one hand. "There's a reason, Jamie—"

"Greg made it very plain."

He winced. "I wish I had a way to—"

"Timon," Cassius said, striding up behind him. "It is time to go."

"What about the body?" Jamie asked.

Cassius regarded her as if he had totally dismissed her from his mind. "It will be taken to our headquarters to be examined by the medics."

"How many actual Opir medics do you have?"

"If we require your help, we will ask for it," Cassius said.

"Cassius," Timon said, a low growl in his voice.

"Hold yourself ready to give testimony, Ms. McCullough," Cassius said, gripping Timon's arm. Timon shook himself free and faced Jamie.

"Be careful," he said. "Stay in your camp."

Then he was walking away with Cassius, and Jamie was left to wonder why Cassius was so hostile to her and so skeptical about a Rider who was unquestionably loyal to him. Surely he couldn't believe that Timon could have done it.

Something was very wrong here, Jamie thought. And she wasn't going to stand idly by and let Timon get blamed for whatever was going on.

It was no easy matter to get Nereus's body.

Entering the Riders' headquarters the next morning wasn't a problem. There were dozens of humans and a few Opiri with complaints for Conclave Security, each waiting their turn for an interview with Riders manning several desks in the large tent.

When an Opir left his hooded cloak behind on the chair where he'd been waiting, she picked it up, hurried out of the tent, pulled it on and found a place in the shadows to hide. Such a disguise would hardly fool a real Opir, who could smell the human in her, but it might allow her to get a little closer to the back of the tent, where the body was probably being held for examination.

She hadn't gone more than halfway to the rear of the tent when a hooded Opir gripped her elbow firmly.

"Let go of me," she said softly.

"I'm here to help," the Opir said. He tilted up his head just enough for her to see his face under the hood. "Do you remember me?"

"Orpheus," she said, recognizing one of the Riders who had escorted the San Francisco delegation.

"Yes. Timon asked me to look after you while he's confined."

"Is he in jail?" she asked, meeting Orpheus's shadowed eyes. "Have they—"

"Cassius is behaving strangely," Orpheus said, "but that's not your worry. What are you doing out here?"

Jamie hesitated, wondering how much she dared tell Orpheus. "Are you truly Timon's friend?" she asked.

"If I weren't, I wouldn't be here."

"Then listen to me. I need to see the body. Timon's been accused of harming Nereus, but I think there's something else going on. Someone is out to blame him for something he didn't do."

"It sounds as if you're talking about a conspiracy. Why would anyone want to get him into trouble?"

"I know how it sounds. But obviously Cassius is taking it seriously."

Orpheus's head dipped. "What exactly do you want me to do?"

"Get me to wherever they're keeping Nereus's body, and buy me a few minutes to examine it."

"We'll both be in trouble if we're caught."

"I only ask this for Timon's sake."

Orpheus sighed. "All right. Come with me."

He led her around to the back of the tent, where there was a smaller rear entrance. It was unguarded. Orpheus continued to guide her through the door flap and into a darkened area divided with sheets of canvas into rooms and short corridors.

"There shouldn't be anyone back here now," Orpheus whispered. "This way."

The area they sought was another canvas-walled room, empty except for a flat board on which Nereus's body lay. It was already beginning to show signs of decomposition, and Jamie couldn't imagine they'd leave the corpse here much longer. She had to work quickly.

Pulling out her notebook and a pencil, she moved around the body, examining it from all angles, lifting the limbs and examining the skull and neck with particular care.

"Anything?" Orpheus said, staring toward the opening that served as the room's sole doorway.

"He wasn't physically hurt," she said. "No broken bones, no lacerations or bruises. I can't find a single mark on him."

"Then Timon couldn't have hurt him," Orpheus said.

"But something did. Nereus was very ill." She began to feel for his internal organs, remembering the many things her father had taught her.

"Some of his organs seem to have shrunk," she said, "and his legs are swollen with edema. His muscle is badly wasted, and there's barely an ounce of fat on his body."

"What does that mean?"

"It's difficult to tell without an actual autopsy, but some of these symptoms suggest starvation. And given the way he looked even before he died…" She set down her notebook and reached into her pocket for the capped syringe. "I'm going to take a blood sample and see if I can analyze it at the human med clinic."

"You think there's something wrong with his blood?" Orpheus asked.

"I know what Opir blood is supposed to look like, and examining it may give me a clue."

"Take your sample quickly," Orpheus said. "I think someone's coming."

Jamie worked carefully but swiftly, drawing the blood and recapping the syringe. It would have to be refrigerated, but the human medical clinic had solar-powered units that could keep it at the right temperature until she could get it under a microscope.

"We have to go," Orpheus said. He took her arm again and half carried her out of the tent and some distance away from the Security headquarters, putting her down only when he seemed certain that no one had seen them leave the tent.

"Where now?" he asked.

"I can get there myself."

"I told Timon I'd watch you."

"Then follow me."

This time, she led Orpheus across camp to the human clinic on the border of the precinct.

"You'll have to stay outside," she said. "I'm a certified medic, and no one is likely to question me."

"How long?" Orpheus said.

"I don't know. Don't shirk your duty because of me. I *can* take care of myself."

"Unless you meet another Nereus."

"It's broad daylight. Worry about Timon, not me."

She entered the tent with a confident step, as if she belonged there. Both Akesha and Don were on duty and greeted her with mild surprise; she made up a plausible story about the blood sample, claiming it was human, and found an open station in the area reserved for medical equipment.

There was a chance she might learn something through a complete blood count and chemistry panel. She ran the necessary tests and waited for the results.

What she saw was far from normal. The hemoglobin

count was dangerously low, indicating severe anemia. The chem panels showed an enormous reduction in certain enzymes essential for the digestion of blood.

No wonder Nereus had looked as he had. It was a miracle he'd been able to function at all.

Nereus had indeed starved to death.

Chapter 23

Meet me by the river.

There was no signature on the note, but Timon knew who had written it. Not only by the message itself, but by the subtle scent rubbed into the paper by tidy fingers, the neat way it had been folded, the precision of the handwriting.

Orpheus had carried the note to him earlier that day, and from that moment on Timon could think of nothing but Jamie. He'd been thinking of her since he'd been relieved of his duty, hoping she was safe, that she wouldn't do anything foolish.

She'd believed him when he'd said he hadn't hurt Nereus; she'd been prepared to testify, though as far as Timon knew she'd never been called in for further questioning.

But he couldn't forget their last conversation. She'd reminded him that they hadn't spoken in two weeks, and he'd heard the subtle pain in her voice; pain and anger he hadn't known how to assuage. He'd spoken of reasons, but how could he deny what he'd told Cahill? How could he explain that his absence was all for her sake?

Because it wasn't, he thought as he made his way through the encampment toward the river. Oh, he'd convinced himself that she'd only be hurt if he continued to see her...because he couldn't return her feelings, because being near her would only reveal to her that he was in desperate need of *her* blood, and no other's.

He'd been able to observe Jamie from a distance for

those previous two weeks; at least he'd known she was all right, even when his heart beat fast with jealousy when he thought of her with Cahill, hearing her former fiancé tell her of Timon's rejection.

But his brief confinement had separated him from her in a way beyond his control, prevented him from protecting her, forced him to wonder what she was doing, and with whom. Those thoughts had been far worse than the mere fact that he'd been held in detention because Cassius was actually willing to believe he'd kill a delegate.

That made no sense. Neither did his shifting feelings about Jamie, or why he was afraid he wouldn't be able to keep his hands off her when they met again.

As they were about to meet now.

She was standing beneath one of the tall trees, her back to the trunk, her gaze fixed on something in the distance that Timon couldn't see.

He approached cautiously, half-afraid that he'd startle her. She turned to look at him before she could have heard his silent footsteps, almost as if she felt his presence.

Their eyes met. She smiled. "Timon," she said, walking toward him with one hand outstretched. "Thank God they let you go."

Her hand shook a little when he took it. It was so delicate in his grip, yet firm enough to remind him of her strength and stubbornness. He could smell her blood, but he refused to let it influence him in any way. He still had no intention of telling her about the blood-bond...nothing to make her feel obligated to the man who had seemingly abandoned her.

"They cleared you?" she asked, letting her hand fall.

"They examined the body," he said. "They found no evidence of physical attack."

"They never called me in," she said.

"The Opir scientists were satisfied with whatever they learned," he said.

"And why was Cassius so quick to believe you had something to do with Nereus's death, when he had no evidence beyond that one man's accusations? Did they talk to the supposed witness?"

"They never found him," Timon said. She had no idea how out of character Cassius's actions had been, or how deeply they had affected Timon. His own captain, his mentor, believing the worst of him so easily…

"Are you all right?" he asked.

"Yes." She looked around them. "But there are things I need to tell you about Nereus."

She explained how, with Orpheus's help, she had broken into the Rider's tent and found Nereus's body. She described her examination and how she had taken blood from the corpse…and how, given the state of that blood, she'd been able to determine the cause of his illness and death.

"Starvation?" Timon repeated, stunned. "Are you sure?"

"The signs were all there."

"Do you know what you risked?" he asked, grabbing her arms. "How could you be so foolish?"

She held very still, her muscles unyielding. He dropped his hands and began again. "What is your theory?"

Gesturing for him to follow, Jamie led him behind a screen of bushes close to the water and sat down on the bank. "This is explosive information," she said. "No one else can know about it, Timon. No one."

"Why is it explosive? Is whatever killed him contagious?"

"I don't know. That's what I need to find out."

Timon closed his eyes, trying not to listen to the rush of blood through the veins of her neck. "No one will hear anything from me," he said.

"I believe you." She shifted her weight. "There are very

few illnesses among Opiri. What happened to Nereus makes no sense to me. There's only one mundane way I know of that he could actually starve to death…if he couldn't get enough blood from the donor stations. And the only way that could happen is if he refused to go or was turned away by the donors."

"If he was as brutal with them as he was with you…"

"It had to start somewhere. If donors refused to serve him, there would have to be a very good reason, or there'd be chaos at the Conclave."

"He would have told someone," Timon said.

"Yes. And his fellow Tenebrians made no such accusations when we spoke to them. They wanted to hide him away."

"We don't know what *they* thought was wrong with him," Timon said.

"When we first met the Tenebrians before we reached the Conclave, he appeared much as you do now."

Timon gave her a blank look. "What are you talking about?"

"Your eyes. Your skin." She reached out, her fingers barely brushing his cheek. "My God, Timon. Are you ill?"

"Of course not." Her touch almost made him tremble, but he hardened his resolve. "What could be wrong with me?"

"The same thing that attacked Nereus."

"Then you are suggesting a disease of some kind."

"All I can tell you is that his blood values were way out of normal range. His ability to digest blood must have been severely compromised. Something caused that to happen. I need to know if it's happening to you, too."

"I can't believe it."

"I'm serious, Timon." She laid both her hands on his arms. "You can always talk to me. I'll always be your friend."

Friend. No matter what came between them, she was prepared to accept whatever he could give.

If he told her the truth, she would be the one doing the giving. But her entire body sang to him, dancing to the rhythm of her heartbeat, bathed in her lush female scent.

"Tell me," she urged him, leaning close.

It was too much, after so long away from her. He gripped her wrists and pinned them against the tree trunk above her head, breathing in the warm fragrance of her neck.

"I'll let you walk away now," he said, "if you don't ask any more questions. If you stay away from me."

"It's you who've stayed away," she whispered, looking into his eyes. "You need something, Timon. What is it?"

He released her and stepped back. "Go," he said.

"Answer me," she said. "What's wrong with you?"

Turning away, he kicked a stone into the river. "I'm addicted to your blood."

He could feel her stare burning into his back. "Addicted?" she asked. "Like a drug?"

"Not nearly so tidy," Timon said.

Jamie put it together quickly. "You developed this simply by drinking my blood? How often does it happen? Nereus took my blood, too. Could he have had this problem, as well?

"It isn't that usual, or every Opir would eventually become addicted."

"Then what happened to Nereus can't be the same thing." She brooded silently. "How long since you've fed?" She grabbed his arm and pulled him around. "You haven't taken any blood since we last…since you—"

"No," he growled, trying to frighten her, to make her leave before he gave in.

"I see what you're doing," she said, undeceived. "It won't work."

"You've seen the worst side of Opir instincts…"

"Are you saying you *are* becoming like Nereus?"

"It's my fault. I should be able to force myself—"

"What's wrong with other blood? Timon, what happens?"

"My body rejects it." He looked toward the encampment, gathering his composure before he spoke again.

"I didn't want it this way," he said. "I don't want you involved."

"How can I not be involved if it's my blood you need?"

Timon shook her off. "Do you know what it's called, Jamie? A blood-bond. It usually happens between full-blooded Opiri and humans from whom they feed frequently. But now it's happened with me. I have no control over it, and neither do you."

"A purely physical bond," she said. "Not psychological?"

"Even the wisest Opiri don't know."

"Then you're starving because of me?" she asked, her eyes widening. "Are you so horrified of the idea of being tied to me in any way?" She inhaled sharply. "You're afraid to owe me anything, aren't you? You can't bear the thought of ever being dependent on me."

"Do you want to be responsible for my life for the rest of yours?"

"Will you die if you don't take my blood? Will you go mad, too? Become like an animal, and expect me to stand by and watch it happen?"

"If I give in," he said, "if you were to let me feed now, there might be no going back."

"But you've just said the bond has already been made," she said. "You know it's no horror to me, Timon. We can manage this in any way we have to. But don't fight it."

Chapter 24

With a harsh groan, Timon folded Jamie in his arms. He took just enough time to numb her skin before he bit, and felt Jamie tremble and sigh as he fed. The experience was intensely sensual…not only for him, after weeks of hunger, but he knew it would be for her, as well. The bloodbond went both ways.

Almost before he finished, she was beginning to remove her clothing. He didn't try to stop her. She shed her shirt and pulled down her pants, kicking them off impatiently. She removed her undergarments and stood before him, a wood nymph with moon-gilded skin and hungry eyes.

The sensible part of Timon went silent, driven away by the bond. He dropped his pants just enough, pinned Jamie against the tree and thrust inside her, pulling her legs up around his hips. She bit her lip on a moan of pleasure and excitement, driving Timon to a possessive frenzy. He thrust again and bent to suckle her breasts, the nipples peaking under his tongue, while she made little whimpering sounds in her throat.

He settled into a steady, hard rhythm, supporting Jamie with his hips and one arm while his other hand searched between them and found her swollen clitoris. He stroked it in time to his thrusts, and she turned her head from side to side, her mouth half-open, panting raggedly.

He continued to kiss and lick her nipples, taking them whole into his mouth, tracing her areoles with the tip of his tongue. Her thighs tightened around his waist, allowing him to move still deeper, up to the hilt.

When she came, it was explosive, sending shocks throughout her body that Timon felt in his own. She arched her back and cried out softly, a little fist deep inside her clenching and unclenching around him.

He finished a moment later with several urgent thrusts, and dropped his face into the curve of her neck. He withdrew and eased her down gently, letting her find her feet, running his hands over her hips and legs as he kissed her mouth.

It was over. And it had just begun.

"The captain of the Riders has asked to see you," Amos said.

Jamie looked up from her plate, half-dazed, and slowly pieced together what Amos had said. "The captain?" she asked.

"Maybe it's about giving testimony regarding the incident with the mad Opir," Greg said, swallowing a mouthful of soup. "They let Timon out too soon."

Jamie felt a chill from the base of her spine to the top of her neck. Surely they couldn't have new doubts about him, after he'd already been cleared?

"Is something wrong?" Greg asked in a solicitous voice.

He didn't know, Jamie thought. He had no idea of what she and Timon had done last night, or how everything had changed.

Yet. But it *would* come out into the open eventually; she was certain. Timon needed her blood. And he wanted her as much as he needed her.

"Is there some other reason the captain would want to talk to you?" Amos asked, pushing his bowl away.

Rising, Jamie automatically collected the dishes and stacked them in the basket that would be carried to the communal sinks. "I have no idea," she said, though her heart banged out a warning.

"Well, you'd better get it over with," Amos said, getting up from the small table. "I'll need you later this afternoon." He eyed Jamie thoughtfully. "I wonder if you can find out what *did* kill this Nereus? I've heard a few rumors that he died of some kind of disease rather than violence. That seems pretty farfetched for an Opir."

"It does," Jamie murmured. "But I'm sure Captain Cassius won't share that information with me."

"They'd prefer to keep it a secret," Greg said, joining them. "What does that say about how much they can be trusted?"

"At least they didn't accuse our Jamie," Amos said.

Greg laughed. "As if *she* could hurt an Opir."

"I'll go," Jamie said, concealing her trepidation. She left the tent and retreated to her own, where she changed into more formal clothing.

Amos had spoken of rumors of disease. Her own theory, but no longer a secret. *Did* the Riders and Tenebrians know what had killed Nereus and were hiding the truth? Maybe she could find out.

She was just about to leave the Enclave camp when Amos intercepted her. "Jamie," he said, "forget what I said about trying to learn what killed Nereus. It's none of our concern, and the Riders have dealt with the situation." He rested his hand on her shoulder. "In fact, I advise that you put it from your mind. It's strictly an Opir matter now."

He let her go with a smile, but Jamie was left wondering why he'd so quickly changed his mind.

The Rider headquarters was as busy as it had been before. Jamie was ushered right past the reception desks and into the back, where she'd so recently been sneaking about to examine Nereus's body.

This time, she found herself in a canvas-walled office

just big enough for a simple table to serve as a desk—currently piled high with papers—and three camp chairs, along with a map of the tent city hung on the side of the tent. She sat down opposite the desk to wait, and Cassius arrived a few moments later. His face was all sharp angles, his bearing rigid with military precision.

"Ms. McCullough," he said, sitting behind the desk. "Thank you for coming."

So it would be this way, Jamie thought. He hadn't bothered to offer his hand, and his disapproval was evident. Whatever he wanted to discuss with her, it would be less than pleasant.

"Why did you want to speak to me, Captain?" she asked, following his lead.

His hard gaze met hers. "You have been seeing my band leader, Timon."

The way he said the words left Jamie in no doubt as to his meaning. There was no point in trying to deny it now. "Timon guided me across two thousand miles of wilderness, Captain," she said. "It's only natural that we continued our acquaintance afterward."

"Your 'acquaintance,'" Cassius said with a curl of his lip. "Do you think I'm unaware of what goes on with my people? Especially when one of the best of them flouts the rules and oaths of our Brotherhood?"

She rose. "Captain, I know that Riders don't ordinarily make friends outside of—"

"Friends," Cassius said with the same contempt. "No, Riders do not make 'friends' outside of the Brotherhood. We maintain our efficacy and our honor through self-sufficiency and unquestionable neutrality. Or hadn't Timon made that clear to you?"

"I know how your Riders are supposed to behave," she said, holding his gaze. "But they aren't machines."

"Nor are they human," Cassius said.

"Half-human," Jamie said. "And Timon—"

"Sit down," Cassius commanded.

"Timon is excellent at what he does. You called him one of the best. If he manages to function so well and still maintain connections to the outside world, he must be doing something right."

"Sit *down*, Ms. McCullough."

Unwilling to engage in childish games, she sat. "Let me get this straight, Captain. You're afraid that Timon's friendship with me will interfere with his work."

"His work, and the reputation of all the Riders," Cassius said heavily.

"You think everyone in the Conclave will stop trusting you to do your job because of one Rider?"

"We are the Brotherhood," Cassius said. "The reputation of one is the reputation of all."

"Is that all there is to it," she said, "or is there more personal reason?" She tilted her head. "Timon is more than just a subordinate to you, isn't he?"

"I see I am not making myself clear, Ms. McCullough," Cassius said. "I am speaking of Timon's welfare. His life. You may care nothing for our rules and oaths, but perhaps Timon's personal fate is of more interest to you."

Jamie sat forward, her fingers curling into fists. "Are you threatening Timon because of me?" she demanded. "Are you suggesting that   "

"I suggest nothing," Cassius said. "I merely tell you that the situation cannot continue. Our laws are very specific. Once one of our Brotherhood proves that he cannot maintain neutrality and becomes tethered to something or someone outside us, he is no longer fit for the Riders."

Chapter 25

Cassius's words hung in the room long after he had spoken them, but Jamie wasn't shocked. Timon had already told her much the same thing. Cassius wasn't literally threatening Timon's life, but he *was* telling Jamie that Timon would lose his livelihood, the world to which he had devoted so many years, the Brothers who had become his family. Being a Rider *was* his life, and Cassius was willing, and able, to take that from him.

"You can prevent the inevitable, Ms. McCullough," Cassius said. "Timon has been temporarily blinded to the gravity of his transgression. But you can make him see. You can reject him so that no doubt remains, and he returns to us."

He doesn't know about the blood-bond, Jamie realized once Cassius's demands sunk in. If he did, he would know it wouldn't simply be a matter of rejection. The bond would still be there, and Timon would still suffer from it.

Numb down to her bones, Jamie tried to find an answer. Maybe the Opir had a cure for the blood-bond, and they could give it to Timon. She was certain that Cassius would do everything within his power to help Timon break free of it.

But Timon had to know exactly what would happen if the blood-bond were discovered. It wasn't her business to tell his captain; *he* would have to inform Cassius, if that was his choice. And so far, he obviously hadn't done it.

"Have you spoken to Timon about this?" she asked. "Did you warn him to stay away from me?"

"Until recently, I thought he would escape from this madness."

"You don't want to force him to make the decision, do you?"

Cassius curled his fingers around a piece of paper on his desk and crumpled it into a ball. "You think he would choose you. But he would come to regret it. You would become a burden to him, a memory hung around his neck to torment him for the rest of your mortal life."

For the rest of your mortal life. Cassius was speaking of the future. A future in which Timon and Jamie were together, in a way she'd hardly dared to consider.

Did *Cassius* believe that Timon was in love with her?

"I would never steal his life from him," she said, standing up again. "It has nothing to do with your threats, Captain. I want what's best for Timon."

"Then you will do as I ask."

"I'll consider what you've told me," she said. She started for the doorway. "I wonder what he would say if he knew we'd had this conversation."

Cassius stood. "Are you threatening *me*?"

"Don't worry. I won't deliberately plant any barriers between you and Timon. But I will do as I think best, Captain. Goodbye."

"Wait." He followed her and stopped just inside the doorway. "Consider this, Ms. McCullough." His expression softened, startling Jamie with the change. "Timon has been like a son to me. I brought him into the Riders when he was only seventeen, a skilled traveler and fighter, but completely at the mercy of the bands of human and Opir savages in the wilds. I taught him how to turn his natural skills into work for the greater good—the work of allowing communication between far-flung Opir and human cities and settlements. Without that communication, this

Conclave could never have taken place. Without the Riders, there would be no hope of peace."

"I don't deny that," Jamie said softly.

"Then grant Timon the chance to continue serving the greater good. Don't confine him to a static life in an Enclave or one of the colonies. Let him do what he was born to do."

Cassius held the door flap open for her, and she stepped through. She found her way through the maze of temporary corridors to the front of the tent and rushed outside. Her legs were unsteady, and she had to stand very still to regain her orientation.

Once she could make her feet move again, she headed back to camp. Timon was waiting in her tent.

"Timon!" she said, stopping at the entrance. "You shouldn't be—"

"It's all right," he said, pulling her into the tent. He took her into his arms and kissed her fiercely, the tips of his cuspids pressing gently into her lower lip.

Jamie broke away, her hands on his chest. "Timon," she said. "I've been thinking—"

"I've been thinking, too," he said, covering her hands with his. "I've been selfish, Jamie. I've been worrying about myself and ignoring your pain."

Am I to have so little time? Jamie wondered. Was it going to happen so fast, the decision she had to make?

"What pain, Timon?" she asked, slipping her hands from under his. "I'm fine."

"But you weren't," he said. He took her chin between his thumb and forefinger. "I abandoned you. I led you to believe that our relationship was over, that there couldn't be anything more between us."

"But I...I understood, Ti—"

"I was wrong," he said, looking deep into her eyes. She saw what was in *his*, the warmth and passion and honesty that had nothing to do with the blood-bond. "I need to tell you now, so that there can't be any question."

"Stop," she said, pressing her hand over his mouth. "If you don't want to hurt me, don't say anything more."

His brows drew down in confusion. "Jamie? I wouldn't—"

"It was my mistake," she said, desperately clinging to her resolve. "I thought I…felt things… I misled myself, and you."

Timon took a step backward, his gaze moving over her face. "What are you trying to tell me?"

"I know what you were about to say," she said. "But you can't have thought it through, Timon. I'm human, and you're virtually immortal. You have your way of life, and I have mine." She half stumbled back toward her cot. "We're too different, Timon. This can't go anywhere."

For a moment, she was sure he hadn't accepted her act. His lips parted, and he drew breath to speak.

Then, suddenly, he seemed to understand. The warmth in his eyes drained away. "What happened, Jamie?" he asked.

She knew she couldn't tell him the truth. Not when he'd been about to speak the words she'd longed to hear. Words he was unlikely to repeat ever again.

"I came to my senses," she said, looking away. "I care about you, Timon. I accept the blood-bond, and I want to continue giving you blood as long as you need it. But if you know of any kind of cure, maybe you should consider trying it, so when the Conclave is over—"

"I won't need you anymore," he said coldly.

"I'm sorry, Timon. I'm—" She turned her back on him, afraid he might still see the lie. Her vision was blurred with tears. Timon made no sound at all.

When she turned back toward him, struggling to think of something to say, he was already gone.

* * *

Timon didn't believe it.

He strode away from the camp toward the corral, his guts churning along with his thoughts. Jamie had known exactly what he'd been about to say, and he'd expected her to welcome his words, to fall into his arms and whisper them back to him. Nothing else would have mattered.

But she had made *other* things matter, things he had already decided were of little importance. It was true that they'd never discussed the even the possibility of a future together; until Timon had come to his senses, there'd been no reason to.

Perhaps it was impossible for Jamie to accept that he couldn't love her once she grew older, slowly changing in strength and appearance as he remained the same. Perhaps she truly thought that they were too different—that he could never give up the Riders, or adapt to her way of life.

Yet if she believed those things, she would have considered them from the beginning. She would never have let their relationship get this far, well before she knew of the blood-bond. He hadn't misinterpreted her feelings.

No, something was wrong. Perhaps Cahill had gotten to her, or even her godfather.

Timon stepped in the middle of the main thoroughfare, his jaw clenching and unclenching. Why hadn't she been honest with him? What had become of his earnest, straightforward Jamie?

You waited too long, he thought. *You weren't honest with* her.

Timon reached the corral, where an eager Lazarus was waiting for his daily exercise, ears pricked and head extended. He nickered and bumped Timon's chest as Timon entered the gate.

"Who is it, boy?" Timon said, scratching the horse behind the ears. "Cahill is too obvious, and she'd never listen to him."

Lazarus bobbed his head.

"Councilman Parks didn't see us together after we reached the Conclave," Timon said. "Who else could have that much influence over her?"

The horse stamped, reminding Timon that Lazarus was ready to be on his way across the rolling desert plain. He was a true Rider's mount, never content to stay in one place for long, bred to remain with the Brotherhood until old age claimed him. Like the Riders themselves.

"I never thought I could leave," he said to Lazarus. "If not for Jamie…"

If Jamie were out of the way, he'd naturally remain with the Riders until he was no longer capable of staying in the saddle. There would never be another like her to tempt him. His life would be simple again.

Why look for explanations? he asked himself with a flash of anger. *Take her at her word.* "Cassius was right," he said while Lazarus snuffled at his jacket. "He said that there's a reason we don't have relationships outside the Brotherhood. It makes us weak. As it's made me."

Lazarus slobbered on his shoulder. Timon pulled the horse's head down and rested his forehead against Lazarus's face.

"Timon?"

He turned to find Orpheus at his shoulder, his hand resting on Lazarus's back.

"Orpheus," Timon grunted. "I'm not in the mood for talking, and I need to exercise Lazarus."

"I can see that," Orpheus said. "But I thought there was something you should know about Ms. McCullough."

"What about her?" Timon asked, a strangling fist taking hold of his heart.

"She asked me to steal the official report on what happened to Nereus."

"When?"

"After I helped her get into headquarters to examine Nereus's body." He cleared his throat. "I had the feeling that she didn't plan to tell you."

Why? Timon thought. *Because she was afraid I'd warn her not to get further involved?*

She would have been right.

"Did you get it for her?" he asked Timon.

"Not yet," Orpheus said. "She asked me to keep trying. Since you've been so worried about her—"

"Thank you, Brother," Timon said, gripping Orpheus's shoulder. "Don't do anything else she asks of you. I'll take care of this."

Orpheus was obviously relieved. "Good. I wasn't looking forward to fielding questions from Cassius if I was caught."

Especially, Timon thought, after *he* had been under suspicion.

"Will you do me a favor and exercise Lazarus?" Timon asked. "I have other business to attend to."

"Of course," Orpheus said, taking hold of the horse's halter. "Don't be too hard on her, Timon. She was trying to help clear you."

Trying to help the man she'd declared she couldn't share her life with. Timon exhaled sharply and strode out of the corral. Evidently Jamie was prepared to be cautious with their relationship, but not where the incident with Nereus was concerned. She had a bee in her bonnet, and Timon's gut told him that she was still on a collision course with trouble.

She said she'd still let him take blood from her. If that was the only excuse he had to see her, it would have to be enough.

He made it to headquarters in half the usual time, pushing through the people waiting at reception and continuing deeper into the warren of corridors and temporary rooms. He stopped at the door flap of Cassius's office.

"Captain," he said.

"Come," Cassius said.

Timon entered and stood in front of the desk. Cassius was slow to look up.

"What is it, Timon?" he asked in a clipped voice.

"I have a request to make."

The captain stopped what he was doing and met Timon's gaze. "And what is that?" he asked.

"Cast me out of the Brotherhood."

Chapter 26

"What?" Cassius said, his voice cracking with surprise.

"You must know that I never stopped seeing the human woman, Jamie McCullough."

"I am aware of this, yes."

Timon chose his words carefully, determined not to let Cassius guess at his true feelings. "I've been intimate with her since we arrived."

Resting his hands flat on the desktop, Cassius stared at the stack of paper to his left. "I seem to remember that we discussed this when you first returned."

"Yes," Timon said.

"And you said you had not developed an emotional attachment to her beyond admiration, respect and perhaps a little affection. Do I take it that you were lying?"

The words were harsh, but Timon had been prepared for them. "I didn't plan for it to go on. She gave her blood to me, and we fell back into the pattern of our journey."

"I see." Cassius looked up again. "You said that you were with *us*, with the Brotherhood. Are you now saying that you wish to abandon us for this human female?"

"No, Captain. That was never my intention."

"Then guilt has driven you to this? Are you asking for punishment?"

"I may deserve punishment for my errors in judgment," Timon said, "but that isn't why I want you to cast me out."

The captain waved him toward one of the two free chairs. Timon sat on the edge and held Cassius's gaze.

"You sent my band to find out if the San Francisco delegation was hiding a secret that might be dangerous to the Conclave," he said. "I told you I hadn't found any such secret. But I have since learned that I may have been mistaken."

"Why?" Cassius asked, a spark in his pale eyes.

"Subtle things, bits of conversation. My intimacy with Ms. McCullough has allowed me to observe her delegation a little more closely, but I haven't been able to get far enough to prove anything." He hesitated. "She's broken off with me because she sees no future for us. If she thinks I'm no longer with the Brotherhood, her attitude may change. And I may get the chance I need to expose whatever they're hiding."

Cassius returned his attention to the stack of paper, his silence so long and heavy that it seemed he had forgotten that Timon was present.

"You ask me to take a great risk," Cassius said at last. "You ask me to trust you, when you have already broken that trust by continuing to see this woman."

"If I betray your trust again," Timon said, his chest tight, "then you can cast me out in fact, not merely as a pretense. And I don't want to lose the Brotherhood. Or you."

Pushing his chair away from the desk, Cassius rose. "I have no desire to lose you, either. But make no mistake—I *will* see you expelled if I ever have reason to believe that you've asked this for personal reasons rather than for the good of the Riders and the mission assigned to us."

"I understand," Timon said, inclining his head. "Will I be permitted to keep Lazarus?"

"I doubt he'd be of use to anyone but you."

"When will you announce the expulsion?"

"Tonight," Cassius said. "I'll make it known to all the Brotherhood, and let the words spread from there. You will feel the disgrace, Timon, but it will not be real. This time."

"Thank you for giving me this chance to complete my mission," Timon said.

Cassius waved a hand in dismissal. "Go now. Play your part well, and I will arrange a way for you to get messages to me as you gain additional information."

Acknowledging the dismissal, Timon left the office. He had acted recklessly, knowing that he might have put himself on the path to losing both Jamie and the Riders.

But he'd made his decision, and now it was only a matter of waiting until the entire Conclave knew that he was no longer worthy of being a Rider.

"I wonder what he did?" Greg asked Jamie, making no attempt to smother the grin on his face. "It must have been pretty bad for him to be ejected from the Brotherhood."

Jamie sat at the table in the central tent, working to control her emotions. Timon, cast out of the Riders. She could hardly believe it, and all she wanted at that moment was to find Timon and ask him what he'd done.

It has to do with me, she thought grimly. His exile had been announced the night after she and Timon had quarreled, if that was the right word. Had she hurt him so badly that he'd done something his fellow Riders couldn't accept?

She had no way of knowing all the rules by which the Riders lived their lives. But if she *was* to blame…

"Excuse me," she said, getting up from the table. "I think I'll take a walk around the encampment."

"Worried about Timon?" Greg asked. "He was the one who rejected *you*, remember?"

Greg had been so eager to tell her of his conversation with Timon, but he had no idea what had happened afterward. How *she* had done the rejecting.

"Don't go near the Opiri," Amos called after as she exited the tent.

That was the last thing Jamie intended to do. She half ran

out of the circle of tents, following one of the lanes between delegate camps toward the main thoroughfare. The hot July sun seemed to beat against her body. Without thinking, she found herself walking toward the eastern perimeter of the tent city, where the camp followers, tinkers and Wanderers had made their temporary home.

She sat down on a patch of dry grass at the edge of the dusty road and caught her breath. She wondered if she'd come in this direction because she expected Timon to have left the Conclave. But it would have made more sense for him to go by way of the corral, if he'd been permitted to take his horse with him.

She could scarcely blame him for leaving without saying goodbye. But maybe he was still here, making preparations.

Rising unsteadily, she was just about to turn back for the Hub when she saw a man walking away from the Wanderers' camp, his head down and his shoulders slumped. She froze as she recognized him.

"Timon?" she called out softly.

He looked up, his expression shifting to a wary mask. "Jamie," he said. "What are you doing here?"

She looked past him at the wagons. "I thought you might have left."

"Not yet." He stopped in front of her, his eyes searching hers. "I went to ask some advice from a friend."

But not from me, she thought. What on earth could she tell him? That she was sorry for his loss?

"I know you might not want to talk to me," she said, suppressing her sudden desire to flee. "But I just… I—" She shook her head. "What did you do, Timon? How could this have happened?"

His gaze shifted away from hers. "I made a mistake," he said.

"What mistake?"

"Do you want to know the truth?"

"Yes." She hesitated. "Was it about me?"

He met her eyes again. "I continued to pursue a relationship with you," he said. "I broke the rules of the Brotherhood."

Oh, God, Jamie thought. *Why did Cassius warn me to stay away from Timon if he already meant to do this?*

She couldn't bring herself to tell Timon about that conversation, even now. But was it possible that Cassius had also spoken to Timon, and that Timon had defied him?

The only reason he would have done that was because of her. Because he hadn't given up on her, in spite of what she'd told him.

"I'm sorry," she said, feeling ill. "This is my fault."

"No." He reached out and brushed her cheek with the tips of his fingers. "I knew what I was doing. I was trying to balance the two things most important to me, and I failed."

Jamie's heart beat sluggishly. She could admit that her feelings for him hadn't changed, that she'd deceived him in order to save him. But now that he'd been expelled from the Brotherhood, would he still want her?

"What do you plan to do?" she asked, her voice not quite steady.

"I'm not leaving," he said, dropping his hand. "There are a few loose ends I need to tie up."

"Loose ends?"

"I'm still the only one who knows your secret, Jamie. We both had to deal with Nereus. And now I hear that you aren't done with your investigation."

"What? But I—"

"You asked Orpheus to help you sneak into the Riders' headquarters, and now you've asked him to steal medical records. I can't have you putting him at risk. I, on the other hand…" He smiled. "I don't have much to lose."

"But you disapprove."

"Because you're investigating something that may not turn out to be what you expect."

"What do you mean? Do you know something I don't, Timon?"

"What do *you* know, Jamie?"

She struggled to find words for something she couldn't explain even to herself. "I may be crazy," she said, "but I know there's something else going on behind Nereus's death. Something's wrong at the heart of the Conclave."

"How can you be so certain? What evidence do you have?"

"Only what you already know about." She bit her lip. "If you're still willing to work with me—"

"If your instincts are correct, maybe I can still do something to help this Conclave succeed."

"Does that matter to you now, Timon?"

"*Something* has to matter," he said quietly.

"And this *does*, Timon. For all of us."

"Then if you still trust me—"

"I've never trusted anyone the way I trust you."

Timon looked away. "We're friends, aren't we?"

Relief flooded through her. She hadn't lost him. She'd pushed him away, but he'd accepted her decision. "Of course." Her tongue and lips felt stiff, as if they knew she was telling a half-truth. "That will never change, Timon. Not from my side."

"Then it's settled," he said. "I can't stop you from pursuing whatever it is you think is wrong, but at least you won't be doing it alone."

Chapter 27

Jamie longed to kiss Timon, but she cut the thought short. He'd lost something he'd cherished…a life he would never have again. Something even her love could never replace.

Taking hold of herself, she turned her thoughts to more practical matters. "You need somewhere to stay," she said. "They can't drive you out of the encampment, can they?"

"No," he said. "My Wanderer friend offered me free room and board, if I choose to accept it."

"Your Wanderer friend?" she asked, glancing beyond him at the wagons.

"Caridad. You remember her?"

Oh, she remembered: lush lips and black hair and eyes that sparkled as they caught some stray light.

"I remember that you took her blood," Jamie said, deeply uncomfortable. "Have you found a way to break our blood-bond?"

"There is an antidote, but it works slowly. If you can give me a little more time…"

"Of course. You can continue to take my blood whenever you need it."

"Perhaps."

"Will you stay with Caridad, then?"

"If you'd rather, I can set up my own camp just outside the perimeter."

Does he still think I'm jealous? Jamie wondered. If he was playing games with *her*, it was nothing less than what she deserved. But if this was some kind of test…

"You should do as you think best," she said.

"Then I'll camp to the south of the wagons. It's closer to the human side, so you won't have to go near the Opiri when you visit. I don't know if—"

He broke off, turning toward the west and the center of the encampment.

"Something's going on," he said, narrowing his eyes. "People are shouting."

Jamie could barely hear anything above the wind, but she didn't doubt Timon for an instant. "Let's go," she said.

Together they jogged along the central lane toward the Assembly and Administrative tents. Others were running alongside them, and groups of humans and hooded Opiri, on either side of the road, were talking in hushed voices.

At last Jamie and Timon reached the edge of a crowd gathered around a place near one of the donor stations. Timon pushed his way through, making room for himself and Jamie.

A body lay at the center of the crowd—Opir, his face uncovered and badly burned by the sunlight. But his position was not that of an Opir attempting to shield himself from deadly light. He was simply sprawled there on the packed dirt, arms and legs splayed.

And he bore all the physical attributes that Nereus had had before he'd attacked Jamie…exactly as if he'd starved to death.

Timon met Jamie's gaze, took her arm and pulled her away from the mob.

"Did you see?" Jamie whispered. "He looked like Nereus. Gaunt, sickly."

"Yes," Timon said. "Something *is* wrong here. And now that there's been a second death, the problem won't just go away."

"Then we need to find out how it happened," she said.

"Let's meet at the med clinic tonight, when I can sneak back in without anyone asking questions."

"Why there?"

"Maybe I've missed something, and being in the lab may help. Three a.m. should be safe enough. Wear a daycoat, just as a precaution."

Timon turned and left immediately. Jamie watched him go, struck again by his stoic ability to accept the loss of the way of life he'd known for so many years, the people he had worked with, his friends, his mentor.

The lab was quiet and dark, save for a single lamp just bright enough to read by. Jamie pulled her mother's journal from inside her jacket. Some memory pressed in on her, only a scrap of recollection, one connected in some way to the writings she had carried since Eileen's death.

"I told you that my mother was a biologist," she said to Timon as she thumbed through the journal. "She worked with human diseases."

"Human diseases." Timon rested his hand on her shoulder, and she almost forgot to breathe. "What are you looking for?" he asked.

"I don't know," she said. She paused at a page near the center of the journal and studied it intently. "Not here. But somewhere..." She riffled through the pages and stopped abruptly. "Here!"

She showed the book to Timon, who crouched with his cheek nearly touching hers. "Look at this drawing. It's my mother's work."

"What is it?"

"An infectious agent called a virus. In this case, a retrovirus." Trying to ignore Timon's earthy, masculine scent, she read the tiny notations next to the sketch. She read them again and then a third time, blinking to make sure she was seeing the words correctly.

Her hand trembling, she let the journal fall into her lap.

"Jamie," Timon said, turning her face toward him. "What did you find?"

"The virus," she said. "I think it's what killed Nereus."

"A virus in an Opir? Illness among Opiri is virtually unknown."

Jamie lifted her head. "I know. It seems fantastic. But *this—*" she pointed to the neat sketch on the page "—was almost certainly what caused Nereus to starve to death, and it's probably the cause of the other Opir's death, as well."

"How can you be so sure? Can you see it in his blood?"

"It takes special equipment for that. But I can put two and two together." Tears spilled out of her eyes. "This virus isn't some unknown disease. Timon, it was created to kill Opiri."

He pulled back, and she could feel his stare. "Created?" he said.

"By humans. Humans who held the belief that they could only survive in this world if all Opiri were wiped out."

"You're talking about genocide."

"Only a few in the Enclave would ever have been a part of such an abomination."

Timon went very quiet. "I've heard of this," he said slowly. "Rumors, whispers of a deadly disease that affected only Opiri. No one ever spoke of it out loud."

"I only knew what my father told me," Jamie said, folding her arms across her chest. "The pathogen was supposed to have been wiped out before it could be used—destroyed at a secret lab facility by a team of Enclave agents."

"And your mother was involved?"

"No! My mother had nothing to do with it."

But Jamie had no way to be sure. Here, in her mother's writing, was a full description of the virus, and a notation that Eileen had had access to a sample after it had supposedly been destroyed.

"No," she said, more softly. "My mother was a good person. She would never have accepted what those people did. And she was only a child when they made the virus."

"I believe you."

Timon's quiet words brought the world out of its wild spin. She met his gaze. His eyes were sympathetic, but there was calculation in them, too, as if he didn't completely trust her.

"How does this virus work, Jamie?" he asked.

She swallowed several times. "It causes the infected Opir to starve to death by altering and destroying his digestive enzymes so that he or she can no longer take nourishment from blood."

Turning his back on her, Timon strode across the tent, passing the row of microscopes and lab equipment. "Then the virus wasn't destroyed," he said. "It's here." He spun around to face her again. "How does it spread?"

She stared at the ground, afraid to meet his gaze. "It can be administered directly, but it can also be transmitted through human blood. A human is infected but doesn't suffer any illness. An Opir who takes blood from him or her not only becomes ill but passes the virus on to any other human he bites. And that human also becomes a carrier, able to infect the next Opir in turn."

"Then this was done deliberately, by humans, just like before," Timon said.

Jamie swiped at her cheek. "Judging by Nereus's symptoms, he was already infected before you and I met with him."

"By whom? Did he and his delegation meet with infected humans before we found them?"

Horrified by the idea that sprang into her mind, Jamie studied her mother's notes again. She jumped up and made the necessary preparations to test her own blood. Timon watched with eerie patience as she examined the sample carefully.

"My mother made a brief notation of what to look for in infected human blood," she said, sinking back into her chair. "I think *I'm* infected, Timon."

They stared at each other as all the implications raced through Jamie's thoughts. The San Francisco Enclave had created the virus, and apparently not all of it had been destroyed. Someone still had it. Eileen McCullough was dead, but if there had been one sample that survived, there could have been others. Hidden away, until the right time came to use them.

And there was another, terrible consequence.

"You took my blood," she said, nearly gasping. "Timon, *you* could be infected, too."

Chapter 28

Timon froze, head tilted and eyes closed as if he was taking stock of his own body. "There was nothing wrong with me that taking your blood again didn't fix," he said. "I'm fine now."

"You could be infected and not know it," she said. "You're a half-blood. That could make all the difference. You attributed your own problems to the blood-bond, but since you're deriving benefits from my blood, that doesn't prove anything. The virus might not directly affect you, just as it doesn't affect humans. But you could be a vector for the virus, like any human."

Timon crouched, his arms folded across his knees. "Then I might pass on the virus to other humans?"

"As long as you take blood only from me or another infected human, you aren't a danger to anyone."

"But every time an infected human gives blood to an uninfected Opir, or an infected Opir takes it from an uninfected human, the virus spreads." He met Jamie's eyes. "Is this what you sensed, Jamie? This disaster looming over the Conclave?"

She shivered. "I'm not psychic. Nereus's death… I just couldn't accept it as some kind of natural occurrence."

"And it wasn't." He reached across the space between them and laid his hand on her knee. "You're a scientist. We both need all our analytical skills to figure this out."

"And stop it," Jamie said. There had to be some kind of

faction behind this, as there had been behind the original creation of the virus so many years ago.

"Let's take it one step at a time," Timon said, steady and calm. "Who could have done this? When could you have been infected, Jamie?"

"If you do have the virus—and I think we have to work with the assumption that you do—then I had to be infected back at the Enclave. Someone involved with the delegation, or the planning of it, had to play some part in this. I was infected without my knowledge, maybe when they inoculated us against several illnesses before we left."

"Then we have no idea if any of the other San Francisco delegates actually know what's happened, or if they're infected, as well."

"No. The only way for me to learn more is to check the blood of every member of the delegation."

"And if one of them is in on some kind of conspiracy, they might object."

She jumped up from the chair again. "I can't believe it," she said. "It had to have been started by someone who wanted the infection spread at the Conclave, where nothing could stop it."

"Is there a cure?"

"If there was, there's nothing about it in my mother's journal."

Timon rose. "Jamie, there must be someone in your delegation who knows what's going on. Cahill. Your godfather…"

"My godfather? Never."

"But you can imagine Cahill involved in this."

"*You'd* have no trouble imagining it," she snapped, and then immediately regretted the words. "We don't have nearly enough information to begin making accusations. I refuse to consider anyone guilty without proof."

"Who in your party hates Opiri enough to commit genocide?"

She sank back into the chair. "No one. We're here on a peace mission."

"A perfect pretense."

"Do you *want* to find one of us guilty?"

"If it will help us stop this somehow." He paused. "We know that Cahill and the rest of your delegation met the Tenebrians the day before we did."

"And you think Greg could have arranged to—" She couldn't complete the sentence. "That would make him worse than evil, Timon. I've known him all my life."

"Will you follow where the facts lead you?"

"Yes. Will *you*?"

He came up behind her chair and rested his hands on the back. "I was a Rider," he said. "I won't let personal feelings cloud my judgment."

"Then you have to consider that I might be guilty, too."

"I know you aren't."

His certainty warmed her chilled skin. "You aren't being objective," she said. "But thanks, anyway."

Kneeling before her chair, he took her hands. "I'll stay by your side every moment until this problem is solved."

"That means finding a cure. My God, Timon, we don't have the resources here to make one!"

"But maybe whoever started this has a way to stop it."

"Why would they want to, when humans aren't harmed?"

"I don't know. But we'd better hope they do."

"Yes." Jamie realized that she was gripping Timon's hands too tightly and let go. They rose at the same time.

"The first thing we have to do is search this clinic," she said. "We don't have much time."

"What are we looking for?"

"Anything that might suggest intensive research—

obscure notes, equipment out of place…whatever catches your eye. I'll check the stored blood samples myself."

Working separately, they covered the clinic in less than an hour. Timon found nothing of interest. Jamie tested all the blood in the refrigerator unit and found no more of the virus.

"It's not here," she said when she finished. "If a supply of the virus is at the Conclave, it's hidden somewhere else."

"Or maybe enough humans are already infected that they don't need a supply," Timon said grimly.

"I'm going to invent an excuse to test the blood of all my colleagues. I can tell them that I'm afraid they might have been exposed to some kind of parasite on our journey from San Francisco." She met his gaze. "You have to leave before it gets light. Do you need blood?"

Timon hesitated. She stepped up to him and offered her neck.

"You have nothing to lose," she said, bracing herself.

He put his mouth to her throat, his tongue laving her skin to numb it. A great wave of sexual pleasure rushed downward and settled between her thighs. He bit, and the pleasure increased to the point that she thought if he touched her she might come right there.

He's not doing this on purpose, she told herself. *It's natural.* But she wanted him so badly then that she didn't dare react. It was life in the face of death. She was giving life, but if she wanted something in return, she could never ask for it.

Jamie bore the throbbing discomfort of her desire until Timon was finished, and then she stepped quickly away. He had a sated, almost dazed look about him, but when his gaze focused again, the full weight of it fell on her. She didn't have to look hard to see that he was aroused.

"You'd better go," she said, trying to control her voice. "I'll come find you as soon as I have anything new to report."

"And I'll try to learn more about this recent death," Timon said. "Be careful, Jamie. Be very careful."

Was this the secret all along? Timon thought, adjusting his daycoat as he strode away from the tent. Was the *virus* the thing the Riders' employers had been looking for, the hidden danger Cassius had sent him to find?

But if these anonymous employers had any idea, he thought as he left the area of the clinic, why would they have left it for the Riders to discover on their own?

Those employers must have heard rumors, but needed evidence.

And now they had it. *He* had it, quite possibly in his own blood, and it was only a matter of reporting to Cassius. There was no question of keeping this horror a secret; Cassius had the resources to investigate far more thoroughly than Timon and Jamie could do on their own.

Someone bumped into him, and suddenly he found himself surrounded by humans emerging from their night's rest. How many of them were infected? Surely not too many, or there would have been far more Opiri deaths. Perhaps the virus hadn't spread far yet. Testing and quarantining humans…

Would cause utter chaos, Timon thought. The entire Conclave would be undermined just as surely as if he had stood before the Assembly tent and announced what he had learned.

And what would happen to Jamie?

Timon stood by the side of the central thoroughfare, recalling the thrill of taking her blood. It had nearly killed him to hold her in his arms and refrain from kissing her. To smell her, taste her soft skin and know that he couldn't let his feelings show.

She wanted to be friends, and they had to remain close allies. He wouldn't risk stepping over the line, for both their sakes. No matter how often he had to remind himself that she could see no future for them.

And there would be no future at all if they didn't succeed in exposing those behind the virus and halting its spread.

He continued toward headquarters, covering his head with his hood to hide his identity.

A short time later he was ushered into Cassius's office. The captain was giving orders to a pair of Riders Cassius didn't know well, and when he entered Cassius dismissed them.

"Well?" the captain asked as Timon stood before the desk.

"I have information," he said. "I've learned the secret."

Cassius met his gaze. "What is it?"

"Before I tell you," Timon said, "I require an assurance from you."

"From *me*?" Cassius asked. "You may still be a Rider, Timon, but if you think you can be insubordinate and suffer no consequences—"

"I don't care about the consequences to myself," Timon said. "There is serious trouble in the Conclave, and I want to see Ms. McCullough protected at all costs."

"Then she has something to do with this trouble."

"I know she has done nothing wrong. But she'll be in danger, and I want your promise that no action will be taken against her by you, the Riders or the employers who had us looking for the secret."

"I can make no such promise. But I can see you arrested, and questioned in such a way that you'll be glad enough to share what you know."

Timon leaned over the desk. "I want the freedom to continue working with Ms. McCullough and the authorization to protect her. That, and your assurance that you'll conduct any investigation as discreetly as possible until you have absolute proof. The alternative is to see the Conclave destroyed."

Timon had never seen Cassius so angry in his life. The captain's eyes were cold stones, his face carved of granite, his mouth as taut as a bowstring.

"I will grant you leave to protect your human female. That is all I will offer."

Curling his fists on the desk, Timon nodded. "I will protect her against anyone who attempts to harm her. *Anyone*, Captain."

And then he told Cassius about Jamie's theory about the virus in Nereus's blood, leaving out any mention of her mother's notebook. He also didn't mention that Jamie was almost certainly infected herself. Cassius would find out soon enough, but maybe the withheld information would buy her—and Timon—a little more time.

Chapter 29

"Nearly finished." Jamie withdrew the needle and pressed a piece of gauze over the tiny bead of blood. Corporal Delgado helped Jamie bandage the puncture and scooted off the chair.

"Are you sure you can tell if we have this parasite?" Delgado asked with a shudder.

"Yes," Jamie said. "And we have the treatment here."

"Thank goodness," Delgado muttered. He looked around at the others who had lingered after their testing. "Have the Councilman and Senator already been tested?"

"Not yet," Jamie said. Because, over the past two days, they were both unavailable every time she looked for them, meeting with some other delegation or involved with negotiations that didn't require Jamie's presence.

Could it be coincidence? Jamie was willing to believe it *was* in Amos's case, but not in Cahill's. He could be avoiding the test.

Or was he? Jamie still didn't have enough information to force the issue. Though she did know Greg hated Timon, seemed to dislike Opiri in general and had the rank, influence and means to carry out this kind of evil project. With Amos it was different. She had thought about it ever since she and Timon had discussed their next steps. It was conceivably a dangerous move, but she was convinced that they needed an ally from within the delegation…an ally who had the authority to help them. And she wasn't sure she'd get a chance to discuss the decision with Timon.

That afternoon she finally caught Amos in camp and suggested that he take the blood test.

He invited her into his tent and asked her to sit down. "What is this all about, Jamie?" he asked with great seriousness. "Why this sudden suspicion about some parasite that's never been mentioned before?"

Jamie hesitated, praying that she wasn't about to make a mistake. Slowly, she told him about her and Timon's investigation of Nereus's death, the retrovirus and her speculation as to its origin.

Amos seemed genuinely shocked. He got up and paced around the tent, his hands clasped behind his back.

"I have heard about the virus," he said. "There are few in the government who don't know the story of the humans who hoped to wipe out the Opiri. But that was long ago, and even if someone in the Enclave resurrected the virus, they couldn't have gotten such a conspiracy past me."

"Are you sure?" she asked. "All it would take is one person working for someone high enough in the San Francisco government to make it happen. And there are people in the Enclave who still hate the Opiri."

"But they're greatly outnumbered," Amos said, "or this delegation wouldn't be here at all. There must be another explanation."

"What if there isn't, Amos? Who could have done this?"

He turned to face her. "You have a suspect, don't you?"

"Is there anything you can tell me about Greg that I don't know? Anything that might suggest he'd fall in with this kind of plan?"

"Greg," Amos said heavily. "You think he's behind this? The man who wanted to marry you, who still loves you?"

"He's been the most hostile to the Opiri, or at least to the Riders. And I've noticed that he leaves nearly all the meetings with Opiri delegates to you, though he has a position almost equal to yours." She shrugged uneasily. "And I also have a feeling. An instinct."

"And Timon has this instinct, too?" Amos sat down and stared at her. "I know you have feelings for him. But to trust an outsider half-blood more than your own people..."

"Not more, Amos. But I *do* trust him with my life."

Sighing deeply, Amos slumped in his chair. "I can tell you this much, Jamie. Greg's great-uncle was one of those originally involved in creating the virus."

Jamie covered her face with her hands. In spite of all he suspicions, she hadn't wanted Greg to be involved. What could have driven him to such extremes?

"We have no proof," Amos said. " I can't have you accusing him of something he may not have done."

"I don't plan to," Jamie said, rising. "If the virus really is loose in the Conclave, punishing the perpetrator now won't stop it. And if someone decides he's the source, the entire delegation will suffer."

"Who else knows about this?"

"Timon and I have been careful," she said. "But we can't assume that Opiri won't figure out why their own people are dying. I'm testing the other members of the delegation to see how many are infected. If we all are..."

"We could all be considered guilty." Amos rose, as well. "I'll do whatever's possible from my end. See what more I can learn from Greg. But, Jamie—I don't want you further involved. In fact, I'd like nothing better than for you to get out of this camp. Perhaps Timon will agree to take you."

"Out of camp? You mean run away? I'm infected, Amos. I could spread this far beyond the Conclave if I run across Opiri who decide to take my blood."

"But Timon will be there. Jamie, I don't want you hurt."

"I'll stand by the delegation," she said. "I don't think that more than a few of our people could know about this, even if Cahill's behind it. If something terrible happens, I'm going to be here with the rest of you to face it."

Amos only shook his head. Understanding that her godfather needed to be alone to absorb what she'd told him, Jamie left his tent.

That night, she went to Timon's little camp. A small fire was burning. Timon looked up, red glittering behind his eyes, and held out his hand.

Grasping it lightly, she sat beside the fire. His fingers were firm and warm.

"I spoke to Amos this morning," she said, slipping her hand from his. "I told him everything."

Timon stared at her. "Why? We still don't know—"

"I trust Amos implicitly."

He was quiet for a long time. "I saw Amos once, alone with two Erebusians," he said.

"What?"

"I saw them meeting at night, in secret. I didn't think much about it at the time, but now—"

"The Erebusians were the original targets of the virus years ago," Jamie said. "They have no love for our Enclave. Did this happen before or after Lord Makedon insulted us at the reception?"

"After."

"The Erebusians might have been offering an apology for their behavior earlier."

"A strange time and place for an apology." He stretched his long legs out before him and looked up at the bold pattern of stars in the night sky.

"Hmm," Jamie said, her thoughts moving ahead. "I did find out that Greg had a great-uncle involved with the creation of the original virus."

A savage gleam flashed in Timon's eyes. "I know you want him to be guilty, but it still isn't enough," she said. "We have to think this through carefully."

Timon didn't answer. He moved closer to Jamie, his shoulder touching hers. His warmth and the scent of him made her catch her breath.

"The moon is full tonight," he said, tilting his head back to study the sky.

She followed his gaze.

"In ancient Greek myth, the moon is associated with the goddess Artemis," he said, interrupting her thoughts. "She was the goddess of the hunt. My stepmother has the same name."

Jamie glanced at Timon's face. It was cast in shadow, but she could see the tension in it, hear the suppressed emotion in his voice.

"Was your stepmother a huntress, too?" she asked.

"As a matter of fact, she is," he said. "Very skilled with a bow. She was a Freeblood exile from a northern Citadel, living on her own outside of the usual packs of hunters. My father met her while he was on his way to rescue me."

"Rescue you?" Jamie said, sitting up straight.

"I was a child," he said. "There was a Bloodlord in the north collecting half-blood children for future troops to pit against the Citadels and, eventually, the Enclaves. He'd already gathered an army of Freebloods who resented the power of the other Bloodlords in the Citadels."

"You were kidnapped by this Bloodlord?"

"He sent his Freebloods to find children like me," he said. "We were kept in a castle on the other side of the old Canadian border."

"I'm... I'm terribly sorry, Timon," she said, lightly touching his knee.

"You know what it is to be taken against your will," he said, still gazing up at the sky. "I survived."

"I guess we both did."

He turned his head to smile at her, and she nearly melted under its warmth.

"We have something else in common I never mentioned before. My father lived in the mixed colony from which I was stolen, but he was originally from your Enclave."

"From San Francisco?"

"He was one of the convicts sent to be a serf in Erebus. He escaped, and my mother, a powerful Bloodlady, left her Citadel to be with him. She died before I was taken."

"I'm sorry," she said quietly.

"I remember what it was like," he said, still staring up at the moon. "I know how difficult it was for you to lose your mother."

"How did your father and your stepmother meet?"

"She was a Freeblood who believed that other Freebloods could abandon their lives of hunting humans and join together in a peaceful civilization free of dependence on human blood. She helped my father find me and fight off the Freebloods working for the Bloodlord. He was pulled down, and his followers…my stepmother decided that they could be redeemed, and my father had already let himself be changed into an Opir to help save me. He joined her in establishing a peaceful band of Freebloods who lived exclusively on animal blood."

"And you went with them."

"I wanted to be with my father, and I trusted Artemis from the beginning. They took up a nomadic life, gathering more Freebloods and converting them to Artemis's philosophy. For me, it was normal to move constantly, like the Wanderers."

"Or the Riders," Jamie said.

He smiled wryly. "I couldn't imagine settling down anywhere. But the time came when I wasn't content with my father's life, either. He and Artemis were devoted to their philosophy, and they wanted me to be like them. I didn't want to dedicate my life to a cause. I quarreled with them, stole a horse and rode away."

"Then you dared what I never did," she said. "I never rebelled."

"It isn't all it's cracked up to be," he said. "I found another family in the Riders, one that didn't require me to fight for some noble goal. I don't have them anymore, either."

"Timon, I'm so sorry—"

"I know." He got up. "Jamie, you should go back to the delegation. There are a few things I need to take care of."

And just like that, he brought their moment of intimacy to an end. He behaved as a good friend would…no more, no less.

"Sleep," he told her, guiding her away from the fire with the lightest touch on her elbow. "You still have human needs."

"So do you," she said, meeting his gaze. "Half-human, anyway."

He smiled unexpectedly, and her heart gave a jolt. "Human enough," he said. "When you wake, I hope to have more information."

Jamie backed away, afraid that she was missing some signal from him. But he only returned to his fire, leaving her to walk along the brightly lit lane toward the San Francisco camp.

Back in her shared tent, she slept deeply and dreamlessly, only to be awakened when Akesha shook her shoulder.

"Jamie!" Akesha whispered. "Nobody can find Senator Cahill. He's disappeared."

Rubbing her eyes, Jamie threw her legs over the side of the cot. "Disappeared?" she said thickly. "What do you mean?"

"No one has seen him since last night, and it's dawn now," she said. "The Councilman is worried about him. He asked me to ask you when you last spoke to him."

Jamie got up, reaching for her robe. "We've barely spoken at all in the past few days."

"You'd better come talk to the Councilman."

Jamie found Amos fully dressed and pacing outside his tent.

"I haven't seen him," Jamie began. "When I—"

"It's worse than that," Amos interrupted. "More Opiri have died, and I don't know what's going to happen to us."

Chapter 30

Cahill wouldn't speak. No matter what methods Timon used—everything short of torture—the human refused to admit that he'd had any part to play in the spread of the virus.

Nor would he expose anyone else in the San Francisco delegation, even to clear himself.

"I know nothing," he insisted for the dozenth time, straining at the ropes that bound his hands behind him. "If the virus came from our delegation, it was distributed without my knowledge."

Recognizing defeat, Timon pulled Cahill off his knees and stood him up. The desert air was cool, though the various earth-colored birds and occasional more striking quail were already going about their business. The mountains to the west were looming shadows. In the distance, the tent city was also beginning to stir.

"You won't get away with this," Cahill said behind gritted teeth. "You're no longer a Rider, and this is kidnapping."

"But you won't tell anyone," Timon said, cutting through Cahill's bonds with his knife. "You're in too precarious a position."

"And you aren't?" Cahill spat.

"We're both on shaky ground," Timon said, pushing Cahill toward the borrowed horses. "We'd better keep things stable as long as we can."

Cahill was no fool. "As things stand now," he said, "you're safe. But the moment my delegation is cleared—"

"*If* it is cleared," Timon said, mounting Lazarus. "I'm on Jamie's side, and that means I'm on yours unless you prove to be the instigator."

"You believe me?" Cahill asked in obvious surprise.

"I don't know," Timon said. "You ride ahead. I'll follow in a few minutes."

With a poisonous glance at Timon, Cahill kicked his horse into a canter. By the time Timon reached the perimeter of the Conclave, he could already see that something was wrong. The tent city hummed like an enormous hive disturbed by a child with a stick.

He rode into the encampment and dismounted. People were talking in groups, humans and Opiri strictly separated from each other. In the few places where the two groups mingled, they exchanged ugly looks.

"Murderers," one hooded Opir hissed as he passed.

With Lazarus in tow, Timon headed straight for the San Francisco delegation. Cassius, along with several Riders, was speaking intently with Amos Parks. Several members of the delegation observed anxiously from the sidelines, including Jamie.

Timon tied his mount to the nearest tent and slipped in among the watchers, though he had no doubt that Cassius had seen him arrive. As he made his way toward Jamie, two of the delegation soldiers arrived with Cahill between them.

"What is this?" Cahill snapped. He stared at Cassius. "What do *you* want?"

"We've been told you were out all night," Cassius said.

"I was riding in the desert," Cahill said. "Is there some law against it?"

Cassius signaled to his Riders. They walked around Amos and took custody of Cahill, displacing the delegation soldiers.

"We'll need to question him," Cassius said with a hard glance toward Timon. "He won't be harmed."

"But this is—" Amos began.

"Our job," Cassius finished.

"Because of wild rumors?" Amos said.

"It is our intention to find the origin of these rumors," Cassius said. He nodded to the Riders. They marched the protesting Cahill away. Cassius lingered.

"I would advise you to take great care, Councilman Parks," Cassius said. "Stay close to your camp unless you have no other choice."

The Riders left without further explanation. The members of the delegation broke into bewildered conversation.

Timon pulled Jamie aside.

"What's happened?" he asked.

"More Opiri deaths," she said, still staring after Cahill. "The rumors have started. Someone has leaked information about the virus." She met his gaze. "Did you tell anyone, Timon?"

Timon thought of Cassius, in whom he had so trustingly confided. The captain would never have spread the rumors himself; he knew as well as Timon what chaos would result.

Could Cassius have shared the information with someone *he* thought was trustworthy? He might have contacted Opir scientists to confirm what Timon had told him about the virus. Could one of them have spread the information in the Opiri precinct?

It didn't really matter who had done it. The consequences were only beginning, and somebody had already decided that Cahill had some part in what had happened. Timon was frankly amazed that the entire delegation hadn't been arrested en masse.

But Timon hadn't told Cassius anything about Cahill in particular. Someone had convinced the captain that the Senator, not the delegation's leader, was the best member of the Enclave to question.

Perhaps someone within the delegation itself.

"No," he said at last, "I didn't tell anyone."

The lie choked him, but he couldn't afford to lose Jamie's trust now. Not when he might be her only protection. He could no longer count on Cassius's keeping *his* word.

"Did anyone else here in camp know?" he asked Jamie.

She looked toward Parks, who was trying to calm his people. "No," she said. "We don't have much time left, if we have any at all."

"I'm not leaving you from now on," Timon said under his breath. "As far as they know, we're lovers who won't be parted."

Later that same afternoon, Jamie learned that Councilman Parks had been called to an emergency meeting with the Conclave's Administrative Committee. Jamie had expected to attend as Parks's aide, but she was more than surprised when the Rider messengers asked Timon to come, as well.

She had no time to ask for an explanation. Their Rider escort, six strong, guided them through an ever-shifting crowd of nervous humans and, near the end, visibly hostile Opiri. Timon stuck so close to her that their bodies were always touching, and that gave her comfort.

As soon as they entered the Committee tent, Jamie felt the tension. The Administrative Committee, sitting behind a long table on a low dais with Rider escorts watching from the sidelines, was made up of six Opiri and six human delegates, led by Opir Committee President Pheidon. They began to question Amos almost immediately.

"Rumors of the virus's existence spread among the Citadels fifty years ago," Pheidon said, "but it was thought to have been destroyed. How did it survive?"

Amos admitted that he had no idea, and denied knowing anything about the virus's being at the Conclave. He asked to speak to Cahill and was refused. The Committee members continued to question him, and he answered plausibly without mentioning Jamie or Timon in any way.

"So you believe it was Senator Cahill who brought the virus from the Enclave, and insist that you knew nothing about it," a human Committee member said.

"I can't speak about the Senator," Amos said in a quiet, respectful voice. "That is your claim, not mine."

"But does it make sense that none of the rest of you knew of the virus?" another Committee member asked.

"Did Cahill suggest we did?"

The members of the Committee consulted with one another. Timon held Jamie's arm, refusing to let her move away from him.

"Timon," Pheidon said. "Please step forward."

With a grim glance at Jamie, Timon let her go and walked toward the dais. Cassius appeared and joined the Committee members beside the table.

"Tell us what you learned from the San Francisco delegation," Cassius asked.

Jamie's stomach tightened with dread. She stared at Timon as he met his captain's eyes, his expression as implacable as the desert sun.

"I don't understand the question," he said.

"We know that you were sent to observe the delegation and gather information about any secrets they might be hiding," Cassius said. "Do you deny this?"

Timon looked back at Jamie, devastation in his eyes. "I still don't know who hired the Riders to uncover these supposed secrets," he said. "Was it the Committee?"

"No," Pheidon said flatly.

"Then who was it?"

"You are not here to ask questions," Cassius said.

"And we have proof of the virus's existence," Pheidon said. "We need to know who else in the delegation had previous knowledge of it, and who kept it quiet when they should have reported it to us immediately."

"I know of no such persons," Timon said, standing very straight.

"Did you not take Cahill out into the desert to question him?"

Jamie closed her eyes. Timon had been sent to spy on them. But when? Before or after he'd helped her identify the virus? Why hadn't he exposed her earlier, or told her about Cahill?

He isn't exposing you now. He's lying for you.

"I learned nothing from him," Timon said. "You arrested him shortly after I returned."

"And it was *your* interest in him that led to his arrest," Cassius said.

"You were watching me."

"We couldn't be sure of your loyalty. You have a chance to prove it now."

Chapter 31

"I did suspect Cahill," Timon said to the council. "But he was the only one."

"You have nothing more to add?"

"No."

Holding very still, Jamie tried to maintain her composure. Timon had withheld important information from her, but now he was withholding it from his captain. He'd put himself in an untenable position.

It would have been so easy for him to tell the Committee everything he knew. That was the thought Jamie clung to. He had spied on her, but he wasn't going to betray her.

But what would the Committee do with him?

Pheidon signaled to Cassius, who dismissed Timon with a wave of his hand. Timon retreated to a point halfway between the dais and where Amos and Jamie stood, as if he still meant to defend the San Francisco delegates from attack.

"We believe we know why the virus was released here," Pheidon said. "It was meant to weaken the Opiri delegations by reducing their numbers. Whoever did this does not want peace, but slaughter, just as the original makers of the virus intended. If it spreads beyond the Conclave, it could conceivably kill every Opir on this continent." He glared at Amos. "It is possible that the instigator did not intend total genocide, in which case he may also have a cure. We must learn if such a cure exists."

"We will do everything we can to cooperate," Amos said.

"I hope that is true, Councilman," Pheidon. "We will be taking preventative action to reduce the risk of infection. Until we find answers, the Conclave is suspended."

Amos inclined his head. "I understand."

"You had better look to your own," Cassius said. "We will have to assume that members of your delegation are infected with the virus. You are forbidden to donate blood, and we can't guarantee your safety if you wander far from your camp."

"If they're innocent," Timon said, "you can't leave them undefended."

Cassius gave Timon such a look of contempt that Jamie winced. "You've thrown your lot in with the humans," Cassius said. "You have my permission to defend them."

Timon backed closer to Amos and Jamie. "We should go," he said softly.

"You're not welcome," Amos said coldly.

"Let him come," Jamie whispered. "You said you owed him a debt, and he can't go back to the Riders now."

Amos must have known this was no time to argue. He preceded Jamie and Timon to the tent entrance, Timon pressed so closely behind Jamie that they were virtually breathing the same air.

As soon as they stepped out into the light, Jamie felt how everything had changed. The nervous, sometimes hostile attitudes of the other delegates, which had seemed disturbing but not alarming on their way to the Committee tent, now seemed much worse. There were far fewer humans out than would normally be seen in daylight, and several packs of hooded Opiri followed closely alongside or behind Jamie, Amos and Timon.

Timon's presence seemed to keep any chance of physical danger at bay, and the Opir gangs contented themselves with muttered curses.

The Enclave's soldiers were waiting for them at the edge of the human precinct, their eyes darting left and right as they closed in around Jamie and her godfather. Timon stood a little apart, following them to the Enclave tents with his face half turned toward the Opiri, who had finally ended their pursuit.

They stopped in front of Amos's tent. Amos spoke to one of the soldiers, who trotted toward one of the nearby tents.

"I thought I'd made clear that you're not welcome here," Amos said to Timon.

"I don't plan to leave Jamie's side," Timon said, holding her godfather's stare.

"Let me talk to him, Amos," Jamie said, taking Timon's arm. She dragged him around to the side of the tent.

"You spied on us for Cassius," she said. "Was it all a lie, your being thrown out of the Riders?"

"It was then," Timon said. "But I suggested it so that I could stay close to you."

Jamie knew she shouldn't take his word for anything, but her heart betrayed her. Timon had said that they would share the same fate from now on. She wanted so badly to believe him.

"What were you supposed to tell him?" she asked.

"He sent me to learn more about the virus."

"Then he already knew our delegation might be responsible. The Opir scientists must have been studying the dead Opiri, just as we suspected."

Timon hesitated. "Cassius didn't confide in me," he said.

"You didn't expect to be exposed so publicly, did you?"

"It's obvious that Cassius doesn't trust me," he said. "He wanted you to know I'd been deceiving you."

"And if you'd told him we were all involved, he'd have arrested us on the spot?"

"I trusted *him*," Timon said. "I expected him to handle this with discretion, considering the stakes." He searched her eyes. "I don't blame you for doubting me. All I ask is to stay by your side and do what I can to help you."

"And I have no way of knowing if this is another ruse. How can you expect me to convince Amos that—"

Timon silenced her with a kiss. He pulled her to his body and pressed his mouth hard against hers.

Jamie responded as if she had no control over herself, melting into his arms and clutching his jacket almost violently. She heard nothing but her own pulse pounding in her ears. Every nerve in her body felt exposed and raw.

She pushed him away, holding him at arm's length.

"You think it'll be that easy?" she demanded, her lips throbbing.

"Easy?" He barked a laugh. "You can push me away, Jamie, but I'm not leaving. Tell that to your godfather."

"And if he sends the soldiers to eject you?"

"I wouldn't want to hurt them," Timon said. "You know I would."

"I know." She took a step back. "I can't stop you. But you may still have a chance to salvage your relationship with your Brotherhood, if you go back now and—"

"It's too late," he said. "I wouldn't go back even if Cassius begged me to. I've made my choice."

If Jamie allowed herself to interpret his words the way she so desperately wanted to, she might dare think they could truly start over, that he loved her and she could allow herself to love him.

But the uncertainty was still there. She didn't dare give way to her own emotions. The distraction could be fatal.

"If you're going to stay here," she said, "you'd better get your things."

With a brief nod, Timon turned away. Jamie touched her lips and watched him disappear. Then she circled Amos's tent and went inside to join the meeting the President of the Administrative Committee had convened for the entire delegation.

* * *

The mob had nearly surrounded the Enclave camp by the time Timon returned.

He'd packed his basic supplies and clothing in a duffel and carried it slung over his shoulder, moving as swiftly as he could. The idea of being apart from Jamie even for half an hour haunted him, and when he saw the mass of hoods, seething like beetles on hot sand, he knew the worst had happened.

Dropping the duffel, he charged into the crowd. He shoved Opiri aside and found the Enclave soldiers standing to either side of Amos Parks, who was clearly trying without success to calm the yelling Opiri.

Timon strode out into the narrow space between the mob and the humans. He stopped in front of Amos. "Where is Jamie?"

"Inside with the others," Amos said. "How many are there out there?"

"At least fifty," Timon said.

"They seem to want our blood," Amos said with a hard smile.

"You spread the virus!" one of the nearest Opiri shouted.

"Genocide!" another cried.

"I've tried to reason with them," Amos said, "but I fear it's gone beyond that."

"Go inside the tent," Timon said.

"And what do you expect to do?"

"Fight."

"Do what he said, Councilman," Sergeant Cho said, shifting his weight. "We can hold them off until help arrives."

"Help?" Amos grimaced. "The human delegations around us aren't going to take on so many Opiri barehanded."

"Riders will come," Timon said.

"And that should comfort us?"

Timon scanned the crowd. "It's not yet sunrise. Until they can move freely without their daycoats, they won't attack."

"We will search the tents!" a female Opiri called. "Move out of our way, or you will be hurt!"

"There's nothing here!" Jamie cried, pushing her way from the tent to Timon's side. "An investigation is already being conducted! You can't—"

Two Opiri surged forward. Timon shoved Jamie behind him and rushed the Opiri. He kicked the legs out from beneath one of them and struck the other across the face, almost dislodging his hood.

"Get inside the tent!" he snarled over his shoulder. Then he took a deep breath and howled.

No Rider who heard the cry of the prairie wolf would ignore it. It meant a Brother in distress, and Timon knew whoever responded wouldn't guess who had made it before they arrived.

Everything went still. Opiri stared at each other. Some recognized the call and began shuffling backward. Others moved forward to replace the two Timon had knocked down.

"I'm not leaving you here to be killed," Jamie said, moving up beside him. "If Cassius or the Committee sent these Opiri—"

Her words were cut off by the sound of hoofbeats. The mob began to split apart as the first mounted Riders began to disperse the Opiri. Timon could hear them ordering the protesters to return to their camps.

"However the Riders may feel about us," Timon said, "they won't let us be murdered."

He grabbed her arm and steered her back to Amos and the soldiers. Then he took up his place in front of them again. A Rider—Orpheus—broke through the closest ring of Opiri and used a long, crooked staff to drag them back. The first rays of sun broke over the mountains, and the Opiri began a disorganized retreat.

When they were gone, Timon released his breath and turned back to Jamie. "You won't be safe from now on," he said. "There are too many who know about the virus and blame you for it."

"If we can buy a little time," Amos said, "we can gain the help of the other humans here. They won't stand quietly by while Opiri work to destroy a human delegation."

"Then it will be all-out war," a new voice said.

Cassius, who had dismounted from his own horse, approached them with long, aggressive strides.

Instinctively, Timon positioned himself between Cassius and Jamie. "War the Riders have a duty to stop," he said.

Cassius looked at him the same way he had in the Committee tent. "We will not be forced into the middle of this," he said. "But we will have justice." He signaled to the Riders behind and around him. "These people are to be taken into protective custody."

Chapter 32

"This isn't necessary," Timon protested. "A few Riders on duty here will stop any outside interference."

Cassius ignored him. "Gather your things, Councilman Parks. We will provide you with new accommodations near our headquarters, where no one can harm you."

"Are we under arrest?" Parks asked calmly.

"You will be safe," Cassius said.

"No," Jamie said. "You can't believe—"

"Jamie," Timon said. He guided her away from the others. "Cassius won't back down now. Fighting them will only turn all the Riders against you."

"They aren't against us already?"

"Cassius is our—*their* captain, but every one of them follows him by choice. If they see Cassius treating you with anything less than complete neutrality, there may be disagreements among them, to our benefit."

"You called the Riders with that howl, didn't you? You knew what would happen."

"I knew there was no other choice but to have the protection of the Riders, one way or another. The Administrative Committee may have ordered this, in any case."

"And you? What would you have done if you led the Riders?"

He held her gaze. "I would have taken you away from here."

"Regardless of who might be guilty?"

Orpheus found them before he could answer and nodded briefly to Timon. "I'm sorry, Ms. McCullough. You must come with us."

"We're coming," Timon said. He took a firm grip on Jamie's arm and led her to the delegation members who stood waiting with their duffels and packs. Leading their horses between the tents, the Riders escorted Timon and the group through the human precinct to the central Hub. They continued on to the smaller of the two meeting tents.

"This will be your residence for the time being," Cassius said, addressing Amos. "Guards will be assigned to this tent. You will be safe." He then turned to Timon. "You have no place here."

"I can choose my own place now," Timon said.

Cassius gestured for Orpheus and another Rider to take charge of Timon.

"What will you do to him?" Jamie said.

"He will not be harmed, unless he resists," Cassius said, turning to walk away.

"Don't fight them," Jamie said urgently to Timon. "Get outside. Try to find out what else you can."

"I can't leave you here."

"And I can't leave the others."

"Come on, Timon," Orpheus said. He looked at Jamie. "Don't worry, Ms. McCullough. Timon still has friends."

Timon took Jamie's hand and squeezed. "I will be back," he said.

To Timon's considerable surprise, Orpheus let him go once they were out of the tent, and Timon wasted no time surveying the area.

Small groups of Opiri lingered in the daylight, muttering under their hoods, and humans moved among their various delegations, concern and anger in their voices.

As the day wore on, things began to change. Donor stations were closed down. Mounted Riders moved through both precincts and picked up both small groups of humans and of Opiri, herding them toward Rider headquarters. Word soon spread that humans and Opiri believed to be infected were being quarantined. The mood in the encampment deteriorated from suspicion and anger to a smothered sense of panic, with humans and Opiri lined up on opposite sides of the thoroughfare hurling taunts at one another.

No human had yet been charged with introducing the virus, not even Cahill…at least not publicly. But the Conclave was falling apart before Timon's eyes. More Opiri were found dead. The first human fatality was discovered in the late afternoon, a man's body with his throat torn out.

Timon had seen enough. He strode to the Wanderer's camp, whose members were packing to leave, and spoke with Caridad. Within the hour he had traveling gear and enough food to last one human for at least two weeks.

Wearing his Rider's jacket, he easily made it to the corral and separated Lazarus and one of the spare horses from the rest. He led them beneath the canopy that served as shade for the animals, saddled them and tied on the packs. Any Riders passing by afterward would assume that the horses were to be used in a foray away from the tent city. It wasn't as easy getting near the Enclave's new "quarters." The tent had been set up to take in some of the quarantined humans, and Riders were everywhere. Timon donned a hooded daycoat as sunset approached and slipped among the Opiri and humans swarming around Rider headquarters, each group staying well apart from the others. Raised voices demanded answers and hurled accusations.

Then Timon waited outside Rider headquarters, watching for Orpheus. He'd almost given up hope of finding his friend when the Rider arrived at the Hub with three frightened humans. As he dismounted, other Riders took charge of the humans and led them away.

"Orpheus," Timon hissed. "I need your help."

"I don't think I'm going to like this," Orpheus said with a weary expression.

Timon had known the risk was considerable, but Orpheus heard him out. The Rider was obviously disturbed by the work he'd been assigned, rounding up humans and Opiri like cattle, and Timon's worry that Orpheus might betray him quickly passed.

"How do you think you can get away?" Orpheus asked when Timon finished sharing his plan.

"A distraction is all I ask. I'll take my chances with the rest of it."

Two hours after nightfall, Orpheus created the necessary distraction. Riders were pulled away from their posts, and people recently taken into custody took the opportunity to run off.

Carrying his Rider's coat under his arm, Timon walked boldly through the milling crowd and ducked in between two quarreling Opiri at the last moment, running at a crouch toward the back of the quarantine tent. He pulled his knife and cut a slit in the back of the tent, just large enough for a person to pass through.

He squeezed through the opening and scanned the inside. It was overcrowded, and most of the humans remained with the groups they'd arrived with. Timon quickly spotted the San Francisco delegation.

Discarding his daycoat and hiding his jacket, he moved casually among the humans, none of whom paid him the slightest attention. Jamie and Amos were seated on one of the risers, locked deep in conversation.

"Jamie," Timon whispered. "I need to speak to you."

She broke off, glanced at Timon and touched Amos's hand. "I'll be back soon," she said, climbing down from the riser. Timon took her hand and led her to the rear of the tent.

"We have to go outside," he said. "Act normally. Don't call any attention to yourself."

"What's going on, Timon?" she asked.

He pulled her through the tent's slit without answering. Once they were outside, he shrugged into his jacket, seized her hand and started toward the Riders' corral.

"Where are we going?" Jamie asked.

The area around the corral was one of the darkest in the tent city. A dozen Rider horses stomped and shifted uneasily inside the fence, disturbed by the noise and the tension in the air. Timon's two horses were still tied beneath the canopy.

"We're leaving the encampment," he said, opening the gate.

Jamie held on to one of the gateposts. "I can't leave. Not while Amos and—"

Timon swept her up in his arms, carried her to the spare horse and tossed her up onto the animal's back. He was on Lazarus before she could dismount. He grabbed her horse's reins and rode through the gate.

Jamie could have ruined it all by shouting for help. But she remained quiet, her face pale and set, while Timon guided both horses around the outside of the corral and turned north. He kicked his mount into a canter, and Jamie's mount willingly followed.

After a moment she took control of her horse and caught up with him.

"What are you doing?" she asked. "We have to go back!"

"Not if you value your life," he said. "*I* do."

After an hour of fast riding and no sign of pursuit, Timon brought the horses to a halt. He lifted Jamie out of the saddle, left her near a tall cottonwood and walked the horses to cool them down and let them drink from the river.

"Here," he said, offering Jamie his canteen. She turned her face away.

"We're not going back," he said roughly, "so you'd better resign yourself."

She glared at him. "Why are you doing this?"

"Your life is in danger. I think that Cassius leaked the information about the virus to the camp, in order to create the chaos that's tearing the Conclave apart."

Her eyes widened. "How do you know that?"

"I honestly believed he could be trusted with knowledge of the virus and carry out a reasonable investigation. Instead he's allowed the rumors to grow and become dangerous. He's rounding up humans and Opiri, confining them under guard without explanation." He hesitated. "He's not the man I knew."

"What could he have to gain by this?"

"I don't know. It makes no sense to me."

Jamie was quiet. "Do you think he was going to claim that *I* released the virus?"

"I think there's a distinct possibility he'd put the blame on you, and on Cahill."

"Do you have doubts that Greg is guilty?"

"I have doubts about everything, at this point."

"Where *is* Greg?"

"I don't know, but the fact that Cassius hasn't released him is telling. My guess is that he planned to formally arrest you very soon."

"To appease the Opiri?"

"It's too late to stop what's happening. But if he put you on trial, I don't think all the other humans would stand by and let him mete out punishment, whatever the Committee's agreement with the Riders. The chaos would only increase." He crouched before Jamie. "I should never have trusted Cassius, Jamie. I won't ask you to forgive me. But I do ask that you let me save you."

Chapter 33

All the fight went out of Jamie…at least all the desire to fight Timon. She studied his face in the moonlight, remembering everything she had loved about him. And still loved. He had saved her life again.

"If you help me, if you go against the Riders, you can never go back to them," she said at last.

"I know." He offered her a canteen, and she drank. His gaze never left hers. "But that doesn't mean I don't still have friends among them. One helped us escape, and most of the others believe strongly in fairness and justice. If I can get to them—"

"And tell them what?" Jamie asked with a feeling of despair. "We still don't know who *did* spread the virus. There must be a clue, somewhere…"

She reached inside her jacket's inner pocket and withdrew her mother's journal. With a sense of desperation and futility, she began searching through it again, straining to read Eileen's minute handwriting on the pages before and after her notations about the virus.

"Let me look," Timon said. He reached for the journal before she was ready to let it go, and for a moment each of them held one half of the cover. Jamie gasped as the binding tore, and the back cover was ripped off.

Timon let go immediately. "I'm sorry. I wasn't—" He broke off and stared at the ground. On the weedy clay soil lay a tightly rolled and flattened piece of paper that had fallen out of the journal's damaged spine.

Snatching it up, Jamie unfolded it with shaking fingers. "It's from my mother," she said, her gaze sweeping over the page.

"What is it?" Timon asked, leaning toward her.

"Take it," she said.

He accepted the browned paper carefully and read the notes. "Your mother had access to a sample of the virus after it was supposedly destroyed," he said slowly. "We already knew that. But here it says that she gave it to the Erebusians so that they could formulate a cure should the virus ever be recreated." He met Jamie's eyes. "She wasn't the only one who had it all this time."

"Maybe the Erebusians *did* invent a cure," she said, getting to her feet. "Timon, a majority of Erebusians have always opposed peace. They suffered when the Enclave cut off their supply of blood-serfs, but they wouldn't settle for any compromise. What if *they* had something to do with the deaths in the Conclave?"

"Killing their own kind?" Timon said, rising to face her.

"Except for a brief time when a more liberal government took over," she said, "Erebus has always lived by the traditional rules of Opiri—challenging, killing and being killed in order to rise in rank and power. If they could justify it, they might return to the old ways of raiding human settlements for blood. Why shouldn't they kill to put an end to a peace they don't want?"

Timon stared at her. "You know what you're implying?"

"Yes. Maybe we've been looking for the culprit in the wrong place." She took the paper from him, folded it up again and grabbed both his hands. "Think, Timon. The Riders travel all over the West. Have you been to Erebus recently?"

His breath erupted in a curse. "Yes. Four months ago, my band traveled to Erebus with a message from the Citadel of Ambrus in old Arizona. We didn't know the contents of the message, but we spent several days camping outside the walls."

"Was there anything strange about your stay there?"

"Yes. The Erebusian government had released about fifty of their serfs and had given them a settlement outside the Citadel where they could live in relative freedom. They were still asked to share their blood, but they weren't living as slaves."

"That is completely out of character for them," Jamie said. "The Bloodlords would never voluntarily give up their serfs."

"It seemed so to me. But these humans offered blood to my band. Including me."

Jamie blinked. "If Erebus had access to the virus…"

Timon finished her sentence. "They could have infected the humans, and by extension infected the Riders, as well, knowing that half-bloods would become carriers without suffering any ill effects."

"And if you were infected at Erebus, you could have infected *me*, Timon. Considering that our delegates have been contributing blood at the donor stations, it's possible that they *didn't* get the virus directly at the Enclave."

"You're right, Jamie," Timon said, moving his hands to her shoulders. "Now we have something concrete to work with."

With a grin she couldn't suppress, Jamie flung her arms around Timon. She felt his instant of hesitation, and then his arms were around her, as well, and he was kissing her. The flood of relief turned to raw desire, and she ground her mouth against his.

Like the last time, there was urgency in their lovemaking. They were still fugitives, and might be found any time.

Jamie didn't care. She wriggled out of her clothes as quickly as she could, and soon both she and Timon were naked.

She pushed him down onto his back and knelt with her knees to either side of his thighs, taking his cock in both hands. She caressed the satiny head with her thumb, and Timon groaned.

"You like that," she said, a little shyly.

"Do you want me to prove it to you?" he asked, beginning to sit up.

She forced him back down with her hands on his shoulders. "*I* like it this way," she said, keeping her grip on him as she leaned over, her breasts brushing his chest, the tip of his cock stroking her stomach.

"Do you like this?" she asked, trapping his cock between them as she offered him her breast.

He caught her nipple in his mouth and suckled hungrily. Jamie felt in control and yet helpless, feeling as though she couldn't get enough of the sensation of his tongue on her nipple, the licking and tugging as his hands came up to cradle her breast.

She adjusted her position, sliding forward so that his cock came to rest between her spread thighs. The friction was intensely pleasurable. Just a little shift, a little movement on Timon's part…

He raised his hips, and his cock pushed inside her, impaling her as she settled on top of him. It was different than the other times, a strange and heady feeling of dominance. She lifted her body and came down on him again, accepting him deep inside.

They worked in tandem, refining their rhythm until they seemed like a single being. When he moved too fast, she slowed him down by easing away; she teased him by hovering over him, only to impale herself again. He kissed her, thrusting his tongue inside her mouth when she bent over him, and he cupped her breasts in his hands when she leaned back again.

She recognized when she was coming close to completion and felt the tension in his body that gave him away. But she didn't want it to end so soon. As if he'd heard her thoughts, Timon grasped her waist and lifted her off, rolling to the side until he was on top.

But he didn't stop there. He lifted her again and positioned her facedown, on her hands and knees. She knew immediately what was to come, and the idea of him dominating her made her even wetter. He knelt behind her, caressing her buttocks, bending to kiss and lick them. Then his finger was inside her, testing her, making her ready.

She pushed back into his hips, and he withdrew his finger. He gripped her hips with his spread hands, held her still and thrust into her from behind, rocking her forward. She gasped, and he covered her with his body, his lips close to her ear.

"Do you like that?" he asked.

"Yes," she moaned. "Please, don't stop."

Gripping her hips more firmly, he thrust again, as deeply as her body could take him. She felt almost at his mercy, and the thought only increased her erotic excitement. He always seemed to know how to be forceful without causing her the least discomfort, and her body wept for more.

When his fingers found the place of their joining and slid up to stroke her clitoris, she knew the waiting was over. She came wildly, gloriously, closing around him and releasing in rapid, ecstatic spasms. He followed a second later, his breath coming in broken grunts as it warmed the back of her neck.

He held her a moment longer and then pulled her back into his lap, licking her neck several times before biting her. She came again, shuddering against him.

When he was finished, he lowered himself to his side, her body still cradled within the curve of his. She rolled over to face him, to see the sated gratification in his eyes and the flush of his skin. She ran her fingers through his mussed hair. He smiled and kissed the tip of her nose.

"I wish we could stay like this forever," she whispered. "Or at least long enough to do it a few more times."

"So do I," Timon said. He stroked her cheek. "But we have a decision to make."

"Do we?" She closed her eyes, willing the world to go away. It didn't cooperate. "I know what you want to do," she said. "Take me somewhere 'safe.' But that place doesn't exist."

He rested his forehead against hers. "If I could," he said, "I'd lock you away in one of your labs, where the only danger you'd face would be pricking yourself with a needle."

"And what if that needle were attached to a syringe with the virus in it?" She turned her face into his shoulder. "You know I can't let this go."

"I know."

"We still need so many answers. Does Erebus really want to destroy the Conclave? Even if that was their intention, they'd have to have the cure or risk destroying every Opir who takes human blood. They'd have to have a way to distribute it after the Conclave falls."

"And assuming they have the cure," Timon said, "how far would they go to attain their goals?"

Jamie rested her lips against his collarbone. "Whatever our theories, we know from the blood work that some members of our delegation were infected. But we don't *how.* I don't see how the Erebusians could have done it before we left the Enclave."

"Unless they already had an ally within the Enclave."

"Greg? But you said you weren't sure about him anymore."

Timon was very still for a very long, uneasy minute. "Your godfather *did* meet with the Erebusians in private," he said.

Jamie rose up on her elbow. "Amos couldn't have had something to do with this. Why in God's name would *he* cooperate with the Erebusians to end any hope of peace?"

"We won't be able to get the answers out here."

"So we have to go back."

"They'll take us into custody the moment we return. If the Erebusians are in on this and they find out you suspect them, they may not wait for Cassius to accuse you."

"Then we'll need your Rider friends, the ones who will be loyal to you, not Cassius. Can you contact them without giving yourself away?"

"If I know you're as safe as you can be. But Cassius—" He broke off, his jaw tightening. "It may seem crazy, but the idea has been haunting me ever since Cassius began acting so strangely. What if he's working with the Erebusians?"

Jamie was truly astonished at Timon's suggestion. "Why would *he* want to see the Conclave destroyed?"

Timon dragged his palm over his face. "I have no idea. But we do need to know how much the Administrative Committee really understands about what's going on. Someone could be manipulating them to take a certain stand."

"Approaching your Rider friends is one thing. Letting the Committee *see* you—"

"Quiet," Timon ordered. He tilted his head and turned it toward the mountains in the east. "There are horsemen out there."

"How far away?" Jamie asked, pulling on her discarded shirt.

"Close, and riding parallel to the river," he said. He looked at Jamie. "If they're Riders, I need to get to them and make them listen to me."

Jamie tugged on her pants. "I'm almost ready," she said.

He stared at her, cold calculation in his eyes. *He's thinking about whether or not to leave me here*, Jamie thought.

"If something happens to you," she said, "where will that leave me?"

"Perfectly safe," an unfamiliar voice said, "as long as you come with us now."

Chapter 34

Timon shoved Jamie behind him and faced the tree from which the voice had come. A white-haired Opir emerged from behind it, his arrow nocked and aimed at Timon's chest.

"Run, Jamie," Timon whispered. "I'll take care of this one."

"You can try," another voice said, this time behind Jamie. "But we'd prefer to do this without violence."

"Who are you?" Jamie asked.

"Freebloods," Timon said in a normal voice. "I recognize their kind."

"Rogues?" Jamie asked, remembering the Freebloods who had attacked the delegation before Timon and his band had come to escort them.

"We consider that word something of an insult," the bowman said.

"What do you want?" Timon asked.

"Only to make sure you're not hostile," a third, female voice said. A woman appeared out of the shadows, graceful, ivory-haired and beautiful. "One can never be too careful out in the desert."

Timon froze. "Artemis?"

Jamie remembered his stepmother's name.

"Timon?" the Opir woman said. Her face split into a broad smile. "We wondered if we would ever see you again. When your father hears—"

"Is Garret well?" Timon said, his voice unsteady.

Artemis's smile faded. "You'll see for yourself soon enough." She looked past Timon and met Jamie's eyes. "You have nothing to fear from us," she said. "Our scouts were just a little overzealous." She gestured for her men to fall back. "May I ask your name?"

"Jamie. Jamie McCullough."

"And I, as my stepson already mentioned, am Artemis."

"What are you doing here?" Timon asked.

"We came to investigate the Conclave, though of course we were not formally invited," Artemis said as Timon gathered his and Jamie's gear and horses. "And you?"

What a strange reunion, Jamie thought. Timon hadn't seen his stepmother since he was seventeen, and yet it was as if they'd barely been apart. If they'd ended their last meeting on a quarrel, you couldn't tell it now.

But you *could* tell that Artemis was a woman who might lead Freebloods to a new way of life.

"We were also at the Conclave," Timon answered. "It's a complicated story."

"If you're headed there now," Jamie said to Artemis, "you'd better wait until Timon tells you what's happened."

Timon gave a brief nod. "You may want to turn around and ride in the opposite direction," he said.

"I doubt that very much," Artemis said, an odd note in her voice.

Leading the horses, they walked out from beneath the trees and into an open area broken by the foundations of fallen buildings, shrubs and a few saplings. Three horses waited, two of them already carrying the scouts. Artemis leaped into her saddle, and Timon and Jamie did the same.

They didn't have to ride far to reach the others. On the other side of a broad ditch stood thirty or so horses, each one accompanied by an Opir Jamie assumed to be a Freeblood. Most were armed with rifles, as well as bows and knives, though Jamie sensed no hostility as she and Timon approached. To the contrary; a number of the Freebloods called out to Timon, and others obviously recognized him.

One among them stood out, an Opir with short-cropped hair and way of carrying himself that seemed subtly different from the others. After a moment, Jamie realized that his face was very thin, and there were dark shadows under his eyes.

"Garret," Timon said. He kept a firm grip on Jamie's hand as he left their horses with the others and started toward his father.

"Timon." Garret's features flooded with emotion as he grabbed Timon in a firm embrace. Timon stood still for a moment and then returned the hug, only briefly releasing Jamie's hand.

"My God," Garret said when he let Timon go. There were tears in his eyes. "I wondered if I'd ever see you again."

Timon took a step back and studied his father's face. "I'm sorry," he said.

"No," Garret said, gripping Timon's arm. "I'm not going to waste the time we have now on past regrets." He smiled as Artemis joined them. "Please introduce me to your friend."

"Jamie McCullough," Timon said before she could speak.

"A very *good* friend, I think," Artemis said, a glint of mischief in her eyes.

Timon shifted his weight from one foot to the other. "She's from the San Francisco Enclave, one of the delegates sent to the Conclave."

"About which Timon apparently has much to tell us," Artemis said, resting her hand on her mate's shoulder.

"You're in trouble," Garret said, with a parent's keen perception. "Out in the middle of nowhere… I don't even know where to begin."

"Neither do I," Timon said, drawing Jamie to his side. "But you aren't well, Father."

Garret raised his brows as if he found the statement ridiculous, but he couldn't conceal the telltale signs. Timon's father had been infected with the virus.

"I'm a little tired," Garret admitted with self-deprecating smile. "It's nothing."

Obviously prepared to argue, Timon shook his head. Jamie put her arm around his waist and leaned her head close to his ear.

"Maybe we'd better tell them what's happened before we discuss it," she said very softly.

Timon's profile was tense with worry, but at last he nodded. As many as possible gathered close to Timon and Jamie as the two of them began to speak, laying out the bizarre occurrences at the Conclave and their own tentative theories as to the causes. Timon recounted his time with the Riders, and how his membership in the Brotherhood tied in with the events that might prove to be so deadly.

"The Erebusians," Garret said, his body struck by a shiver as he spoke. "They seemed to agree with the changes for a while, but the improvements obviously didn't last long after Ares and Trinity left them to their own devices."

"*If* they're guilty," Timon said. "We have no absolute proof. We have to get it, and either clear Jamie's delegation or find out if a citizen of the Enclave is part of the conspiracy."

"The Opiri could even be framing my people," Jamie said.

"There could be dozens of possibilities," Timon said, "and we have to find out which is the right one."

"By going back?" Garret asked. "They'll take both of you prisoner."

"I believe I can sneak into the encampment and get some

of the other Riders on our side," Timon said. "Jamie can remain with you."

"You know I won't stay behind," Jamie said. "We have to rescue the rest of my people, Timon, before everyone is convinced they're guilty."

"We won't be able to do it without a small army. If I can find enough Riders—"

"There is another way that might not end with your arrest," Jamie said. She turned to Artemis. "Will *you* help us?"

Artemis's eyes seemed to see right into Jamie's heart. Jamie felt herself drowning in memories of her own mother, lost to her so long ago.

"I know it's a lot to ask, especially since you don't know me or my friends," Jamie said. She met Garret's gaze. "You need it, sir. You have the virus."

Timon flinched, and Jamie could see his jaw flex over clenched teeth. "How long have you been ill, Father?" he asked.

"A week," Artemis said. "We did not know what it was. We met two groups of travelers on the way here, one of them human. You know we don't ordinarily take human blood, but they were so gracious. . ."

"Then it's already spread beyond the Conclave," Timon said.

Artemis and Garret conferred in silent communication. "What would you like us to do?" Garret finally asked.

"Get my delegation out of the encampment," Jamie said. "An incursion from outsiders like you won't be expected, and while you're doing that, Timon can look for his Riders and I'll find a way to speak with the Committee. If I can get them to consider our alternate theories for what's happened at the Conclave—"

Timon folded his arms across his chest. "There's no

guarantee that the Freebloods can get you out again once you've seen the Committee…if you even make it that far."

"I'm not letting you go in alone."

"This sounds familiar," Artemis murmured, with a half smile for Garret. She sobered again and turned to Timon. "I won't ask our people to risk their lives without consulting them."

"Understood," Timon said. "But if you're willing, I have an idea that might protect Jamie even if your band isn't able to help us."

"Timon—" Jamie began.

"Right now you'll be wanted as a suspect," he said to her. "That's all you are to the authorities—a possible human criminal subject to temporary laws that can easily be twisted to the advantage of our enemies. But what if you were more than human, protected by different laws even the Erebusians can't ignore?"

Artemis looked at him sharply. "Are you suggesting Conversion?" she asked.

"Turn me into an Opir?" Jamie asked in sudden understanding. "Of course. Any Opir who Converts a human essentially owns the new Opir until she chooses to release her vassal."

"And the patron is entirely responsible for the vassal until that time," Artemis murmured. "Only an Opir prepared for a deadly fight would attempt to break the bond, or take you away from your lord or lady."

"Any previous acts on her part would be erased by the change," Timon said. "Even Cassius couldn't touch her."

"And what about the danger to the patron, if someone should challenge him to get at me?" Jamie asked.

"Challenge is a risky proposition at any time," Artemis said, showing her teeth.

"Do you understand what my son is telling you?" Garret asked Jamie. "Once you're Opir, you can never turn back.

Your human life will end. You'll be confined to darkness unless you wear a heavy daycoat, and you'll rely on blood for nourishment."

"I *do* understand," Jamie said, her heart beating faster. "I know I won't belong in the Enclave any longer, and I'd never go to a Citadel…"

"But you won't be alone," Garret said, looking pointedly at Timon. "Not unless you want to be."

Chapter 35

Jamie followed Garret's gaze. Timon was staring fixedly at the ground, high color in his cheeks, and Jamie wondered if he was embarrassed because of his father's bluntness or because he didn't really feel what Garret obviously assumed he did.

"I'll go along with the plan if it means I can go back to the tent city," she said. "Conversion means that I would also become stronger and faster, better able to fight."

"Jamie—" Timon began.

"She's right," Artemis said. "You're a fool if you think she'll be willing to hide among us for her own safety."

"That means whoever does this will have to give me the freedom to take necessary actions," Jamie said. "Timon can't Convert me, because he's a half-blood. It would take a full-blooded Opir to do it."

"Yes," Timon said, glancing up. "And that Opir—" He stopped, his expression darkening as if he'd experienced some terrible inner revelation. "I'm an idiot," he said. "It won't work. Jamie carries the virus, so any Opir who changed her would be infected, as well."

"I'm already infected," Garret said. "I'll do it."

"No," Artemis said. "You don't have the strength." She met Timon's gaze. "I, too, am infected."

Timon sat bolt upright. "No. You look normal, not—"

"Garret and I are not the only two in our band who suffer the affliction," she said evenly. "We have found that this virus takes a different course with each individual. One of our people has already died, but I am barely showing the signs even though I have experienced the symptoms."

"But you're already starving," Jamie said. "I can't ask you to—"

"As long as I am strong enough to be of help, I will be," Artemis said. She gave Garret a pointed look. "It will do no good to argue. If Jamie does not object…"

"No," Jamie said, feeling deeply humbled. "I trust you."

"I will not abuse the privilege," Artemis said. "When this is finished, I will set you free."

"I know," Jamie said. A new thought struck her, and all at once her certainty evaporated. "Excuse me, but I'd like to speak to Timon alone."

Hearing the urgency in her voice, Timon got to his feet. He followed her a little distance away and stopped, frowning at her with obvious concern.

"Have you changed your mind?" he asked.

She met his gaze. "I am only concerned about our blood-bond. You won't be able to take nourishment from me once I'm Opir."

Timon gave a short laugh, only a little strained. "I didn't tell you, did I? I was able to get the antidote before things turned sour on us. There's no risk to me whatsoever."

"Thank God," she said. But a small, selfish voice inside her mourned the fact that another bond between them would be broken.

Timon saw the sadness in her eyes and cursed the lie. If he admitted that there wasn't an antidote he was certain she'd refuse to go through with the change. She'd assume the worst—that he wouldn't survive without her blood—but he knew it was possible to break the bond through harsh discipline and suffering. Suffering no worse than that which the infected Opiri had already been forced to endure.

Unlike them, at least he had a chance.

"Is there anything else that bothers you?" he asked.

"No," she said. "It's a good idea, Timon, as long as your mother is strong enough."

"I've never known anyone stronger," Timon said.

"And if she has to fight for me?"

"If she becomes unable to help, she'll tell us. And I'll be nearby."

She searched his eyes, but he refused to let her see even a shadow of doubt. All that mattered now was getting through the next few days, and giving Jamie a place to retreat to if things went wrong. Once her own people were free, she would take fewer risks with her own life, and he could concentrate on finding the cure for Artemis and Garret.

If the Erebusians had it, that would be proof enough of their guilt.

Artemis came up behind them, a silent huntress. "When would you like to begin?" she asked Jamie.

"Now," Jamie said.

"Then allow me a few moments with my son."

Jamie nodded with a brave smile. She touched Timon's shoulder and walked toward the bosk. Timon watched her go, holding himself rigid so that he wouldn't run after her.

"You love her," Artemis said. "Why haven't you told her?"

"How do you know I haven't?" Timon asked coolly.

"Because she doesn't know how you feel about her."

"She guessed, and decided that there was no future for us."

"It didn't look to me as if it was over between you."

Timon turned sharply to face her. "It's far more complicated than you could understand," he said.

"Emotions are always complicated."

"I'm going to find the cure," he said. "All I ask is that

once you're well again, you take care of her for as long as she needs you."

"What aren't you telling me, Timon?"

"I haven't been a boy in a very long time," he said. "Trust that I'm doing the right thing. And be careful with her."

"As if she were my own daughter." She looked toward the bosk. "I will go to her now. We will have privacy near the river."

"I'm coming with you," Timon said.

"I'm sure she will want you to be there." Artemis started toward the trees, showing no signs of illness. Timon followed her to the river's edge.

Jamie looked up with a smile, just a little strained. "I'm ready," she said.

"Sit, and make yourself comfortable," Timon said, taking her arm to help her down beneath one of the cottonwoods. He crouched beside her on one side, and Artemis knelt on the other. Timon squeezed her shoulder as Artemis prepared to bite.

A brief shudder ran through Jamie's body as Artemis's teeth pierced her flesh, but she gave no other sign that she was afraid. Within a minute it was over, and the small wound on Jamie's neck was already healing.

"It's done," Artemis said, meeting Timon's gaze over Jamie's head. "Are you all right?"

Jamie mumbled something in her throat, her eyes tightly closed. Timon bent over her and touched her cheek.

"She's cold," he said, his pulse jumping.

"Every human reacts differently," Artemis said. "Be patient."

But Jamie didn't open her eyes. Timon listened intently. Her heartbeat was slow and her breathing shallow.

"This isn't right," he said. "Jamie, can you hear me?"

Her lips curved up in a faint smile. "I hear you," she murmured.

Timon closed his eyes. "You may feel a little weak," he said. "Don't worry."

"I'm not…worried," she said. "I'm just tired."

"It would be better if we returned to the others," Artemis said.

"I'll carry her," Timon said. But as he reached out to lift Jamie in his arms, she whimpered in obvious pain. He lowered her carefully and cradled her body against his.

"Something's wrong," he said. "She can't be moved."

"Then we'll bring everything she might need here," Artemis said, the first hint of worry in her voice. "I'll go back now."

She left, and Timon released his rigid control over his emotions, holding Jamie as close as he dared. His gut told him what was wrong, though he'd been too blind to see the most terrible risk of all.

The virus. It had altered the Conversion.

Jamie moaned. Timon bent his head close to her mouth.

"What is it?" he asked, gripping her had. "I'm here."

"I won't…get old now, will I?"

"No, Jamie."

"So you and I…can be together."

Timon raised her hand to his lips and told her what she needed to hear. "Yes. As long as you want."

"Good." She gasped, her back arching. "It hurts."

"I know." He stroked her damp hair away from her face. "Stay with me."

She tossed and turned, her skin alternately hot and cold, as Timon waited for his stepmother to return. Artemis finally arrived with several of her Freebloods, leading horses and bearing bedrolls, clean water and a change of clothing for Timon and Jamie. Timon tried to make Jamie drink, but she only turned her head away.

"You know what is wrong with her," Artemis said, settling beside Timon.

"Yes. Jamie already carries the virus, making her react negatively to the change. I never even considered the possibility."

"Nor did any of us," Artemis said. "Not even Jamie." She placed her hand over Timon's. "It has made her ill, but it has not killed her. She is clearly fighting these negative effects with all her strength."

Jamie moaned, and Timon forgot about his stepmother. For the remainder of the night, he stayed beside Jamie, held her, spoke to her of any nonsensical thing that came into his mind…anything but the subject she herself had brought up. *We can stay together.*

Chapter 36

At dawn Jamie was finally still. Her breathing was steady, her heart rhythm normal, but nothing about her had changed. Her hair showed no streaking of white, which usually appeared within a day of Conversion; her teeth, when Timon gently parted her lips, were still flat-edged.

None of that mattered. She was alive, and when she opened her eyes and smiled at Timon, he felt as if he had been given the greatest gift of his life.

Artemis shooed Timon away and examined Jamie in private. When she rejoined him, she was shaking her head.

"I see no signs that the change has taken hold," she said.

"The virus may have delayed the process," Timon said.

"Or it may have stopped it entirely," Artemis said. "We have no way of knowing until we see how she responds to the light, and even then some of the newly changed maintain tolerance for sunlight for as long as several days."

"I'm not letting her go back to the Conclave unless I know she'll be acknowledged as your vassal," Timon said.

"There is one other test," she said, following him back to Jamie's side. She knelt and took Jamie's hand.

"Jamie, look at me."

Jamie turned her head and met Artemis's eyes.

"Try to sit up."

Using the tree trunk for support, Jamie inched her way into a sitting position without apparent difficulty.

"Now I would like you to get up, walk over to the river and throw a pebble into it."

With a grunt of concentration, Jamie planted her hands on the ground and tried to push herself up. Timon fell to his knees at her side.

"Are you crazy?" he demanded of Artemis. "She's in no state to—"

"I know she isn't," Artemis said. "But she would have tried to obey me no matter how difficult it was. She's become my vassal, Timon." She smiled at Jamie. "It's all right. Relax."

Easing Jamie back down, Timon hunched over her as if he'd fight Artemis like an animal defending its prey from an interloper. "Don't do that again," he said.

"I don't intend to. But your question is answered. She may not have visibly changed yet—perhaps she never will, entirely—but she is fully under my protection according to Opir law. No one will be able to touch her without first going through me."

Timon exhaled. "Thank you."

Artemis rose. "I have spoken to our people," she said. "They have agreed to assist us in our mission. Now we must make plans." She looked at Jamie. "Are you feeling well enough to help us?"

With Timon's assistance, Jamie sat up again. "I'm ready," she said.

A half dozen Freebloods joined Artemis, and they all discussed possible tactics to deal with the Rider guards and hostile Opiri while the Freebloods released the San Francisco delegation, and Jamie and Artemis approached the Committee. When they had made their plans, Timon helped Jamie walk a few steps and allowed her to test her strength. She never mentioned the words she had spoken in her fevered state.

Timon helped her into a hooded daycoat, and as they rode back to the Freeblood camp, he explained what had happened to her and what they'd discovered about her condition. She accidentally confirmed that she hadn't changed in essentials when her hood slipped off her head and her horse walked into a patch of bright sunlight. She suffered no ill effects.

"But I may still change more," she said. "I feel strong, Timon. And I'm not talking about recovering from my illness. I think I'll really be able to fight."

He dismounted. "Now isn't the time to test your abilities," he said.

Jamie slid out of the saddle and, without warning, charged at Timon. Her technique was awkward, but she managed to land a blow to Timon's belly and evade his attempts to catch her afterward.

A little breathless, Timon laughed. He feinted one way, moved in another, and finally caught Jamie in his arms.

"You're right," he said, his face very close to hers. "You are stronger."

"Artemis won't have to protect me," she said, a hint of defiance in her voice.

Timon pinned her arms at her sides. "Follow her lead," he said, well knowing that his stepmother would never let Jamie act recklessly, strong or not. "You won't have a choice, anyway."

"Your stepmother doesn't underestimate me the way you do."

"Underestimate you?" He held her back, his hands softening on her arms. "I've never done that, Jamie."

"You underestimate both of us," she said softly.

Timon let her go. "Are you hungry?" he asked.

Her expression went blank. "No," she said. "I certainly don't crave blood."

"Let me know as soon as you feel any kind of hunger or thirst," he said. He glanced toward Artemis, who was speaking intently with Garret and a group of Freebloods.

Beyond them, the others in the band were armed and clearly prepared for a fight.

"As we agreed," Timon said, "we'll be riding among the Freebloods toward the center of the band, so that we can get as close as possible to the encampment without being seen. I'll break off first and try to get the attention of as many Riders as I can. If Cassius is there, I'll get him to chase me. Artemis will be with you when the Freebloods attack the Quarantine tent, and you'll go straight to the Committee. After that, we'll have to make this up as we go along, but promise me you won't—"

"I know. *You'll* be the one in the most danger."

"I wouldn't bet on it." He moved his hands, unsure of what to do with them, longing to hold her again. At last he touched the edges of her hood with his fingers and pulled it down a little lower over her face. "Remember, keep this hood up even if the sunlight doesn't bother you. Even without the physical changes that would mark you as a new Convert, you can pass as one if you behave the right way."

"I won't forget."

"Maybe you should share your secret with the Committee. Knowing we all come from the same stock could knock some sense back into both humans and Opiri."

"Not yet," she said. "I'm afraid it'll make things worse if enough people reject what I have to say. They'll only have my word for it, Timon."

"You still have the research notes that they can read for themselves."

"Not when they're so busy fighting each other," she said. "We'll only get one chance."

One chance, Timon thought. *One chance for so many things*. But it wasn't the time to discuss feelings or a future beyond what the next few hours might hold.

"I wish—" Jamie began.

Timon pressed his finger over Jamie's lips. "You have everything you need to do what has to be done," he said.

She wrapped her arms around him fiercely and buried her face in his jacket. "Thank you," she said.

"For what?" he asked as he breathed in the warm, earthy scent of her hair.

Jamie looked up. Timon stared at her lips. A single kiss wouldn't make promises he might not be able to keep, or claims that she might reject. He lowered his head.

"Riders!" someone shouted.

Timon grabbed Jamie's hand and jogged toward Artemis, who was ready to mount her horse. He helped Jamie into the saddle behind her, and then found Lazarus among the Freebloods who were preparing to mount.

More than twenty Riders were approaching at a gallop, rifles at the ready. The timing could not have been worse. Timon prepared to break off from the others and face his former Brothers alone, hoping that somehow he could lead them away from any confrontation with the Freebloods.

But when Orpheus rode to the front of the line of Riders, Timon waved the Freebloods back and went ahead to meet his friend with cautious hope.

"Timon?" Orpheus called out as Timon approached. "Are you all right?"

"Were you sent to find Jamie and me?" Timon asked, keeping his distance.

"In a manner of speaking," Orpheus said in a dry voice. "But nothing is that clear-cut anymore."

"Did Cassius order you to take us prisoner?"

"If he did, *I* didn't hear him," Orpheus said. "And neither did any of these Riders." He gestured toward the Freeblood band. "Who are they?"

"Freeblood travelers on their way to the Conclave," Timon said.

"They should turn around and go back the way they came," Orpheus said.

"Will you try to stop them?"

Orpheus looked at Timon through narrowed eyes. "What are *you* doing with Freebloods?"

"One of them is my father. We didn't go looking for them. They found *us*."

"Then you should know the encampment is in virtual chaos. Mobs have taken over the Opiri district, and the Administrative Committee is in protective custody."

"Their own idea, or someone else's?"

"Cassius...*suggested* it. He has Rider guards around the tent."

"What about Jamie's people?"

"Still under guard, as well. They're being kept with the quarantined humans. They haven't been given any kind of hearing, but half the camp thinks they're guilty, and there's only a handful of Riders protecting them from the mobs."

"Where is Cassius?"

Orpheus's expression hardened. "He seems to have lost his mind. He doesn't care about restoring peace. He gives conflicting orders and stands by while fights break out, and he's away from camp half the time personally hunting down humans who are trying to leave. More Riders are beginning to notice that he's actively impeding our peacekeeping efforts."

"And the Riders with you now?"

"They doubt that Cassius can continue to lead us. It's as if he *wants* the Conclave to fall apart."

Timon nodded. "Cassius has thrown away his neutrality, Orpheus. He has hostility toward the San Francisco Enclave that has nothing to do with their possible involvement with the virus."

"I believe you," Orpheus said grimly. "I saw him meeting privately with the Erebusians. He obviously didn't want anyone to know what he was doing."

"Did you actually hear anything?"

"I couldn't get close enough. But afterward, I persuaded these men to stand aside and observe before taking any controversial action on Cassius's orders."

"Controversial, as in executing the suspects?"

"It's a real possibility. Our people still need a leader, and I'm not the one to fill that role. They'll hear whatever you have to say."

"Will they?" a new voice called. A horseman burst out from among the others, a familiar face bobbing above the horse's head.

Cahill. He was disheveled but appeared unhurt.

"Will they follow a man who ran away from his duty?" Cahill said, jerking his mount to a halt in front of Timon.

Chapter 37

"I didn't run away," Timon said. He glanced at Orpheus. "How did you get him here?"

"We...*convinced* his guards to let him come with us. We thought you'd want to speak to him."

"They were ready to blame *me* for the virus," Greg spat. "But I had nothing to do with it. It was Amos all along."

"What?" Jamie asked, riding up beside Timon. "What are you saying, Greg?"

"He's behind all of this—infecting us with the virus at the Enclave, covering it up, conspiring with Opiri to destroy the Conclave."

Jamie felt the blood drain from her face. She and Timon had discussed the possibility, but she'd never come close to accepting it.

"How can you possibly know this?" she asked Greg.

"There were clues," Greg said. "I put them together."

"Then you have no proof," Timon said.

"What possible motive could he have?" Jamie demanded. "Amos has always supported the Conclave. He would have no reason to undermine it."

"I only know that there's some kind of conspiracy," Greg said, "and he's part of it." He turned to Orpheus. "I'm grateful for what you did," he said, "but I'm not going back to the encampment. Jamie, since you're free—

"Thanks to Timon," Jamie said, defiantly grabbing Timon's hand.

"Don't go back there for any reason," Greg said, his jaw

set. "Anyone in our delegation could take the fall for Amos, and I know they were looking at you, too."

"Nothing will happen to Jamie," Timon said.

"Of course not," Greg said. He spat to the side, and then rode away.

"Looks like we wasted our time bringing the human to you," Orpheus said.

"It doesn't matter," Timon said. "We have more important things to think about now. Orpheus, the Freebloods have agreed to help me release the detainees and the rest of Jamie's delegation."

"What do you want us to do?"

"Get the other Riders' attention away from the quarantine tent. But only if you're sure you want to set yourself against Cassius."

"Our decision is made," Orpheus said. "We'll do as you ask." He glanced at Jamie. "And Ms. McCullough?"

"She'll be carrying out her own mission."

Artemis rode up behind them. "Is there a problem?" she asked.

Timon quickly made the introductions, and after a moment of sizing each other up, Orpheus and Artemis seemed to approve of being allies.

"We'll find out what's going on," Artemis said. "And we'll make sure this Committee knows about it."

Timon nodded, took hold of Lazarus's bridle and led Jamie away. "Are you sure about this?" he asked.

"More certain than ever," she said, holding his gaze. She longed for him to do what he'd almost done before the Riders had come…pull her close and kiss her, to remind her what she was fighting for.

But it seemed that he had retreated even further away from her. Even his voice was distant.

"Be careful," he said.

"And you." Timon nodded and rode back to the Riders.

Artemis returned to the Freebloods. The Riders left first, heading back for the tent city, and the others followed five minutes later. Artemis and Jamie rode toward the front, ready to break off just before the Freebloods reached the perimeter of the encampment. Jamie blinked when she saw Garret hidden among his people, clinging to his horse's back with obvious difficulty. She knew he wouldn't want Artemis to know that he, too, was risking his life.

But he would give that life for Artemis's sake, as she would give hers for him. And Jamie knew *she'd* give anything in the world to save Timon. She already knew he would do the same for her.

The Conclave was indeed in chaos. No one seemed to notice when Jamie, Artemis and a small contingent of Freebloods rode into the encampment. Starving Opiri roamed about, as sickly as zombies under their hoods, and humans huddled in their tents. In both precincts, Opiri and human bodies were strewn in the street. Where the skin was exposed, the Opiri bodies were so badly burned that the causes of their deaths couldn't be determined.

Riders were in evidence, but they seemed detached, uninterested in the deaths or the squabbles. None of them recognized Jamie under her hood. When they saw Freebloods ride boldly into the tent city on Artemis's heels, they made no attempt to stop the intruders. Instead they dispersed, leaving Jamie and Artemis free to approach the Committee tent while the Freebloods rode straight for the quarantine tent.

Guarded by their small escort, Jamie and Artemis dismounted some yards away from the tent entrance, leaving the horses with one of the Freebloods. At once they were confronted with eight Riders who had been set to guard the tent.

"We need to see the Administrative Committee," Artemis said, her hooded, assessing gaze sweeping over the men.

"We were ordered not to let anyone in," the leader said, looking Artemis up and down. "Who are you?"

"Newcomers to the Conclave," she said, gesturing toward the Freebloods behind her. "I must speak to your leaders on behalf of my people."

"You've come at a bad time. The Committee is not seeing anyone."

"Who runs this camp?"

Before the leader could answer, horsemen rode up behind Jamie and Artemis. Riders, armed with rifles and accompanied by none other than Cassius himself.

"Who are you?" he demanded, addressing Artemis.

"As I told this man, a newcomer to the Conclave," she said, keeping her gaze averted. "They will not allow me to speak to the Committee."

"Are you blind? The Conclave is finished." Cassius said, kicking his horse closer to her in a threatening fashion. "Where are the horsemen who entered after you?"

"I know nothing about them," Artemis said. "I believe they are Freebloods, but I have no idea—"

"You're lying," Cassius said. He turned his gaze on Jamie. "Who are you?"

"My vassal," Artemis said. "She is of no importance."

But Jamie knew the game was already up. Cassius had recognized something about her—her scent, the way she moved. It didn't matter. He reached over and flipped the hood off her head. Sunlight burned into her eyes, but her skin wasn't affected. She was still virtually human.

"McCullough," Cassius snarled. He gestured to his men, a dozen of them, who crowded in close. The guards at the tent door circled Artemis and Jamie from the other side. Jamie prepared to resist.

"Surrender yourself," Cassius said, "and I may let you live."

"You have no right to her," Artemis said. "She is mine."

Cassius hesitated, and his men stilled. "Whoever you are," he said, "you could not have Converted her so quickly. She is obviously still human, and we will—"

"You will do nothing. By Opiri law and custom, a vassal belongs to her patron. If you wish to break law and custom, you will have to fight me."

Dismounting swiftly, Cassius faced her from inches away. "You have no proof."

"Taste my blood, and then taste hers. That will be proof enough."

"I will fight you myself," Jamie said, stepping forward, "if my lady permits. We'll soon see if I'm human or not."

Cassius laughed. "Try me, little girl."

Chapter 38

But Artemis moved faster. She attacked Cassius with hands and feet, fighting roughly and fiercely. With an effort, Jamie held herself back, knowing that her interference would change this from a one-on-one battle to an outright melee that would sweep over her and Artemis like a storm.

As it was, Cassius's Riders kept their distance, and she was forced to watch, her nails biting into her palms, while Artemis defended her. She was certain that Cassius had every advantage in weight and height, but she had underestimated Artemis. While Cassius fought like a wolf, the Freeblood darted in and out like a striking snake imbued with wings, weaving under Cassius's fists and dodging his kicks.

Cassius was clearly taken aback. He had obviously not expected such resistance, and Jamie could see when he began to falter. The moment he did, Artemis pressed her advantage and cut his legs out from under him, falling on his chest and pressing her arm against his neck.

"She is *mine*," Artemis panted.

With a pounding of hooves, another Rider drew up among the observers. He flung himself out of the saddle.

"Opiri are attacking the quarantine tent," he said breathlessly. "We don't recognize them. We think they're trying to free the prisoners."

His mouth curled in a silent snarl, Cassius raised his hands above his head in a gesture of surrender. His men shifted and murmured. Artemis rose and backed away. Cassius scrambled to his feet.

"This is not over," he said. "You protect a criminal, and therefore you are one yourself. We will be back."

He leaped into his saddle and summoned his men with a sharp gesture. The eight guards remained by the tent, as implacable as ever, while the others set off at a rapid pace toward the quarantine tent. Artemis glared at the guards, but Jamie could see her decide not to take them on.

"Thank you for defending me," Jamie said. "But we can't just stand here. We may be able to help at the quarantine tent, provide some kind of distraction."

To Jamie's great relief, Artemis didn't argue, and they headed across the Hub. A huge crowd was gathered around the quarantine tent, mainly hostile Opiri. They were held back by a battle between Timon's Riders and Cassius's, though neither Timon nor Cassius was in sight. There was violent movement and shouting from inside the tent.

Jamie and Artemis looked at each other. As one they rode into the battle, charging in among Cassius's Riders and sowing confusion wherever they could.

It was soon apparent that Cassius's men were less than enthusiastic. As vicious as the fight had looked from a distance, both sets of Riders seemed to threaten and circle each other rather than engage, and though a few were wounded, there was no sign that any had died. *Maybe Timon has more Riders on his side than he realized*, Jamie thought.

Maybe there was still hope after all.

Timon and the Freebloods burst into the tent through the huge rent cut into the back, slicing through the crude repairs someone had made and expanding the opening to accommodate their mounts. They rode in among the detainees, Timon barking orders and reassurances as the prisoners huddled among the risers, frozen in fear and indecision. He saw no sign of Amos.

Timon sent the Freebloods to herd the detainees into the center of the tent, noting for the first time that Garret was among the Opiri. Timon made no effort to confront his father; Garret seemed to be having more success than most in reassuring the humans.

The sound of battle outside the tent told Timon that their time was almost up. Soon either Cassius's men or the Opir gang would break through. The Freebloods hustled the prisoners out the back of the tent, where spare horses waited. Each Freeblood took a human up with him, and soon they were riding pell-mell toward the edge of the encampment.

Timon stayed behind and rode around the tent to rejoin his Riders. Orpheus was exchanging threats with a Rider on Cassius's side, but their horses stood yards apart. Timon was encouraged by the impasse. Cassius's men didn't want to fight, even though the captain had surely given them a direct order.

"Stand back," Timon ordered as he joined Orpheus. "We have no quarrel with you if you stay out of our way."

"You're a traitor!" the opposing leader, Philokles, shouted.

"Are you so sure Cassius isn't the traitor?" Orpheus called. "He's doing everything possible to help destroy this Conclave!"

"Go back to Cassius, if you believe what he's doing is right," Timon said. "If you have doubts, if you wonder how the Riders have fallen so far while Cassius makes no move to protect the people of this Conclave, then join us. We will discover the truth and expose the real traitors."

He had barely finished his appeal when Artemis and Jamie pushed through the Opir mob. Timon's heart leaped into his throat, but the Opiri were listening intently to what he was saying, momentarily distracted from their hatred and suspicion.

All at once Philokles and perhaps a dozen of his Riders turned their horses about and trotted away. Eight of them remained.

"We'll join you," one of them said. "We want the truth."

"Then you're welcome," Timon said. He looked down as Jamie approached.

"We couldn't get in to see the Committee," she said. "Not without a battle we probably couldn't win."

"Then I'm glad you didn't risk it," Timon said, reaching down to grip her hand while he looked for injuries. "You've been fighting," he said to Artemis.

She shrugged. "Cassius came to take Jamie. He didn't believe she was my vassal."

"I could have defended myself," Jamie protested softly.

"Thank you, Mother," Timon said. "Where is Cassius now?"

"Perhaps he's fled," Artemis said.

"Not Cassius," Timon said. "Artemis, will you take Jamie out with the—"

"Will you let me stay with Timon, Artemis?" Jamie interrupted.

Artemis looked from her stepson to her vassal. "I'm sorry, Timon, but she has the right to be with you."

Timon closed his eyes. "Yes," he said. He helped Jamie mount behind him, his body coming alive at the touch of hers, and rounded up his Riders. One of them took Artemis up behind him.

"We don't have the element of surprise on our side now," Timon said, addressing his men. "But one way or another, we're going to get to the Erebusian camp and search their tents."

Murmurs of agreement answered him. Jamie locked her arms around Timon's waist, and he felt the softness of her breasts against his back, her thighs locked to his.

"We may die," Timon said quietly, for Jamie's ears alone.

"I'm not afraid," she said.

He covered her arms with his and squeezed her hands. "I know you aren't," he said.

She pressed her face into the back of his shoulder. He signaled to his men.

"Let's go," he said.

The Erebusian tents seemed to be deserted. A small group of Opiri wandered in the vicinity, but none of them belonged to the delegation. They turned hostile faces toward Timon and his Riders.

"Where is the delegation?" Timon demanded, leaving Jamie on Lazarus as he dismounted.

"We don't know," one of the Opir said sullenly.

"When did they leave?"

The Opir didn't answer, only stared at Timon—and Jamie—with contempt and a glimmer of fear. Striding toward the largest tent of the Erebusian camp, Timon pushed Opiri out of his way and entered the tent. The camp furnishings were in place, as if their owners had left in a hurry. Jamie and other Riders followed him inside.

"It's seems they've fled the Conclave," Orpheus said. "Should we pursue?"

"Not yet," Timon said. He left the tent and began to search another, Jamie at his side. They had still found nothing when they reached the last tent.

Timon cursed.

"Timon," Jamie said. She pointed at a lump in the simple woven carpet that covered the dirt floor. Timon flipped the carpet back to find the earth disturbed. He kicked the loose dirt aside and found a trapdoor to a square hole dug deep into the earth.

"Something was stored here," he said. He ran outside and found solar panels neatly and competently disguised against the back of the tent.

"It could have been a refrigeration unit," Jamie said,

coming up beside him. "How could we not have seen the panels?"

"We never *expected* to see them," Timon said. He took her hand and returned to the Riders.

"I believe the Erebusians have the virus," he said. "They've taken it with them. We need to bring them back to the encampment."

"Our pleasure," Orpheus said with a tight grin.

"I'm coming with you," Garret said, his horse appearing beside Lazarus. He looked even more sickly than before, his body bent and his eyes red rimmed.

"Father," Timon said, hiding his despair over Garret's appearance, "you must rest."

"And what if the Erebusians have the cure with them?" Garret asked.

"Let him go," Artemis said, her usually confident voice nearly breaking. "He has little time left."

Timon knew she was right. And if Garret had to die, he'd want to go down fighting.

He took advantage of the momentary confusion to pull his parents aside. After a whispered conversation, Jamie came to join them. But the plans had already been laid. Timon spoke separately to Orpheus, making his wishes clear.

"Let's ride," he said.

Chapter 39

Before Jamie could protest, Artemis mounted a spare horse and ordered Jamie to ride behind her. She made it a command Jamie couldn't disobey, no matter how much she fought it. Timon could see her trying to resist and felt a momentary rush of guilt, quickly set aside. Artemis had to get back to the Freebloods…not just for Jamie's sake, but because her people had to be ready for another fight.

While Artemis broke away at a gallop, Timon led the others toward the shadows of the bosk, Orpheus and Garret right behind him. He soon found what even the Erebusians couldn't conceal: multiple hoofprints curving away south along the river. They were moving fast, without any wagons to slow them.

But Timon and his men had gone no more than a mile when a large group of Riders led by Cassius intercepted them, every man armed with a rifle.

According to previous plans, Timon's Riders assembled in formation behind him. This was the test, of his Riders and Cassius's, family against family. It would be impossible to avoid casualties.

Cassius made the first move, kicking his horse into a hard run and brandishing his rifle as if he meant to scare Timon off with a display of aggression. Timon rode out to meet him, his own rifle at the ready.

"Surrender," Cassius shouted, "and there need be no deaths."

"What have you done, Cassius?" Timon called. "How many of our beliefs have you already betrayed?"

Cassius aimed his rifle and shot one of the Riders behind Timon. The man fell from his horse without a sound. Timon returned fire, but Cassius had already turned his horse around and was galloping back to his own lines.

There was no order to the battle, no rules. The two groups fell on each other, using their rifles to shoot and club, Brother against Brother. More men fell, some with looks of bewilderment on their faces, as if they didn't understand how things had turned so rotten.

Timon fought with the rest, but Cassius stayed out of his reach. As Timon's numbers thinned, he began to feel as if he were drowning in a merciless sea of death and horror. It was one thing to ask his Brothers to fight their own people, and another thing to see it, see men he knew die one by one.

Then Garret fell, a bullet in his shoulder. Timon jumped from Lazarus's saddle and knelt beside his father, checking the wound.

"I'll live," Garret croaked. But Timon knew that Garret's body was too weak to heal such a wound, and the shock alone might kill him.

He raised his head and looked around him. The knowledge struck him all at once: he didn't have the courage to sacrifice so many when he knew the Freebloods could continue the pursuit of the Erebusians without his Riders. He touched his father's cheek, took Lazarus's reins and went in search of a messenger. He glimpsed Orpheus in the act of beating down one of the enemy, caught the other Rider by his jacket and issued a quick order. Then he mounted, fending off attackers as he continued to look for Cassius.

The Rider captain sat his horse on a slight rise, untouchable and arrogant. Timon rode straight toward him. A bullet whizzed past his ear, and Cassius brought up his rifle.

Timon dropped his rifle to the ground and raised his

hands above his head. "I surrender!" he called out. "Spare my men!"

After a moment of narrow-eyed hesitation, Cassius fired his rifle toward the sky three times. His men broke off the fighting and rode toward him, and Timon's Riders, abandoned in midbattle, stared after them.

"You will spare my men?" Timon asked, continuing toward Cassius with his hands in the air.

"If you give up without resistance," Cassius said, "and accept the punishment coming to you for treason against the Brotherhood."

Timon dismounted and stood very still as two of Cassius's men yanked his arms behind his back and bound them firmly. "My father, the Freeblood," he said. "He's dying of the virus and has been shot. There's no need to take revenge on him."

"Take him, as well," Cassius said, giving another of his men a quiet order. "Command your traitor Riders to follow me, and we will return to camp."

With his guards prodding him along, Timon made the rounds of the battlefield and gave the orders. His men surrendered reluctantly, but at least they would live and be permitted to gather their dead once Cassius and Timon had returned to the Conclave.

As he supported Garret, Timon and his Riders were forced to walk while Cassius's men rode among them. All were silent, as if even Cassius's riders had suffered a shock from the carnage. They took no pleasure in their victory.

When they reached the Hub, Garret was released and Timon was placed under guard in a small storage tent, suffocatingly hot and close. He didn't try to free himself. Cassius seemed a man possessed, intent on making Timon suffer, and would undoubtedly keep Timon from taking blood. He didn't know that Timon was fighting off a blood-bond or he would have been even more pleased at Timon's capture.

Nothing Cassius could do could match Timon's worry for Garret, his concern for Jamie and his despair over the failure of the Conclave. He had come here believing he had no stake in its success, but Jamie had gradually influenced his thinking without his being aware of it, and now there was nothing he could do. Jamie would have to carry on.

He reminded himself that she wouldn't be alone…she would have Artemis and the other Freebloods. And there was still a chance that they would catch up with and overcome the Erebusians. There was still a chance that Jamie, with her courage and determination and her precious secret, could save the Conclave.

He doubted that Cassius would let him live long enough to tell Jamie he would always love her.

Jamie continued to ask Artemis questions, but the Freeblood would not respond. They had not been at the Freeblood camp but a few hours when Orpheus rode in, his mount mottled with sweat and foam.

"Timon's Riders met with Cassius near the bosk, and he was forced to surrender," Orpheus said, panting heavily. "The Erebusians are headed south. He asks your Freebloods to pursue them in his place."

"Artemis, let me go after him!" Jamie said.

"Impossible," she said. "He can take care of himself, and we have another job to do."

"You don't give a damn about him!"

Artemis met her gaze. "He is my son. I love him, as you do."

"Garret is with them!"

"I know. What would they want us to do?"

Jamie knew all too well. She would have to trust in Timon's intelligence, his skill and his instinct for survival.

She would help find the Erebusians. For him. She caught a riderless horse and mounted.

"Go!" Artemis shouted, and half the Freebloods reined their horses toward the river.

Soon they reached a battleground, littered with Rider bodies. Jamie searched for Timon. He wasn't there, but she recognized many of the fallen.

"He was alive when I last saw him," Orpheus said as he rode past her. Ignoring the carnage, the Freebloods continued their pursuit. The scouts riding point found the hoofprints, and then Jamie saw dust rising in a cloud as a ragtag group of hooded horsemen fled ahead of them.

A dozen Freebloods split off from the band and rode at an angle to cut off the Erebusians' retreat. They forced the scattering Opiri to merge together, horses pushing against each other, followed by a scuffle of confusion as the Erebusians attempted to get their mounts under control.

That gave the Freebloods the advantage they needed. They used a pincer movement to trap the Erebusians between them, and gradually closed the jaws of the trap, squeezing their prey into a tighter and tighter line.

It was soon obvious that the Erebusians had guns themselves, but the weapons were nearly useless in such close quarters. Some on both sides resorted to knives, but Artemis ordered Jamie to stay well clear of the fighting.

Forced to obey, Jamie hung back until the Erebusians had been subdued. Once the Freebloods had them off their mounts and on their knees, Jamie dismounted and strode along the line of prisoners.

"Where have you hidden it?" she demanded, stopping before a dusty and defeated Lord Makedon.

"I have no idea what you're talking about," Makedon said, his eyes burning with contempt.

"The cure!" Jamie said. "Where is it?"

"I'm almost certain they don't have it," Artemis said,

joining Jamie. "And that means it's probably back in the tent city."

"Unless someone else managed to take it away," Jamie said.

"If we believe that, we have no hope," Artemis said. "Do you still have hope, Jamie?"

"Always," Jamie said. "We have to go back to the Conclave."

"Agreed," Artemis said. "But this is no time for another frontal assault by an army. You and I go alone."

Chapter 40

The tent city was as hushed as a graveyard. There were no mobs or disturbances; the humans remained in or near their tents, and the Opiri seemed to be in a state of tense anticipation, as if they no longer felt the need to display their anger.

Riders at the perimeter saw Jamie and Artemis approach, and one of them turned his mount toward the Hub. The other Riders closed in, their faces expressionless but their actions less than friendly.

"Where is Timon?" Jamie asked.

The Rider remained silent, and there was no further conversation until the first Rider returned.

"Bring them," he said.

"Where?" Artemis said, maintaining a firm hold on her horse's reins.

"To Cassius," the Rider said. "He's waiting for you."

Cassius was sitting in a camp chair outside the quarantine tent, a faint smile on his cold, pale face. "Ah, Ms. McCullough," he said as two of the Riders gave the women a quick pat-down, seemingly unaware of the knife hidden in Jamie's boot. "I have been waiting for you."

"Where is Timon?" she asked. "What have you done with him and his Riders?"

"See for yourself," Cassius said, opening the tent flap.

Jamie and Artemis entered to find Timon sitting, hands and feet bound, against one of the risers. His body pulled against the ropes, muscles hard and jaw set.

Ready to run straight to Timon, Jamie stopped in her tracks when she saw the other prisoners. They were not bound, but stood in the center of the tent, staring at Jamie and Artemis with expressions ranging from alarm to sorrow.

Amos. Garret, sporting his bullet wound. And a woman Jamie recognized with a shock.

Mother.

There in front of her was Eileen McCullough, who had supposedly died when Jamie was a child. Eileen, so much older but alive and looking well.

"Not the reunion you were expecting," Cassius remarked.

Great sadness filled Eileen's eyes, but she didn't speak. Jamie controlled her first impulse to run to the woman she'd lost so long ago. After a quick glance to reassure herself that Amos and Garret were all right—or at least not near death—she sidled away to crouch beside Timon.

"Are you hurt?" she asked, carefully sliding her knife from her boot and hiding it behind her back.

He looked into her eyes, acknowledging what she was about to attempt. "Whatever he says to you," he said, "don't give him what he wants."

"But her delegation has already given me what I want," Cassius said. "Amos has confessed. All I require now is confirmation of *your* guilt, Ms. McCullough."

"Amos?" Jamie said, maneuvering her knife's blade to align with the knot at Timon's wrists. "To what did you confess?"

Her godfather, dirty and rumpled, closed his eyes. "I had no choice," he said. "I wanted so badly to keep you out of this, but I had to save her."

His sideways glance told Jamie who he meant. Eileen, tears in her eyes, lowered her head.

"Where *were* you?" Jamie asked her mother, torn between anger and joy.

"It's an interesting story," Cassius interrupted, barely noticing when Artemis went to Garret. "When your mother gave the virus to the Erebusians so that they could devise a means to fight it, they realized she would be useful in creating a cure. They kidnapped her from the San Francisco Enclave and made it appear as if she had died in an accident. She has been living with them ever since."

"She's been in this camp all along," Amos said, scraping at his face. "It was part of the bargain. The Erebusians sent a spy to me in the Enclave, informing me that Eileen was alive and offering to return her. In exchange, I was to take the virus they provided and infect members of our delegation with it, making sure that none of our people gave blood to anyone but our Rider escorts so as to keep the spread of the virus under some control until we reached the Conclave. Then, when they took blood at the donation booths, they would spread it via their human donors."

Jamie could hardly believe what she was hearing but continued to saw at Timon's ropes as inconspicuously as possible. "Why would you do this for my mother?" she asked Amos.

"Don't you know?" Cassius said mockingly. "What would *you* not do for Timon?"

All at once Jamie understood. Amos, her godfather, loved his best friend's wife. It was written on his face, along with his shame and despair.

"Tell her why the Erebusians set up the plot, Cassius," Timon said, baring his teeth at his former captain as he strained to pull his wrists apart.

"Because they didn't want their cherished way of life to end, and planned to bring the Conclave down with death and suspicion. All hope of its success would be destroyed once they set Opiri against humans."

"But they put their own people at risk," Jamie said, feeling Timon flinch slightly as the knife slipped. She tried not to react. "They were responsible for killing dozens of Opiri, perhaps thousands before this is over. We *know* you've been helping the Erebusians, against all the laws of the Riders. Why?"

A bitter smile crossed Cassius's face, but he didn't answer. "You have a choice now, Ms. McCullough," he said. "You can obtain mercy for your godfather and mother by confessing to helping smuggle and spread the virus, or you can see them both publically tried and punished for their part in this travesty."

Timon tugged at his wrists again, and Jamie could hear the rope slowly coming apart. "What will you do to them if Jamie confesses?" he asked.

"I will give them, and you, a quick death rather than let you be torn apart by an Opir mob," Cassius said.

Jamie laughed, trying to buy time. "Maybe we'd rather take our chances with the mob."

"He doesn't want you to confess simply to confirm Amos's guilt," Timon said, his shoulders moving almost imperceptibly. "He wants revenge on you, Jamie."

"Why?" Jamie asked.

"You stole what was mine," Cassius said.

Timon, Jamie thought. Cassius believed she had stolen Timon's loyalty to him and the Riders. The man who'd been like a second father to him.

"How can I gain access to the cure?" Artemis asked abruptly, startling everyone. Jamie had almost forgotten she was there.

"Your mate will soon be dead anyway," Cassius said.

"Spare him, cure him, and I will give you anything."

"Bring your Freebloods to my side, and I will see that Garret gets the cure."

"Let me go," Artemis said, "and I'll do it."

After a few moments of hesitation, Cassius nodded to his men. They escorted Artemis to the entrance.

"If you betray me," he said, "I will make certain that Garret dies a painful death."

Artemis and Garret exchanged a long look, and then Artemis was gone. Jamie had no orders, no instructions. She had no idea what Artemis would do.

But she knew what Timon was about to do. He held his hands together behind his back, but they were no longer bound; the last shreds of the rope had parted. Though there was blood on his wrists, he seemed not to notice. Jamie could feel him preparing, the tendons in his neck standing out, muscles sliding under his skin.

Jamie shot to her feet and rushed toward Eileen, as if she couldn't bear to be parted from her mother a moment longer. The guards moved to stop her. At the same moment, Timon sprang up from kneeling position and charged Cassius.

Jamie stopped and turned to observe, her fingers digging into her palms. She knew as well as Timon did that the guards might interfere at any instant.

But as Cassius hurled himself forward to meet Timon, not one of his Riders moved. Instead they backed away to form a loose circle, only one guard remaining to watch Garret, Amos and Eileen.

They were giving Timon a chance, though Jamie didn't know why. She pushed the question aside and focused on the battle that had just begun.

Timon grappled with Cassius like a savage predator, a side of him that Jamie had glimpsed only a few times before. His clothing couldn't hide the flex of muscle and the perfect harmony of body and mind as Cassius tried to fend him off, clearly shocked at Timon's attack. He seemed unprepared when Timon butted him in the stomach and carried his former captain halfway across the room.

Suddenly Cassius was fighting back with equal viciousness, his fingers curled into claws, his mouth gaping to bite and tear. He sank his teeth into Timon's arm, but Timon shook him off as if he felt no pain, shoving Cassius away.

Cassius didn't hesitate to strike again. He lashed out with his feet, but Timon gracefully leaped up and out of the way, catching Cassius's leg and flipping the captain head over heels. He flung himself after Cassius, snapping at his opponent's neck like a wolf. His teeth grazed flesh, and Cassius scuttled backward on hands and feet.

He wasn't fast enough. Timon followed him, pinning him down and lunging again for Cassius's throat.

This time he succeeded. His teeth clamped on Cassius's neck, and he held the captain to the ground with the threat of tearing Cassius's throat out.

The silent, watching Riders closed in around the combatants. Jamie tensed, prepared to rush to Timon's aid. But the Riders stopped, and one of them, a tall man with dark hair, began to speak.

"We have been loyal to the Brotherhood, and to our captain," he said. "We, too, have had doubts, but we did not act against the Riders' law. We said nothing when Cassius broke it instead. Now we suffer the dishonor of knowing we were wrong."

Chapter 41

Cassius tried to gurgle a reply. Timon let go of him and leaned back, blood on his mouth. Exhaustion grayed his skin.

"Ask him why he let the Conclave fall to chaos," he said, his breath coming harsh from his chest. "Ask him why he chose to aid the Erebusians rather than stop them."

Clamping his hand over his throat, Cassius cursed the Riders who stood over him. "I was trying to save us, save the Brotherhood." His gaze shifted to Timon. "You were too blind to see what a victory for the Conclave would mean for us. If there was a true peace, the need for our services would be gone. Humans and Opiri could move freely without fear of attack, create their own forces to hold back the raiders and tribesmen. We would become obsolete."

"You're wrong," Jamie said, crossing the room. "Peace would take years for both the Citadels and the Enclaves. There would always have been a place for your people, a need for them."

"And I should trust the opinion of a weak little human, who would be glad to see the Riders disbanded?"

"She isn't a weak human," Garret said, shuffling forward, a hand over his wound. "She's my wife's vassal, soon to be a Freeblood. The virus altered her transformation, but she *is* one of us now."

"There is no 'us,'" Cassius spat. "You Freebloods are nothing but savages."

"Who is the savage here?" Timon asked. "You are as responsible for the deaths here as the Erebusians." He paused, as if a sudden revelation had hit him with blinding force. "Who were the employers looking for the Enclave's secret, Cassius? It was the Erebusians, wasn't it?"

Cassius only glared, but Jamie understood. "They intended all along to expose us as guilty of carrying the virus," she said. "They would have announced that they suspected us from the beginning, so that it would appear that they were the true advocates of peace, and we were the enemy from the very beginning."

"But they already knew that Amos was part of the plan," Timon said. "They wanted all possibilities covered." He turned to Cassius. "We know how the Erebusians infected some Riders when we visited Erebus. They must also have infected humans and Opiri directly, here at the Conclave."

"Ask the Erebusians. I don't know all their tricks."

"And where are the Erebusians now, to stand up for *you*?"

"With us," Artemis called from the front of the tent. She led four Freebloods clumped around two Opiri—Erebusians, Jamie thought, with their hoods pulled low over their faces.

"Meet Lords Makedon and Lykos," Artemis said, flipping back their hoods to reveal their pinched faces and a few recent bruises. "We caught them as they fled from the Conclave."

Cassius flinched, and Timon nodded slowly. "You lost your only allies, who used your own Riders as vectors for their disease when they were infected at Erebus."

"Where is the cure?" Artemis demanded.

Timon held up his hand and addressed the Riders. "Will you interfere?" he asked.

"Cassius is no longer worthy of the Brotherhood," the dark Rider said. "We follow you now, Timon."

"Then take charge of the Erebusians, free your Brothers from confinement and be prepared to gather the human and Opir delegates." He turned to squeeze Cassius's torn neck. "You will take us to the cure. Now."

All the fight gone out of him, Cassius allowed himself to be dragged to his feet and stumbled ahead of them out of the tent, passing through ranks of Freebloods guarding the remaining Erebusians. As Opiri and human delegates began to emerge from their tents, Cassius led everyone to the Rider barracks, where he revealed a solar refrigeration unit hidden beneath bundles of supplies.

"Distribute this to all the humans in the camp, and every afflicted Opiri, and the virus will be destroyed," he said in a flat, emotionless voice. "Any Opir who drinks from a human with the cure will himself be cured."

"And the people who may have left the encampment?" Timon asked. "We know the virus has spread beyond the Conclave."

Cassius laughed with self-mockery. "Who better to find them than the Riders, led by Captain Timon?"

Timon looked at Jamie, and the expression in her eyes told him that she had understood Cassius's meaning perfectly. The Riders loyal to Timon and the cause of peace would surely expect him to continue to lead them indefinitely. Her despair affected him deeply, but not only because he shared her pain.

It told him all he needed to know.

He took her slender hand. She gripped his palm as if she wanted their very flesh to become one. His need for blood was growing, and yet he wanted to sweep Jamie off her feet and forget the problems of the Conclave, forget the cure, forget everything.

But he was still in possession of his sanity. After a few seconds, he let her go and stepped back.

"Ms. McCullough," he said formally, "will you administer the cure to my father?"

"With great pleasure." She nodded to Garret, who came forward on Artemis's arm. Jamie found syringes and gave Garret the injection. The change was not immediate; the only hint that the cure was working came in the shrinking of the bullet wound in Garret's shoulder, almost too gradual to perceive.

She then used three needles to inject Artemis, Timon and herself, mumbling about acquiring an additional supply in the human clinic.

"We have to get this to the other sick Opiri as quickly as possible," Timon said. "The Riders will gather them, and you can pass the cure among the humans."

"Will they want to help the Opiri after the way they've been treated?" Artemis asked.

"Everyone in the Conclave will know how they have been used and manipulated." He glanced from Cassius to Amos. "You will have to face the consequences of your acts, along with the Erebusians."

"Do you think your threats frighten me?" Cassius asked.

"*I* won't be the one deciding your fate." Timon looked up as his Riders, led by Orpheus, crowded into the tent. "Have the others told you what must be done?" he asked Orpheus.

The golden-haired Rider nodded, though not without a hint of reluctance. "The wounds between Brothers will take some time to heal. But we understand."

"You are in charge of rounding up all the delegates and bringing them to the Hub," he said. "I hope you won't have to fight, but use whatever means necessary to get them in one place."

"Understood." Orpheus signaled to the two groups of Riders, and they left the tent together. Timon wiped his mouth with the back of his hand and looked for Jamie. She was with her mother, their heads bent close together as they spoke to each other. Timon could imagine the strain and emotion of their reunion.

He gripped Garret's shoulder on his way to Jamie, earning a ragged smile from his father and a grave nod from his stepmother. Jamie looked up as he approached, and Eileen met his gaze without flinching.

"You two will wish to talk," she said, gently separating herself from her daughter.

"Yes," Timon said, guiding Jamie away with a hand at the small of her back. He was deeply disturbed to see that his hand was trembling.

"You need blood," Jamie said, stopping to face him. "We need to find you an infected human before—"

"It won't do any good," he said. "I lied to you before, Jamie. There is no antidote for the blood-bond except for avoiding all blood for as long as possible, including the original partner's."

"You mean you've been starving yourself since I changed?"

"It hasn't been that long, and—"

"Long enough."

"It makes no difference," he said. "I have to go through with it."

"If only my blood would still work for you…"

"We have no time for that now, Jamie."

"Timon—"

"The Conclave is about to become a dangerous place again, and we'll need all our wits about us."

"Until the truth is known," Jamie said, lifting her chin.

"That's what I intend to make sure of. If the Riders can't handle the delegates, I'll ask my stepmother to send Freebloods to help them. If your mother is willing, she can help you distribute the cure among the humans."

"Of course," Eileen said, joining them. "It is what I've always wanted."

"Yes," Jamie said, her blue eyes bright with a calm wisdom. "But there's something else that needs to be done. It's time to share my other secret, Timon. When the people have gathered, human and Opiri, I will tell them that they are far more alike than they ever dreamed."

"No," Timon said sharply. "The very existence of the Conclave is hanging by a thread. It's not the right time."

"When will it ever be?" she challenged. Her eyes narrowed. "You think it'll never be safe, don't you? That it should be kept a secret forever? Are you worried those who object to the data will attack me?"

Timon cupped her chin in his hand. "I've let you risk yourself too many times, because I respect your courage. But not this time. Now, let us take Cassius and Amos to the Administrative Committee and tell them what's happened."

Jamie went silent. A little of the tension left Timon's body. She wouldn't fight him on the matter of her secret; she knew what was most important. And he loved her all the more for it.

For the next few hours, he kept Jamie close at his side. He, along with Garret, Artemis, Eileen, Orpheus and their Opir and human prisoners, met with the Committee and the Administrative Committee, where the guilty ones were given the promise of protection from attack by angry delegates in exchange for their confessions. The Committee members were grim; most of them seemed ready to admit that they were partially culpable in allowing matters to proceed so far, especially since they had known that the Erebusians has been the Riders' "secret" employers all along.

With the Committee's full backing, they set Timon's plan into motion. The Riders split and carried the news of the cure through the human and Opir districts, instructing the delegates to gather near thc Hub. Those who didn't believe were gently encouraged to do as they were asked, but there was no violence.

They made a priority of giving the cure to the ill Opiri, and then distributed it to the humans exposed to the virus.

Jamie soon informed Timon that more of it would have to be produced to cover infected humans and Opiri outside the Conclave, but Eileen assured them that she and Jamie could do the work once they had access to a complete lab in one of the Enclaves.

Timon refused to think of what that would mean, just as he'd pushed aside all other thoughts of the future beyond the Conclave. The problems of the present remained pressing enough. Even as the cure was being given, humans and Opiri began to demand to know where it had come from. Timon brought the Committee and prisoners before the delegates and stepped back to let Pheidon explain. At the last minute, the Erebusian lords lost their courage and tried to escape.

A mob of humans and Opiri caught them. There were screams and cries of rage as the two groups fought over the prisoners, each claiming the right to seek revenge.

Timon mounted Lazarus and led the Riders in among the crowd, using his staff to push people aside and away from their prey. But it wasn't enough. In the ability to hate, there was little difference between humans and their enemies.

He was sending out a call for more Riders when someone shouted behind him. The hair stood up on the back of his neck, and he wheeled Lazarus around.

Jamie stood on the dais hastily constructed in front of Rider headquarters, her arms flung wide. She shouted again, slowly gaining the attention of the observers closest to the dais.

Timon started for Jamie, but more people were turning toward her, blocking his path. He used his staff to push his way through. By the time he reached the foot of the dais, half the Opiri and humans were focused on her, and she had begun to speak.

"Do not let them win!" she cried. "Do not let those who would destroy peace speak and act for all of us!"

Chapter 42

A hush fell over the encampment, and even Timon was transfixed. The slightly awkward, uncertain Jamie he'd known at the beginning of their journey was gone. In her place stood a poised young woman with absolute conviction in her voice, drawing all attention to her as if she'd worked some magic spell.

"Humans do not speak for Opiri!" an Opir yelled.

"Nor Opiri for humans!" a human countered.

"Be quiet, all of you!" Jamie said. Timon dismounted and jumped onto the dais, standing shoulder to shoulder with Jamie. He couldn't stop her now. He wouldn't.

"You claim that humans and Opiri can't speak for each other," Jamie said, her voice carrying across the Hub. "But the gap between you is far narrower than you imagine." She took a deep breath. "Science has proven a truth that has been kept secret for many years, a secret that can finally unite our peoples, in the same way the makers of the virus attempted to tear us apart."

"The Opiri tried to kill us!" someone shouted.

"How many humans would have let us die?" another replied.

"Silence!" Timon roared.

"Hear her out!" a woman called.

"Yes, let her speak!"

Jamie glanced at Timon, smiled and stepped forward. "I will tell you that secret now," she said to the crowd. "Opiri and humans share a common ancestor."

The noise of protests and gasps and burst of conversation rose up like a cloud of dust, muffling Jamie's voice again. Timon leaped down from the dais with his staff and stalked into the crowd, glaring and baring his teeth. A ripple of quiet passed over the watchers.

"I have the research," Jamie said. "Long ago, in Africa, one of the early hominid lines split off. The original line of hominids lived by hunting game and gathering edible plants, eventually evolving into Homo sapiens, and the other adapted to feed on blood. There were always far more of the former, but the latter survived, learning to hide from those who would hunt them down, just as humans were hunted by them."

"Impossible!" someone yelled.

"Ridiculous!" said another.

"We have nothing in common," yelled a third.

"You have everything in common!" Jamie said. "You Opiri would like to think you are above human sentiment, but you fall in love with humans and produce half-bloods like the Riders. You humans reject what you see as the savagery of the Opiri, and yet you engage in wars and violence yourselves. It's time to recognize that we can only survive by coexisting as kin!"

There were more shouts. As Timon had feared, many refused to accept what Jamie had told them.

But there were some who remained quiet, who seemed to consider what Jamie had said. One Opir woman looked up and raised a clear, calm voice.

"You said you have the research," she said. "Can you show it to us? Can you prove that what you say is true?"

"Yes," Jamie said. "It will take time to show all of you, but it can be done. It *will* be done."

Timon had never felt such pride. With only a little help from him and the Riders, she had taken control, forced the delegates to listen. And even if many of them rejected the research and left the Conclave, there would be others who would come to believe, who would stay and talk and find common ground.

Jamie had been right.

He had a quick word with Orpheus and the other Rider band leaders, asking them to make certain that the Erebusians were returned to custody and that no more fights broke out. Little by little the crowd drifted apart, humans retreating to their own territory while the Opiri returned to theirs.

Timon found Jamie embracing her mother. As Timon approached, Eileen released Jamie and glanced warmly at him before moving away. Garret murmured something about finding Artemis and disappeared into the thinning crowd.

"It's done," Jamie said, grinning at Timon with unalloyed happiness in her eyes. "And you didn't think I could do it."

"I always knew you *could*," he said, taking her hands. "I was, however, afraid of the consequences. I was wrong."

She touched his cheek. "You only wanted to protect me. That's what you've always wanted."

No, he thought. *It's so much more than that.*

"Let's walk by the river," he said, tucking her hand through the crook of his elbow.

"Now?" she asked, looking around. "There's so much to be—"

"Now," he said. "I don't want anyone to bother us."

She let him lead her along the thoroughfare toward the west and the bosk. The sun was high, but Jamie still showed no sensitivity toward it, nor had her teeth or skin begun to change. Would she ever become fully Opir?

As if in answer to his unspoken question, she suddenly burst into a run faster than any human could manage. She was as graceful as a doe in flight, speeding far ahead of him before he thought to chase her. When he did catch her, laughing and panting, he was in no doubt that she was something new and different come into the world.

He opened his arms, and she fell into them. He silenced her laughter with a kiss, the savage bubbling up in him all over again. She responded with equal urgency, lacing her fingers in his hair and closing her eyes.

"Timon," she murmured against his mouth. "Oh, Timon, we've won."

He held her close, breathing in the sweet scent of her skin, of the blood underneath. She wasn't that naive. But her faith had brought them this far.

Perhaps she was right.

"Bite me," she said, arching her neck backward.

Hunger flooded through him. "You know I can no longer draw sustenance from your blood," he whispered, kissing her ear.

"I don't care," she said. "I want to feel you."

As he bit down gently into her neck, she unbuttoned his fly and put her hand on him. He was already hard, and he wondered how she could expect him to control himself when he was tasting the very essence of her body, becoming one with the beat of her—

He stiffened as the realization struck him. Her blood offered more than intimacy and a sensual thrill. He could taste the wholesomeness of it, feel it course through his body like nectar.

She was *feeding* him, just as she had so many times before. Her blood had not lost the ability to nourish him, and he made a small, triumphant sound in his throat as she continued to stroke him, drawing him toward the inevitable climax.

He drew back, stopped her hand and unbuttoned her pants. With eager fingers he pulled them down, and she stepped out of them. He fell with her to the ground and, without further hesitation, entered her yielding body. She wrapped her legs around his waist and drew him in, clearly aware that he could barely control himself, that he had to have all of her *now.* He moved vigorously, licking the place he had bitten, kissing the underside of her delicate jaw and working his hand between their bodies to caress her tender flesh.

Jamie contracted around him with a cry of pleasure, and he followed a moment later. Then he rolled over and settled her in the crook of his elbow, trying to absorb every part of her into himself.

"How did you know I could feed from you?" he asked her.

"I only guessed," she said, rubbing her palm over his chest. "I hoped, since I don't seem to have become completely Opir…"

"You were right." He sighed, realizing that they'd reestablished the blood-bond all over again. He tried to put the thought out of his mind.

"Tell me about your mother," he said, changing the subject.

"I don't know what to say to her. She's been a prisoner for more than half my life."

"She obviously loves you," Timon said. "And you still love her."

"Yes. But Amos…" She released her breath. "He did what he did because he's loved her all this time. And now he's a criminal, partially responsible for dozens of deaths. How do I begin to understand *that*?"

"Maybe you can't," he said, nuzzling her cheek. "It would be easier if he were an evil man. But I don't think he is. He just made a terrible choice."

"Because, in the end, he didn't really think that Opiri lives were equal to my mother's freedom."

"I'm sorry, Jamie," Timon said, running his hand down her arm. "I wish I could take your pain from you."

"I know." She placed her hand flat over his chest as if she could gather his heart in her hand. "I know."

They lay that way for a few precious minutes. Jamie was the first to rise, retrieving her pants and pulling them on with her back to him, as if she'd suddenly become shy of his gaze.

"We have to go back," she said, her voice wavering.

He buttoned his pants and adjusted his shirt. "The Riders expect me to lead them now."

"Yes." She turned to face him, her expression calm and almost distant. "They're still badly needed."

"To take the cure beyond the tent city," he said.

"And to help us salvage what we can of this Conclave."

"We've lost the right to call ourselves neutral."

"At least you aren't delegates." She started out of the bosk. "The fate of the Erebusians and my godfather have yet to be decided. I wouldn't be surprised if the Committee put it to some kind of vote."

"They'll never get a consensus now."

"But this will not be the last meeting," she said, confidence returning to her voice. "It can't be. Maybe no real decisions will be reached today, or tomorrow. But both Opiri and humans have much to think about, and not only of the fact that we share a common ancestor. The Opiri have seen members of their own kind responsible for killing innocents who came to the Conclave in good faith. Humans have witnessed a similar betrayal, forcing them to be vectors of those deaths. Once they've fully understood—"

"If they ever do."

Jamie stopped to face him. "Believe, Timon. Believe, for my sake."

He laid his hands on her shoulders. "I will. But believing isn't enough."

She moved, but he didn't let her go. She met his gaze.

"We both know what we have to do," she said, her voice constricted and tight.

"Do we?" he asked.

"Of course we do!" she said. "You're the leader of the Riders now. They need you. I've already accepted that."

"And your mother needs you to help produce more of the cure."

"Yes." Her throat bobbed. "It…it was always going to be this way, Timon. Even when I let myself—"

"Let yourself what, Jamie? Love me?"

She tilted her chin up. "Yes."

"And have you stopped? Have I managed to drive you away forever?"

"What difference does it make?" she asked with the despair he'd seen in her eyes before. "Our worlds have always been too different."

"Like the humans and Opiri?" he asked. "I won't take your freedom from you."

He cupped his hand under her chin. "Freedom means nothing to me without you by my side."

She began to tremble. "You…"

"I love you, Jamie." He kissed her very lightly on the lips.

Chapter 43

A full day passed before everyone was sure that the cure was successful. The stricken Opiri were beginning to recover, and the last of the humans had received their injections. The Committee had managed to gather a quorum of delegates to discuss the fate of the Conclave, and of those who had attempted to destroy it.

Jamie sat with the rest of her delegation except Amos, who, like Cassius and the Erebusians, was being held elsewhere until a decision about their fates could be reached. In spite of what she'd told Timon, Jamie had expected the meeting to be boiling over with anger and accusations, but the tent was almost shockingly quiet.

She looked for Timon, who stood with the Riders at the foot of the Committee's dais. His men were alert but relaxed, as if they, too, expected reason to prevail.

Timon had said he would believe, and he did. His gaze met hers across the wide space, and he smiled, the expression all for her.

Her heart beat so loudly in her ears that she almost missed the verdict. It wasn't at all what she'd expected. The Erebusians, Cassius and Amos were not to be executed, as she'd feared.

Instead the Erebusians were to be taken by the Tenebrians, who promised to incarcerate the offenders, and Amos was to be returned to the San Francisco Enclave, where he would also be imprisoned as a murderer. Jamie felt only a twinge of grief now, knowing she had lost a man who, in many ways, had existed only in her own mind.

As for Cassius, he was stripped of his membership in the Riders and would join the Erebusians in Tenebris. The delegates agreed that no others were to be held to blame.

The discussion about the fate of the Conclave itself was far more complicated. There was still enough goodwill to make some kind of peace a reality, but all agreed that the Conclave could only be a beginning. News of Jamie's revelation had to be spread and absorbed; even now, there were some delegates who refused to believe.

But the foundation had been laid. There would be other meetings, in different places; ambassadorial visits between Citadels and Enclaves; visits to the successful mixed human/Opiri colonies; acts of goodwill such as the voluntary sharing of blood.

As for the virus and its cure, there remained the danger that those who'd left the Conclave earlier had carried it with them back to their communities. Every Enclave, Citadel and colony of any kind had to be visited and a sample of the cure offered to deal with any infections that might appear in the future. Led by Eileen McCullough, scientists of the San Francisco Enclave would be responsible for producing sufficient quantities of the cure, making it available to all who requested it.

And the Riders would carry it. The Riders, led by Timon.

It wasn't as if Jamie hadn't seen it coming. The moment the Brotherhood had declared Timon their leader, she had known what must happen. More than ever, they needed a firm and incorruptible leader. They had to re-earn their reputation for neutrality, and Timon was just the man to do it.

He had said he loved her. But love wasn't enough to keep them together, even if he had to go through withdrawal from the blood-bond before he was fully fit to lead the Riders into a new future.

She closed her eyes as the meeting ended, ignoring the remaining members of her delegation as they rose and left the tent with all the others. When everything was quiet, she opened her eyes.

Timon stood on at the foot of the risers, looking up at her.

"Jamie," he said softly.

"I have to rejoin my people," she said, rising to descend some distance from where he stood.

"What's the hurry?" he asked. "It'll be days before anyone is ready to leave. There are still plans to be laid."

She stopped at the end of the riser and looked away. "I know some of your men will be accompanying us back to the Enclave to pick up more of the cure," she said.

"Yes. I've chosen Orpheus to lead them."

Her throat was almost too tight for words to escape. "Good. It'll be easier to work with someone we know well."

Timon frowned. "You and your mother?"

"And all the scientists we can recruit. We built the original virus, and now we have to make sure it can never be revived."

He grabbed her hand. "Have you forgotten already?" he asked.

"No. But you know as well as I do that it isn't that simple."

"When did I say love was simple?" He caressed her palm. "Or are you trying to tell me that you don't feel the same? Was I so wrong?"

"Timon," she whispered, closing her eyes. "My feelings for you haven't changed since the day we met. But we're just two people. So much needs to be done. We've both become too much a part of this, Timon."

"What if you had the chance to see what you've set in motion firsthand?"

"What are you saying?"

He brought her fisted hand to his chest. "You've come too far, Jamie. You deserve to *live*, not hide behind walls."

The beating of Timon's heart passed through Jamie's skin and pulsed through her body. Her mouth went dry. "What are you suggesting, Timon?" she asked hoarsely.

"My parents have offered to have the Freebloods help the Brotherhood spread the cure and escort new teams of ambassadors between settlements. They would be more than happy to let you travel with them. It's very possible to live only on animal blood, as they do the majority of the time—and since you haven't shown any signs of hunger, you may not need it at all. I know you have the strength, and people will respect what you've done here. You could make a difference."

"Of course," Jamie said thickly. "I'm still your mother's vassal."

"That ends today. You'd be traveling as a free person."

"Without you."

"Did you think I would leave you?"

"The Riders…"

"I'm leaving the Riders. I'll tell them they will have to find a different leader now."

She stared at him. "The Riders are your life."

"*Were* my life. Now I have another reason to live."

"I'm barely Opir. What if I have only a human life span?"

"Then we'll make the most of it."

"What if I really want to go home?"

"Then I'll go with you. We'll find a way, Jamie."

She met his gaze. "Will we, Timon? Can we?"

"Anything is possible if you can speak the words."

"What—" She broke off, suddenly understanding. In all her time with him, she had never told Timon she loved him.

If she spoke now, it would be like the blood-bond, a kind of magic that would tie them together forever.

She'd always thought herself a coward. She was still afraid. Timon was offering her no less than everything. Could she accept it?

Raising her hand to his lips, he kissed her knuckles. "If you need more time to think…"

"I've spent enough time thinking," she said. She unfolded her hand and pressed it to Timon's face. "I love you, Timon."

He laughed, grabbing her around the waist and swinging her in a circle.

"Which way do we ride?" he asked.

* * * * *